For Every Girl There's A

Single Girl Summer

A NOVEL

BY DEANNA KIMBERLY BURRELL

Chi-Towne Fiction Books

Windy City Publishers Chicago

SINGLE GIRL SUMMER

Windy City Publishers
1935 S. Plum Grove Rd., #349
Palatine, IL 60067
www.windycitypublishers.com

Published in the United States of America
10 9 8 7 6 5 4 3 2 1

First Edition: June 2011

Library of Congress Control Number: 2011925486

ISBN: 978-1-935766-13-1

Front Cover image by Chevonne Woodard
Chapter Image by: BNP Design Studio/ClipartOf.com/#219019
Cover Production by Don Warner, DoubleD Graphics

Windy City Publishers
Chicago

A NOVEL

BY DEANNA KIMBERLY BURRELL

This book is dedicated to dreamers
Who are pregnant with possibility,
Pursuing passion,
And producing nothing short of phenomenal.

The journey to manifestation
Can be trying and exhausting,
But don't ever stop.

We need your dreams and contributions;
They make life so sweet,
Like a juicy peach on a hot summer day.

April

Chapter 1

Fr: <Henry>
To: <Button>
Sunday, April 19, 2009 11:37AM
Subject: hey sexy

Sorry I had to work all weekend and this week is going to be hectic too. Don't worry, I found the perfect restaurant and gift for Saturday. Miss you.

Fr: <Button>
To: <Henry>
Sunday, April 19, 2009 2:18PM
Subject: RE: hey sexy

Really, Half? Thought you forgot about me. I already have plans for my birthday.

Fr: <Henry>
To: <Button>
Sunday, April 19, 2009 2:22PM
Subject: RE: hey sexy

Don't call me Half. I'm full in this relationship. You're the one who gets in the pool to splash around, but won't swim a lap. Scott and I are meeting at the restaurant at six so I'll see you tonight and Saturday. Save us some ribs.

⁂

Sunday afternoon, just after the brunch bustle and a couple of hours before dinner, was Button's favorite time to arrive. For the regular customers, a Sunday meal at Anand was like going to church, a requirement for starting the week off right. Button sighed and hooked her tartan-pattern umbrella to the host stand, letting the raindrops puddle on the granite floor. She ran her fingers through her pixie haircut. *At least my hair isn't as soaked as my trench and Jimmy Choos. It better not rain like this on Saturday. Between Henry's commitment, my Mom's rants, and this sideways rain, I can't take one more thing trying to ruin my birthday. Mmmmmmm, that's nice.*

Button tilted her head back and inhaled deeply. Her mouth watered. The aroma of caramelized onions and braised beef usurped her problems. When Button finally exhaled, she moaned again and curved her lips into an expectant grin. *At least something's going right. Chef's putting his foot in those ribs. I wonder how many reservations we have.*

As if on cue, Davis floated through the burgundy-velvet drapes into the foyer. The silver brocade on his vintage tuxedo jacket glistened under the spotlights. He stopped in his tracks and smiled adoringly at Button.

Davis gushed, "Ms. Jackson, you're a Burberry wet dream. Now let Davis get you out of that coat." While he took her wet things down the hall to the coatroom, Button admired the place she considered her home away from home. The mahogany walls were adorned with original paintings entitled "Birth of a Gospel Nation," "Black Metropolis," and "Obama's Bronzeville Blues." The high ceilings, hints of plush velvet, bronze chairs, and vibrant artwork representing the breadth of African-American life in Chicago were just some of the design elements that made Anand as stylish as its owner. But it was the food that made it one of the most popular restaurants in the city.

Davis returned with a Louis Vuitton Cherry Blossom umbrella. "Davis brought back your umbrella. He was the envy of all the divas last night. This *pièce de résistance* is the best date he's ever had." He extended the umbrella to Button.

She waved him off. "Keep it as long as you like. I have so many umbrellas and it's going to monsoon all week."

Mouth agape and eyes bulging, he said, "I always thought fairy godmothers had wands. But no, Davis' fairy godmother makes dreams come true with limited edition accessories. He is not worthy." Davis kissed Button's hand and then quickly stashed the prized umbrella in the host stand.

"Making dreams come true is my pleasure." Button winked at Davis and moved closer. "I hope this rain isn't ruining Sunday dinner. How many reservations for tonight?"

"All times and tables are booked solid. A little rain can't keep 'em from our fall-off-the-bone, finger-lickin' short ribs. Oh, and a large wine shipment came in yesterday. Is that the new pairing for the ribs? Davis wants to hear all about it." He popped his elbows on the host stand and rested his chin atop balled fists.

Button's face beamed. She spoke slowly, letting the words fall like the long finish of a deep red wine. "It's a sun-kissed Bordeaux from Maison des Boissons, a quaint French winery I visited last year. This blend of Cabernet, Malbec, and Syrah creates a complex symphony of red cherries, spicy tannins, and dark chocolate. Not only is it a wine of vigor and longevity, it pervades your taste buds and makes the beef flavor pop. You'll love it." Button's eyes twinkled and her voice was breathy with desire.

"Oh, Davis loves to hear you describe wine. You love wine almost as much as he loves gossip." Leaning in conspiratorially and lowering his voice to a whisper, he continued, "Speaking of which, Senator Smith was in here last night all cozy with that woman who's not his wife. He's becoming a regular in that back 'mistress' booth. Scan…de…lous." Davis' eyes danced with the elation that only fresh, juicy gossip afforded.

"I'm not surprised."

"Well, Davis is shocked. *Shocked*! He's supposed to be one of the good ones." Davis tapped the wood stand for emphasis.

Button shook her head. "It's not a question of good or bad. As natural hunters, men are incapable of long-term monogamy. They love to chase. They may stay at one table for a while, but eventually they start sniffing around for fresh meat. Monogamy doesn't exist in a world called reality."

"Ms. Jackson, a man would be crazy not to commit to a woman like you!"

"A woman like me isn't crazy enough to commit to any one man. You know I keep my options open."

"Not if Mr. Henry has his way. That lickable piece of caramel man-candy wants to marry you." Davis looked around to make sure they were alone and then lowered his voice to a whisper again. "Davis isn't supposed to tell you, but he called to ask what to get for your birthday. A little birdie told him a four carat, princess-cut diamond." David was pleased with himself.

"Oh no, you didn't."

"That man-hunk of yours is perfect. Big, strong, corn-fed body and every time he smiles or says y'all, Davis' heart goes a-flutter. He doesn't understand why you insist on playing the field when your Southern Prince Charming is ready to settle down," Davis whined.

Button sighed. "Prince Charming is a bad cliché; not a real person. I've learned my lesson. If he's rich and successful, then he doesn't have any free time. If he's great in bed with a banging body, then he spends more time grooming than I do. If his conversations are stimulating and intelligent, then he doesn't make me feel safe when we walk down a dark street. If he has excellent taste, then he's a cheapskate with bad credit. If he's fun and young at heart, then he has kids with demanding schedules. I could go on and on."

Davis held up his hand. "No need. Davis gets the picture of other men, but not your man. What's wrong with Mr. Henry?"

"If he's a financially stable, good-looking, southern gentleman, like Mr. Henry, eventually he's going to cheat, like all men inevitably do. Once a man knows you love him, it's over. Love and commitment make men lose interest so I'm never giving either. Got it?" Button concluded and shot Davis a look to make sure he understood.

"Then there's no way for Mr. Henry to win," Davis half-stated, half-questioned.

"I don't give a commitment and I don't ask for one. I keep my interest diversified. Henry knows that and is free to do the same."

"But what if Mr. Henry wants more?"

"Of course he wants more." Button rolled her eyes. "That's how they get you. They convince you to settle down and give up your power and then they run all over town on you. A smart woman never dates just one man. A smart woman plays hard-to-get and her men never get bored or complacent. My mother raised me to be a smart woman."

"You always say your mother is crazy."

"She is, but that's beside the point."

"Mr. Henry is a good man and he wants to marry you. Oh, you'd make a gorgeous couture bride." Davis paused as he conjured the image in his head. "And Davis, as maid of honor extraordinaire, would try really hard not to upstage you. He promises."

"Davis, please."

"What? If Davis isn't maid of honor, who is?"

Button sighed with exasperation. "*No one*! I'm not getting married."

"Mr. Henry isn't going to play this game with you forever. Don't let him slip through your French manicure."

"My dear, men come. Men go. It's the circle of life. I'm off to sample my new Bordeaux. Can you get someone to clean up this water?" Button threw him an air kiss, turned on her heel, and disappeared through the velvet drapery.

Davis stared, shaking his head. "Damn, you're cold," he finally yelled after her.

"That's right, cold as hell," she tossed back over her shoulder and laughed.

CHAPTER 2

Fr: <Mom>
To: <Button>
Saturday, April 25, 2009 10:52AM
Subject: HELLO?????

BUTTON TAMIKA JACKSON, YOUR VOICEMAIL'S FULL AND YOU DON'T NEVER ANSWER YOUR PHONE. HAPPY BIRTHDAY AND GUESS WHO I SAW? YOUR FATHER. AIN'T SEEN HIM SINCE I WAS SEVEN MONTHS PREGNANT WITH YOU AND HE RAN OFF WITH THAT TRAMP WHO WAS SUPPOSED TO BE MY BEST FRIEND. SAID HE FEELS BAD ABOUT WHAT HAPPENED. I CURSED HIM LIKE THE DAY'S LONG. HE AIN'T NEVER BEEN NO GOOD AND AIN'T NEVER GONE BE NO GOOD. I ALMOST POPPED A VEIN. YOU SHOULD CALL THE WOMAN WHO GAVE YOU LIFE AND HOPEFULLY I AIN'T DEAD BY THEN.

Fr: <Button>
To: <Mom>
Saturday, April 25, 2009 11:35AM
Subject: RE: HELLO?????

I just finished this book on the power of forgiveness. It said it's not healthy to hold onto hurt feelings, anger, and disappointments because eventually those things start to eat away at our insides. By holding a grudge, we think we're hurting the other person. But in reality, we're only hurting ourselves. Maybe it's time to forgive.

Fr: <Mom>
To: <Button>
Saturday, April 25, 2009 11:36AM
Subject: RE: HELLO?????

SOME SHIT YOU BETTA NOT FORGIVE AND SURE AS HELL DON'T FORGET. THIS IS IT. DID YOU FORGET WHY YOU'RE NAMED BUTTON?

Fr: <Button>
To: <Mom>
Saturday, April 25, 2009 11:38AM
Subject: RE: HELLO?????

No, I didn't forget. You never let me.

* * *

A Spanish guitar strummed softly in the background while Henry and Button took turns feeding each other bread dipped in warm cheese and fruit dipped in orange-chocolate liqueur. Henry waited patiently for Button to notice it was her turn to feed him, but she was lost in thought again. To finally get her attention, he leaned over, kissed her on the cheek, and said in his sexy, Texas twang, "Happy thirty-first birthday, Cocoa Button. You get more and more beautiful every year."

Button and Henry both landed in Chicago from their respective small, southern towns right after high school. Button enrolled in a college with a prestigious hospitality management program and Henry took an electrician's apprenticeship under his uncle. With hard work and savvy networking, they both excelled in their fields and opened successful businesses. They met a couple of years ago when Henry was having dinner with a client at Anand. The entire night, he couldn't take his eyes off the statuesque beauty sauntering through the restaurant like she owned the place. As he was leaving, he caught her alone by the host stand. "Ma'am, all night I was wondering what Anand means. Do ya' know?"

Button drank in his olive skin, curly hair, and bulging muscles. Her eyes roamed over his crisp, white dress shirt, Levi's jeans, snakeskin boots and stopped at his Lone Star belt buckle. The rugged stranger towered over her and she could imagine how good it would feel to be wrapped in his powerful arms. "It's a Sanskrit word that means bliss and happiness. This restaurant is my Anand." Button's own accent was stronger than usual.

"So, you're the owner?" He leaned casually on the host stand. His smile flashed beautiful, white teeth.

"Owner and sommelier. Button Jackson from Augusta, Georgia." She smiled flirtatiously. Henry's ears picked up her drawl and he was smitten.

Henry James was a gentleman with excellent manners and easy conversation. He planned interesting dates, was dependable, built like a football player, and great in bed. Ultimately, he wanted to get married and have a family. Of all the men who had held Button's "half-boyfriend" position, he was by far her favorite, and she knew he'd be a wonderful husband—for someone else. Lately, she could feel another woman's growing presence in his life, and even though she wasn't ready for their relationship to end, she refused to date exclusively and definitely didn't want to get married.

"Thanks." Button responded absentmindedly and reached over the table to check the beef tenderloin sizzling in hot oil.

"What's wrong?" Henry studied Button's face. "You don't like the restaurant? The website said fondue's romantic."

"Nothing's wrong, Baby. This is great." Button dipped a piece of bread in the cheese and popped it in her mouth. "This Gruyère is my favorite."

"You don't have to pretend. Cooking your own food and getting grease burns isn't sexy." Henry took the napkin from his lap and wiped grease splatter from Button's arm.

"Henry, I love it. Snuggling in a curtained booth and feeding each other is very sexy and very thoughtful. Thank you." Button returned his kiss on the cheek.

"So, what's wrong? And don't say nothing," Henry asked.

"Nothing." Button shrugged innocently.

"You're distracted. You're messing up our dip-and-feed rotation. After two years of living in Button's world, I know a lil' something something. Tell me what's wrong," Henry pressed.

Button's eyes searched thoughtfully. "Nothing," she said unconvincingly.

"Tell me."

Button speared a piece of pineapple, twirled the utensil, and then dropped it on her plate. "Well, I may have a small case of the birthday blues," Button admitted.

"What's messing up my baby's birthday? Tell me and I'll fix it." He winked at her.

"My mother's in the middle of one of her crazy episodes. She got me good this morning with an all-caps email rant."

"Was it the usual?"

"Yup, did I forget how I got the name Button? Nothing new. I emailed her back and suggested it's time she practiced some forgiveness. That didn't go over well. She's getting crazier as she gets older and she refuses to let go of the past. And I have your voice stuck in my head saying I'm doing the same thing and I'm going to turn into my mother. I don't want to turn into her. And then..." Button's voice trailed off and she shook her head. "Nothing." She dipped the pineapple from her plate in the chocolate and chewed slowly, signaling she was done talking.

Henry leaned back in the booth to get a good look at the birthday girl. "And then...what else?"

Button shook her head dismissively.

"What else happened?" Henry insisted.

Button took a deep breath. Unlike the other men she'd dated who were always trying to change or control her, Henry truly cared about her happiness. When he gave advice, it was always spot-on and unselfish. His favorite strategy was to follow up his advice with a self-help book or be-a-better-you project. Button respected his perspective and subtleness, but she wasn't sure if she was ready to discuss what happened to her earlier today.

"This looks serious. If you want to talk, I'm here. Whenever you're ready," Henry sipped his beer.

"Well, my mother also wrote that she saw my father for the first time since he ran off and left her pregnant with me. Then when I got to work," Button lowered her voice to a whisper. "There was a letter from him." She looked around to see if anyone had heard.

"Did you open it?"

"No, I was too afraid."

"You should open it."

"I never open any."

"He's sent you letters before?"

"In college. I told my mother and she demanded I send it back unopened. I got a few from him. I never opened them."

"You should open it."

"And betray my mother? She's crazy, but I owe everything I am and have to her. She sacrificed a lot raising me. My father put her through hell."

"All good parenting is defined by sacrifice. He may have put her through hell, but she chooses to stay there. And you—you've been letting her issues be your issues for too long. You should open it tonight and see what he has to say."

"That letter is a Pandora's box. Once it's opened, all hell could break loose. This isn't a decision I want to rush into. I need some time to think it over."

"Why didn't you tell me about the letters before?"

"It's not important. He ran off before I was born. He's never cared about me and I don't see any reason to care about him."

"Like it said in that book I gave you, forgiveness is a powerful healer."

"I don't need to forgive anyone. I don't care. Forgiveness is my mother's problem."

"No, Baby. That's your problem, too. Your father ran off with your mother's best friend, but that doesn't make all men dogs and all women rivals. You say she's lonely and doesn't trust anyone. Right?"

Button hesitated, wondering where Henry was going with this conversation. She finally answered, "Yeah."

"Cocoa, you need to work on your fear of commitment. It's unhealthy."

"What's unhealthy?"

"You think not depending on anyone makes you strong, but it doesn't. You're afraid. You're afraid to commit to me. Hell, you don't even have any girlfriends 'cause you're afraid of other women."

Button cut her eyes and raised her voice. "That's just mean and untrue. I have Davis." Henry stared at her incredulously.

"Davis is not your girlfriend. He's never even been to your house and you don't hang out outside of work."

"Again, that's not true. We work out together."

"You got him a job teaching a class at your gym, which was cool, but also self-serving because he saves your favorite bike for you. Outside of the restaurant and gym, you don't hang out. Not to mention Davis is a he. Girlfriends are your female equals and you should have some." Button folded her arms on the table and sighed while she processed what Henry was saying.

"Women are messy. I don't want or need any more mess. I have enough with my mother."

Henry stroked Button's arm and looked in her eyes. "Baby, I have three sisters and in my opinion there's nothing more beautiful than seeing them together.

They love each other. They laugh together. They support each other. And when one of my sisters is tripping, they call her on her shit. They provide balance and the necessary reality checks we all need once in a while."

"I'm an only child," Button countered.

Henry continued to stroke her arm. "Cocoa, I know that. Your only-child qualities are obvious. But just because you weren't given a sister in blood doesn't mean you don't deserve sisterhood. Girlfriends are the sisters you get to pick and a blind man could see you really need someone, besides me, calling you on your shit." Henry smiled slyly at his underhanded dig.

"Whatever, Henry. Can we drop this?"

"No, I'm serious. You're not ready to open the letter from your father. I get that it's complicated because you don't want to hurt your mother. But you can find a girlfriend. Let's make that your goal. How long do you need...a month?"

"Baby, I'm too busy and too old to make new friends."

"Please, I know you make new friends all the time. You can do this. You're fun and friendly. You're a little mouthy, but we can't all be perfect." Henry winked mischievously.

Button rolled her eyes at Henry, but he continued anyway, "I got it! My big summer party is the last weekend in May. Your goal is to bring a girlfriend to the party. That gives you a solid month."

"That's the stupidest thing I've ever heard." Button laughed until she suddenly pulled her arm away and her face went cold. "No wait, I get it! You're inviting your new girl to the party and you need to keep me busy and out of your way. That's what all this shit is about," she accused.

Henry snorted and shook his head. "Button, this half-boyfriend crap is your idea, so don't be that way. *All the fun of a boyfriend, and none of the responsibility*," he mimicked Button. "You've been clear with me from the beginning and I accept that. I love being with you, but I want more. If you won't give me more..."

"No, you're right," Button interrupted. She knew she'd crossed the line.

"I can't not invite her to the party. This is the fifth year I've done it. Everywhere I go, it's all people talk about. Cocoa, I didn't plan on telling you on your birthday, but yes, she'll probably be there, so it'll be good for you to have a friend to hang out with."

"Whatever, Half. Can we move on to the next subject?"

"Don't Half me. You know I hate that. Last thing I'm going to say is that I love you. I cut you a lot of slack because you've inherited your mother's trust and attachment issues, but you can't hide behind her sob story forever. You're a grown woman with your own mind and it's time you start acting like it."

Button exhaled deeply. "Fine. Now this conversation is closed."

Henry laughed at Button. "This conversation is closed when I say it's closed."

"If you keep this up, I'm not going to let you stay at my place tonight."

Henry shrugged, unconcerned. "We'll stay at my place."

Button reached for a strawberry. Her tongue traced the red, fleshy fruit and she devoured it seductively. She and Henry watched each other intently. Then she leaned into Henry's broad chest and nibbled his earlobe. Her hand slid up his muscular thigh and she whispered in his ear, "If you like the way I eat strawberries, you'll love the way I eat you."

Henry's leg tightened and a sexy smirk crossed his lips. "Conversation closed. Check, please."

Button threw her head back and laughed. Henry continued watching her. When she stopped laughing, he gently cupped her face in his hand, traced the dimple on her right cheek, and drew her mouth to his. Button melted like the orange-chocolate liquor into his strong arms and soft lips.

CHAPTER 3

Fr: <Caroline>
To: <Dawn>
Cc: <Carlisa>
Sunday, April 19, 2009 8:05AM
Subject: Martin Sister Sunday

Here's the plan for today. Carlisa and I are dropping all the kids at Mom and Dad's house. We'll catch a movie at noon and have brunch at Anand after.

Dawn, do you want to meet at Mom & Dad's or at the movies? ATTENDANCE IS MANDATORY!

Fr: <Carlisa>
To: <Dawn>, <Caroline>
Sunday, April 19, 2009 8:08AM
Subject: RE: Martin Sister Sunday

Can't wait! Who the hell told me to have twins? Damn genetics. Dawn, you better be there!!! Haven't seen my big sis in forever.

P.S. Do we have to go to Anand? It's kind of pricey and Dawn goes there all the time.

Fr: <Dawn>
To: <Carlisa>, <Caroline>
Sunday, April 19, 2009 8:15AM
Subject: RE: Martin Sister Sunday

Twins, don't be mad. Slight change of plans. Rick told me last night he's taking me out for a special dinner on Friday and I need a new dress. I'm traveling next week so I have to shop this morning. Stores open at 11. You guys go to the movies and I'll meet you at brunch. Anand is fine. I'll even treat since I'm messing up the plans.

Fr: <Carlisa>
To: <Dawn>, <Caroline>
Sunday, April 19, 2009 8:17AM
Subject: RE: Martin Sister Sunday

Special dinner with Rick Stallings. Sounds "engaging?" Since you're paying, no problem about the show.

***

Even though she wasn't going into the office, Dawn was dressed in a smart pinstriped suit with her hair pulled into a neat bun. It had rained all day, but Anand was packed. She followed Davis through the bustling restaurant to a table where her twin sisters were sipping mimosas and chatting.

"Look who Davis found! Told ya' she wouldn't melt in the rain. Sisters reunited." Davis pumped his fists in joy. Dawn hugged and kissed her sisters as he pulled out a chair, and she sat.

"We just ordered our food," Carlisa informed Dawn.

Davis handed Dawn a menu. "Ms. Martin, have you ever eaten brunch with us?"

"No, just lunch."

"Davis recommends the watermelon-glazed chicken. The kitchen marinates chicken quarters in watermelon puree, lemon zest, and red chili flakes overnight. Chef grills the chicken along with watermelon and pineapple slices over an open flame. The chicken and fruit are served warm with a delicious glaze on the side.

It's to die for. I'll send your waiter over ASAP."

"Sounds delicious. Can you tell the waiter I'm having that and a mimosa? Thanks." Dawn handed the menu back to Davis. He bowed and disappeared from the table.

"Did you find a dress?" Caroline asked.

"Did I ever. It's short and fire-engine red. My dress is so hot, it burned a hole in my shopping bag." Dawn buttered a piece of bread and leaned back happily in her chair.

"The trend for summer is to go bold with your color. I hope Rick Stallings is ready," Caroline said.

"Don't we all," Carlisa murmured under her breath. "What's the special occasion for dinner?"

"Rick's going to propose on Friday," Dawn bubbled.

"Really? Why do you think that?" Caroline asked skeptically.

"Hellooo. I'm a lawyer. It's my job to read people and notice the signs," Dawn answered.

"What signs?" Carlisa sipped her mimosa.

"He's been back and forth to Houston working on this huge oil deal for the past six months and it's finally wrapping up. This is the biggest venture capital project he's ever done. Men always like to wait until they're at the apex of their career to settle down."

The waiter interrupted by bringing Dawn's mimosa. "Ladies, would you like another?"

"Yes, keep 'em coming," the twins answered in unison.

"Is that it?" Caroline turned back to Dawn.

"No. That's not it. I can tell he's planning something. I've caught him whispering on the phone a few times. And yesterday, he told me to clear my calendar for Friday evening and dress to impress." Dawn danced in her chair and looked back and forth between her sisters who calmly swallowed the rest of their drinks. "Don't all speak at once or get too excited for me."

Caroline and Carlisa exchanged looks. "Dawnie, you're a fantastic lawyer, but reading Rick Stallings is not your strong suit," Caroline said.

"Maybe I've been wrong a couple of times before, but this is it. I can feel it. Nothing says ready to get married like success and a fancy dinner. Why do both of you keep looking at me that way?" Caroline and Carlisa exchanged looks again, but didn't say anything. "What?" Dawn demanded.

"First, there was the dinner on the top of the John Hancock..." Carlisa began.

"...when you wore the white Grecian dress." Caroline finished her sentence.

"You thought Rick Stallings was proposing, but he was celebrating buying a condo on the Gold Coast. He didn't even ask you to move in with him," Carlisa shook her head as she reminisced.

"Then, there was the shimmery black scoop-neck dress and dinner with his parents. You thought Rick Stallings was going to propose. He announced the new retirement home he gave them in Palm Springs. You were devastated and didn't go to work for two days after that," Caroline reached across the table to take Dawn's hand.

Dawn snatched her hand away and played with the napkin in her lap to avoid eye contact with her sisters. "You two are always raining on my parade."

Caroline sighed. "Dawnie, we love you and hope that right after the dinner rolls hit the table, Rick Stallings is down on one knee popping the question. But with his track record, we're worried that on Friday, the fire-engine red dress will be another false alarm."

"It won't be." Dawn snapped at her sisters.

"You've been with him three years. Rick Stallings needs to piss or get off the pot. You're twenty-nine and not getting any younger," Carlisa blurted out.

"Plus my kids are three and four years old. Carlisa's boys are three. It would be nice if all the cousins were close in age," Caroline added.

"Sorry if I'm not moving fast enough for the two of you. Sorry I didn't meet my husband in college, get married right after graduation, and start having babies. Maybe if I didn't need to work to support myself, I could have timed the birth of my hypothetical children better." Dawn's voice screeched.

"Calm down, Dawnie. That's not what we're saying. You're Type-A. From birth, you always had a five-year plan so instead of playing this guessing game, maybe you should sit down and talk to him," Caroline said.

"You always say everything's negotiable, so when are you going to start this negotiation?" Carlisa added.

"At least find out if Rick Stallings wants to get married?" Caroline suggested.

"Rick wants to get married." Dawn insisted.

"Maybe you should confirm that and get a timeline on when." Caroline exchanged another look with Carlisa.

Dawn's voice quivered. "You really don't think he's going to marry me."

Caroline's shoulders dropped and her voice softened. "We're happy you're a big-time lawyer, but we don't want you to miss out on the joys of marriage and children and we know you don't want to miss out on that either. Sorry, but we're not convinced Rick Stallings wants the same thing."

"But we met a great guy who'd be perfect for you," Carlisa said excitedly. "He doesn't make as much money as you, but he's ready to get married and start a family."

"Rick wants to marry me." Dawn persisted.

"When?" The twins asked in unison.

"He's going to surprise me when the time is right. I just need to be patient."

"You don't have any patience." The twins responded again in unison.

"I don't have a lot but I'm working on it. Rick asked me to be patient with him and our relationship and that's what I'm doing." Dawn explained.

Carlisa shook her head. "Patience is the consolation prize offered by a fool with no plan."

"And impatient is who you are, so what gives Rick Stallings the right to tell you to change?" Caroline asked.

Carlisa co-signed. "Yeah, that's our job. It's also our job to look out for you. It's been three years and he's a nice guy, but..."

"Rick isn't just a nice guy. He's the total package. Men don't get any better than him and if I have to wait a little bit then dammit, I'll wait," Dawn shot back.

"Piss..." Carlisa started the sentence.

"...or pot," Caroline finished.

Dawn pursed her lips and fixed her sisters with an icy stare. "First of all, stop finishing each other's sentences and talking in unison. Your twin talk is creepy. Secondly, stop using Rick's full name like he's some hypersexual porn star. Last, but certainty not least, *stop ganging up on me*!" Dawn slapped her palm on the table with each word for emphasis.

"Hey now. I'm moving as fast as I can," the waiter said, laughing. He set a plate of food in front of each sister. "I know better than to keep hungry women waiting. Are we doing okay here? Need anything else?"

"No, thank you. I'm going to wash my hands," Dawn tossed her napkin in her seat and headed to the bathroom.

Anand was Dawn's spot. After eating lunch there every Friday for the past couple of years, she was on a first-name basis with the staff and always seated promptly, regardless of the wait list. Being there made her feel happy and comfortable. But not today. The suede chocolate walls and the privacy of the individual bathrooms felt claustrophobic. Dawn had to breathe deeply to calm her nerves. Her pounding heart and stilted breath signaled the onset of a mild panic attack, which for the past couple of weeks had become regular occurrences. Dawn loved her sisters, but spending time with them, like waiting for Rick to propose, was a mighty test of her patience. Dawn splashed cold water on her face and looked at her reflection in the narrow mirror.

Another panic attack? What is wrong with me? I graduated magna cum laude from Columbia Law, I'm dating one of Chicago's most successful bachelors, and I'm on track to make partner before my thirtieth birthday this year. My last performance review praised my ability to keep a cool head no matter how much pressure builds on a case or how much responsibility is thrown at me. I'm the go-to girl. So why can't I catch my damn breath?

Rick's voice echoed in her head, "I want to surprise you when the time is right. Please Darling, be patient and stop trying to control everything. You control enough at the firm. Let me do this!"

Dawn had patience. Hell, her patience was another key to her success at the firm. When she was negotiating a deal for her client, she laid out an offer and then waited for opposing counsel's response. She wouldn't keep calling to discuss or get feedback. She'd just wait and let them sweat. She had cracked many a hard nut that way and earned herself the nickname "The Closer." She had the highest settlement-close rate in the firm. But now, she was on the other side and her sisters were no help and this hot, cramped bathroom wasn't helping either. Dawn's heart and thoughts raced like wild horses while she splashed more water on her face.

When it comes to this engagement Rick has all the power and he won't let me rush him which is fine because I'm practicing patience and getting really good at it so why did Carlisa and Caroline have to bring up the white Grecian and shimmery black scoop-neck dresses what the hell do they know this time will be different Friday's fire-engine red number is going to make a great engagement story and I can't wait to rub it in their helpful we-know-a-really-nice-guy-who's-ready-to-get-married-and-have-kids-before-our-kids-are-going-off-to-college faces but right now I really need to calm down catch my breath and get the hell out of this tight-ass bathroom.

Chapter 4

Text Message to Rick
Fr: Dawn
Saturday, Apr 25, 2009 7:12 PM
Where are u?
U cancelled plans yesterday.
U owe me dinner tonight!

Text Message to Dawn
Fr: Rick
Saturday, Apr 25, 2009 7:52 PM
Another meeting running late.
Moved reservation to 9pm.
I'll let you know when I'm on my way.

Text Message to Rick
Fr: Dawn
Saturday, Apr 25, 2009 7:54 PM
Ok.

Text Message to Dawn
Fr: Rick
Saturday, Apr 25, 2009 9:51 PM
Lots going on at the office.
Tell you at dinner.
Hope u r ready to celebrate.

***

Dawn surveyed her elegant condo. With its minimalist design and weekly maid service, everything was clean and orderly. She paced in her underwear, jewelry, and robe, trying to find small tasks to occupy her time but not cause her to break a sweat. The bling from her diamond earrings, tennis necklace, and matching bracelet caught her eye in the hallway mirror. All the pieces had been gifts from Rick. She just needed a princess-cut, diamond engagement ring to complete the collection.

She couldn't wait to put on her show-stopping red dress when she knew Rick was finally on his way to pick her up. Every fifteen minutes, Dawn checked her phone and peeked at the dress in her closet where it hung, far away from her other non-engagement dresses. She didn't want their bad mojo to rub off on her new secret weapon.

I should give those dresses away because I know I'm not going to wear them again. I hate clothes with bad memories. Dawn's stomach growled. *I wonder if I have time to make a snack. No, I'm too nervous to eat and Rick should be here soon. I hope.*

Dawn rummaged through the refrigerator. Instead of eating, she threw out all the old leftovers and organized the canned goods in the pantry so the labels faced forward. She logged in to her work email account and responded to messages until a hunger headache made it impossible to form coherent sentences. She switched to steaming all the wrinkled shirts in her closet and then plopped on the couch to watch her favorite news channel.

The news flashed clips from last night's local fundraising event to which she and Rick had been invited, but couldn't attend. They had become one of Chicago's power couples and their presence was requested at numerous charity and social engagements. As an educated and highly paid lawyer, Dawn knew it was difficult to find an attractive African-American man whose professional success and salary exceeded her own, so she was extremely proud to be dating Rick Stallings, a partner at a venture capital firm. They were both intelligent, hardworking, successful, and driven. They worked long hours, traveled for business, excelled at demanding jobs, and juggled hectic schedules. They were movers and shakers and complemented each other well. Hell, they were perfect together.

Dawn's stomach growled again just as her cell phone beeped with a message that Rick was finally on his way. She slipped into her dress, touched up her lipstick, and checked her reflection in a full-length mirror before heading out the door. Walking down the hallway towards the elevator, the thought popped into her head that she was always waiting for Rick. She waited for him to return calls, pick her up for dates, and, of course, marry her. When Rick made her wait, Dawn felt unappreciated.

What am I doing? Am I really complaining about a little waiting? I'm about to get engaged to Rick Stallings! Gorgeous, successful, rich Rick Stallings. Not only do we love each other, but the sex is amazing. A little waiting is a small price to pay so just get over it. I'm going to be Mrs. Dawn Stallings. My sisters don't know what they're talking about.

Sashaying off the elevator, Dawn's muscular legs glided her across the lobby as the short hem of her dress tickled her hamstrings. Rick whirled through the revolving doors and Dawn stopped short to take him all in. His ebony skin, chiseled features, 6'2" slender frame, broad swimmer's shoulders, perfectly tailored suit, and that smile—he was beautiful. Rick looked like he stepped off the cover of a men's magazine in his slate grey three-piece suit, crisp white dress shirt, and crimson pocket square. He kissed her softly on the lips, mindful not to smear her lipstick, and then hugged her close.

"You look fantastic," he whispered in her ear.

His Vetiver scent filled Dawn with desire. She felt so lucky, happy, and nervous, all at the same time. He escorted her to his exquisite silver Mercedes with gull-wing doors. She melted into the butter-soft seat and smiled. The night was off to a great start.

In the car, Rick rested his hand on Dawn's thigh as they covered the usual small-talk topics of weather and family. The restaurant was French, fabulous, and packed. Dawn and Rick were seated immediately and the chef even came out to greet them. Then the waiter brought a bottle of Veuve Clicquot champagne and two flutes to the table. Dawn loved that classic yellow label. Veuve was her favorite champagne. Rick preferred Cristal. Actually he preferred the taste of Veuve, but thought a bottle of Cristal was more in line with his image. *He ordered Veuve for me. That's a good sign.*

After telling her how fabulous she looked again and ordering his favorite baked onion soup, Rick got lost in his Blackberry. He didn't even offer a toast after the waiter poured the champagne. Thirty minutes later, Dawn's excitement had worn off. She couldn't wait until he finished this oil project because it was the most challenging and time-consuming project he'd worked on since they'd been together. Poking at her niçoise salad, Dawn realized this dinner wasn't going to make a good engagement story if Rick didn't get off his phone. She cleared her throat and looked impatiently at him.

"Sorry, Darling. Let me finish this one message and then I'm turning it off. The rest of the night is all about you." Rick's fingers moved at warp speed then powered off the phone. *He never turns his phone off. That's a good sign*. Rick tucked it in his pocket and looked directly at Dawn. They held each other's eyes. Rick leaned over and kissed Dawn passionately. Any reservations she had about spending the rest of her life with him melted away with that kiss. *I'll be the perfect wife and mother to our beautiful children. I could start looking for a job as a corporate attorney so my hours will be more nine-to-five. I would love to make partner, but I need to put our family first.*

"Darling, you really do look beautiful," Rick complimented sincerely.

"So do you. We're a good-looking couple," Dawn replied lovingly.

"Sorry again for being late. This oil refinery deal is a monster and it keeps morphing into more and more projects, but it's going to be huge. It's a lot more than I expected and, as usual, Brett isn't pulling his weight. If his father didn't have so much money invested in the firm, he wouldn't be a partner. He's such a waste. The only thing he's good at is entertaining clients."

"Brett's a playboy," Dawn chuckled.

"He's supposed to be making these trips to Houston, but it's all falling on me."

"Is the deal wrapping up soon? I'm starting to hate Houston and I was hoping we could plan a romantic getaway for next month."

"The biggest piece wrapped up tonight. There's still a lot more to do, but everything's going according to plan. Darling, I want to share my success with you. I know it's not easy with my crazy schedule, but you stick by me and are learning to be patient. I truly appreciate it. Let's toast our future." Rick's champagne flute clinked with Dawn's.

"Honey, I'm so proud of you." Dawn was giddy. The bubbles tickled her throat. Her heart pounded in her chest. *This is it! Candlelight, champagne, this is perfect! What a great engagement story*!

Rick continued, "And since absence makes the heart grow fonder, I know that our relationship will continue to grow stronger when I move to Houston to work on the second phase of this project."

Dawn was gobsmacked. "You're...*what?*" The sweet taste in her mouth turned bitter.

"The second part of this project; it's really intricate and our investors feel it's necessary to have the project point person, which is me, on the scene for the day-to-day operations. I should only be gone a year. You stay here because I know you're going to make partner this year. We'll do the long distance thing. Time will fly by." He shrugged casually and took a sip from his flute.

"Wait. You're moving to Houston?" Dawn's forehead crinkled. "So you, you aren't proposing?"

Rick's left eyebrow raised in surprise. He reached for Dawn's hand, but she flinched at his touch and jumped out of her chair. Shaking her head repeatedly, Dawn turned beet red. Looming over Rick, she pointed a French-manicured index finger at him.

"No. I object," Dawn shouted. *Whoosh*. All heads turned and all eyes goggled their table. "*I object to all of this*. I've given you three of the best years of my life. I made it crystal clear that I want to get married. I asked you for an engagement timeline, but you told me to be patient. Now, you unilaterally decide to move to Houston, without me. Who the hell do you think you are? *I adamantly object to this bullshit*!"

"I suggest you sit down," Rick demanded.

"I suggest you enjoy your damn soup." Dawn threw onion soup in Rick's lap. All the female diners cheered and clapped as Dawn grabbed her purse and stormed out of the restaurant, indignant but vindicated.

"Dawn. Dawn!" The snap of Rick's fingers cut into her daydream. Dawn blinked hard, surprised at the onion soup still sitting half-eaten in front of Rick. She look around the restaurant, wondering if anyone else could see her heart breaking, but no one acknowledged her. She now understood how a woman could be so enraged with her man that she created a public spectacle, but Dawn wasn't the type of woman who created public spectacles.

"So you, you aren't proposing?" Dawn repeated.

"Darling, I love you. I do." Rick cleared his throat. "But I'm not sure that we're ready for marriage. In fact, I think some time apart will be good for us."

Dawn's chin quivered. She slid forward in her chair to lean toward Rick. "Are we breaking up?"

"No, no." Rick cleared his throat again. "But I was thinking we could see other people while I'm in Houston. It'll help us decide if we're right for each other." Just then the waiter interrupted with their entrees. The tension at the table was thick. He quickly placed the plates, refilled the glasses, and excused himself. "What do you think, Dawn?"

"I think we're right for each other. I don't need to date anybody else to know that."

"Don't you want to make sure you aren't settling to be with me?"

"Do you think you're settling with me?"

"I'm not saying that. I'm not sure I'm ready to get married, but I think the space and perspective of an open relationship will help me figure it out."

"When are you moving?"

"In two weeks."

"Do I have a say in this?"

"The move, no. The relationship, we need to discuss."

Dawn opened her mouth, but no words came out. She slid back in her chair limply as Rick watched her. They sat in silence. Finally he picked up his fork and began eating. She felt like she needed to say something else, but no words came to mind. She blinked back her tears, picked up her fork, and ate.

Shrouded in silence, the meal and the car ride home moved in slow motion. Dawn watched buildings and pedestrians drone by as she kept asking herself, *How did I get here? Really, how did I end up in this situation? I'm successful, beautiful, caring, and loving. I'm a wonderful daughter and sister. Why is he doing this to me?*

Rick's car pulled into the circular driveway of her building and he parked in front. "An open relationship will be good for us," Rick said.

Dawn sighed loudly and looked over at Rick. *I love him. Why doesn't he want to marry me?* She pushed the automatic door opener and let herself out of the car. Though she was a litigator, Dawn was at a loss for words. The idea of starting over at twenty-nine was terrifying. As she waited for the elevator, she did the math in her head. With her break-up rule of at least two months of healing for each year together, that would be six months to recover if she broke up with Rick. Another one to two years to find a new boyfriend, then date him for three years, be married at least two years before trying to get pregnant. If she and Rick broke up, the best-case scenario for finding someone new and having a family put Dawn in her late thirties. That didn't work for her.

Maybe I should wait for Rick. He can be insensitive, but he does love me. He's just confused and afraid of commitment—like most men. Maybe he's right about me being more patient. But maybe my sisters are right and Rick's never going to marry me.

Dawn unlocked her condo door and caught the tail end of a message from Carlisa, wanting to know how the dinner went. Dawn rolled her eyes at the answering machine, retrieved a bottle of tequila from her freezer and poured herself a double. *The twins are going to have a field day with this story. Another dress, another disappointment.* She took a gulp from her glass, closed her eyes, and savored the oaky flavor of the smooth liquor. Then she pulled the red dress over her head, grabbed a plastic garbage bag from the pantry, and made a beeline for her closet. She snatched the white Grecian and black scoop-neck dresses off their hangers and stuffed all three non-engagement dress disasters in the bag. In her red bra and panties, she went back to the front door, flung it open, and threw the bag down the hallway. *Maybe someone else will want them. I can't believe this happened to me again.* She slammed her door shut and leaned against it, heavy with disappointment.

Dawn limped back to her bedroom and kicked her stilettos under the bed. Her breath shortened. Her head pounded. *He's moving to Houston and wants an open relationship.* Climbing into bed, she pulled the covers over her head, and yelled at the top of her lungs, "Why doesn't he want to marry me?" The duvet stifled her wails until she cried herself asleep.

CHAPTER 5

Fr: <Meghan>
To: <Frank>
Saturday, April 18, 2009 9:09PM
Subject: really?

I had dinner with your sister last night. Why haven't you told your family? Can you ever tell the truth? When are you moving?

Fr: <Frank>
To: <Meghan>
Sunday, April 19, 2009 7:25AM
Subject: RE: really?

Moved last week. What did you tell her?

Fr: <Meghan>
To: <Frank>
Sunday, April 19, 2009 7:27AM
Subject: RE: really?

Nothing. You need to do that. What did you do with your keys? Did you lock up?

Fr: <Frank>
To: <Meghan>
Sunday, April 19, 2009 7:31AM
Subject: RE: really?

On the table by the door and put the bottom lock on. Sorry.

***

Six months ago, Meghan Cherry-Henderson separated from her husband and moved into her parents' home. The months felt like years as she waited in vain for Frank to call. Too embarrassed to tell anyone, Meghan isolated herself from her friends and coworkers. She only went to work and sulked around the house. A couple of months ago, Mama Cherry made a request. "Meg, I'm going to hire you to redecorate your room. It's time we updated your bedroom and you've got such a good eye. Let me know how much it's going to cost."

"I can't take your money. And I don't feel very creative," Meghan whined. "Baby, you need a project. You need to get your mind off Frank and get your creative juices flowing. I need a decorator and I'm giving you a budget. You can't say no to your mother."

Looking around her childhood room, Meghan knew of all her design projects, this was one of her best. Monet's garden series was the inspiration. Walls painted creekside green served as a tranquil canvas for a collection of Giverny garden prints. Meghan dressed the queen-sized bed with an ornate gold comforter and flanked each side with curvy, tortoise-gold nightstands. Clinquant grape pillows and wine-colored vases created contrast with the gentle walls and made the vibrant purple, red, and green brushstrokes in the art pop. From concept to finish, it had only taken her a month to complete. Life's tragedy was art's inspiration.

I can't believe what an asshole Frank is. He didn't call for Thanksgiving, Christmas, New Year's, or my birthday. He didn't tell me he moved out of the condo. He hasn't told his family we're getting a divorce. Not that I'm surprised. He never told me anything when we were together. He didn't tell me he was pissing away our money, he didn't tell me why he never wanted to have sex anymore, and the final straw was that he didn't tell me he would do whatever it took to keep our family together.

The first five months of the separation, Meghan defined her days as awful or miserable. Lately, her outlook had brightened to bad or crappy. But today, a combination of the dreary weather and an unpleasant email exchange with her estranged husband had relapsed Meghan to the overwhelming sadness of her worst days. She wondered if her depression had caused the heavy rains and dark clouds or vice versa. It was a classic chicken-or-egg debate, and ironically, those were the very things her parents were eating right now.

Every Sunday after church, her parents faithfully went to Anand. Her mom always ordered the bacon, tomato, and avocado omelet and her dad never strayed from the watermelon-glazed chicken. They were already disappointed this morning when Meghan decided not to join them.

Before they left for church, Mama Cherry came to check on Meghan, who was still in bed. Mama Cherry sat on the edge of the bed, stroked Meghan's back, and said, "I really wish you would come with us."

"Sorry, Mama. I'm not in the mood."

"Baby, I'll never forget the time we went to Fort Lauderdale and you saw a palm tree. You said you wanted to be as tall as that tree when you grew up."

Meghan forced a smile. "I remember. Those trees are so pretty."

"Do you remember when we learned why palm trees grow in Florida?"

"No," Meghan mumbled into her pillow.

"Because monsoons and hurricanes can blow other trees away or snap them in two, but not palm trees. They bend, but they don't break. Flexibility allows a palm tree to bend all the way to the ground and weather the storm gracefully. When the storm is over, it straightens up and is actually stronger. You're in the midst of a storm. Know that you were made to bend and not break. You too will flourish."

"So I can still be a palm tree when I grow up?"

"That's right, Baby. Now, you're not going to make church, but meet us at brunch."

"I'll try."

Mama Cherry kissed Meghan on the forehead and left for church with Papa Cherry. Meghan didn't feel flexible. She and her heart were broken. So broken she didn't have any more tears to cry. All morning, she just lay in bed and stared at the Monet print.

Movement downstairs interrupted the silence. Her parents were home from the brunch she was supposed to attend. They were worried enough already. The sight of her catatonic state and unkempt hair would give them even more gray hair before their time. Meghan took a deep breath, closed her eyes tight, and prayed for strength. She finally pushed the covers back and crawled out of bed. Scowling at her reflection in the full-length mirror kitty-corner from her bedroom door, she hated how fat she looked in her favorite paisley print pajamas.

"They never fit this tight before. Stupid divorce weight," she spat at the mirror before heading off to shower. Meghan put on a touch of makeup and a loose-fitting animal print dress. She used to wear it with a belt to show off her curves. She had never been a thin girl, but she was proud of her shapely size-ten body. The stress of the divorce had ballooned her to a size fourteen and nothing in her closet fit right anymore. With Frank tapping out their savings and not paying their bills, Meghan couldn't afford to buy new clothes at her favorite boutique shops. She squeezed into whatever she could and purchased larger-size clothes at thrift stores. She was lucky she had always been a great bargain shopper with a talent for finding stylish items on a tight budget.

She quietly descended the stairs. The hardwood floors felt cool on her bare feet. Lingering on the bottom step, Meghan watched her parents. Even in the midst of her calamity, seeing them together filled her with joy and love. After thirty-six years of marriage, they were still so in love and comfortable with each other. Her mom sat on a high stool at the kitchen island thumbing through recipe books as her dad doctored up their coffees.

"Taste this, Baby. I'm trying something new." Papa Cherry placed a terra cotta cup in front of his wife and waited with eager eyes.

"Mmmm, delicious. With a hint of ..." Mama Cherry sipped again. "... hazelnut?"

Papa Cherry planted two long kisses on his wife's lips. "You get one for being right and one for being so beautiful."

"If I told you I was making pan-seared tuna with jalapeño, avocado, and mango chutney for dinner, what else would I get?"

"Taken upstairs." Papa Cherry yanked at his wife's skirt while she laughed.

Meghan cleared her throat loudly. "There's a child in the room," Meghan announced.

"Hey, Love. Do you want some coffee and watermelon chicken? I got you an order to go. It's in the oven and still warm if you eat it now," Papa Cherry said.

"Yes and yes! I'm sorry I missed church and brunch. How was service?" Meghan retrieved the Styrofoam container from the oven and some silverware from the drawer before sitting on the high stool next to her mother at the kitchen island. Papa Cherry poured another cup of coffee before continuing.

"The minister preached on the story of Joseph and how his brothers sold him into slavery. That injustice turned out to be the first link in a chain that made him a powerful ruler of Egypt. What they meant for evil, God meant for good. You may not figure out the good right away, but stay encouraged and faithful. Time will bring the lesson and the blessing." He set a cup of coffee in front of Meghan and kissed her on the forehead.

"Thanks, Papa. I needed to hear that." Meghan smiled weakly at her father.

"Did you talk to Frank?" Papa Cherry asked.

"He emailed me that he moved last week," Meghan said in between bites of food.

"Are you going to move back to that condo?"

"Yeah. It'll be easy because I just have to move my clothes. I think I'll go back tomorrow night after work."

"Oh, we're going to miss you. Are you sure his sister doesn't know you're separated?"

"Positive. She asked me for gift ideas for his birthday."

"You couldn't get out of going to dinner with her?"

"I ran into her when I was leaving work. I didn't have to go to dinner, but I wanted to. I love Frank's family. They've always been so nice to me. Once they find out, we may never talk again and even if we do, it won't be the same. I wanted to have one last pleasant memory." Meghan's chin quivered and a tear rolled down her cheek. She set her fork down, dabbed her eyes with her paper towel, and blew her nose. "I hate this. I hate having the saddies and crying all the time. I hate worrying you guys."

Papa Cherry embraced Meghan. "Baby Girl, you're not worrying us. We love you and we love having you here. It makes it easier for us to check on you. We'll get through this together. Stay here with your mother and me as long as you need. Hell, you don't have to move back to that condo right away." He kissed her forehead again before releasing her.

Mama Cherry closed her recipe book. "Meg, your dad and I were wondering if you had decided to file your divorce papers. We're not rushing you, but we want to make sure you're making progress and not getting stuck. Like I always say, if you're in hell, keep going."

Meghan turned her head to look at her mother, seated next to her. "Everything is signed and notarized. My do-it-yourself-divorce book says all I need to do now is file the paperwork, get a court date, and that's it."

"Are you going to keep the name Henderson? It's been six years so I understand if you keep it, but…Never mind. It's your decision." Mama Cherry shooed the question away with her hand.

"I'm changing back to Meghan Cherry," Meghan answered.

"Oh, good. I mean, it's your call, but I completely agree." Mama Cherry nodded her head.

"Why would I keep Frank's last name? It's been months and he hasn't called once. It's time to close this chapter of my life. I'm going to the courthouse to file the papers tomorrow. I can go on my lunch."

"You shouldn't go alone. I'll meet you there." Mama Cherry patted Meghan's hand.

"Thanks, Mama."

"Your papa and I were also thinking you need to get out of this house. Isn't there a Sunday-night party you used to go to with your friend from work?"

"I'm not in the mood to party." Meghan picked up her fork and took another bite of chicken.

"Honey, you need a change of scenery. Hanging out with us will make you old before your time," Mama Cherry continued.

"Divorce is making me old. Actually, that's not true. It's having a weird regressive effect. I'm back to college me. My face is covered with pimples and I've added a freshman fifteen. I'm too fat and ugly to go anywhere." Meghan stuffed another piece of chicken in her mouth.

"Honey, sometimes it helps to go out. Get some fresh air. See new people. Get back out there," Mama Cherry encouraged and looked at her husband for support. He nodded in agreement.

"New people are fine. It's the old people I'm worried about. They always ask 'How's married life?' I'm still telling everyone the 'happy wife, happy life' lie," Meghan explained.

"Tell them the truth. Get it over with," Mama Cherry recommended.

"I hate telling people bad news. Everywhere I go, I'm a rain cloud threatening to ruin someone's good day," Meghan sighed with exhaustion. "I'm not ready to tell anyone else and I don't feel like going anywhere."

"Baby, whenever you're ready. How's your chicken?" Mama Cherry changed the subject.

"Delicious. Thanks guys. I love you." Meghan smiled at her parents and wished their support was enough to take away the pain in her heart.

Chapter 6

Fr: <EastLake Condo Association>
To: <Meghan Henderson>
Saturday, April 25, 2009 1:25PM
Subject: assessments for Unit 805

Thank you for your inquiry. Your account is $3,000 in arrears and there is currently a lien on your unit. Please advise if you can make the account current with a lump sum payment or if you need to work out a payment plan.

Fr: <Meghan Cherry>
To: <EastLake Condo Association>
Saturday, April 25, 2009 2:56PM
Subject: RE: assessments for Unit 805

I'm going to need a payment plan and can you update the name on my account and mailbox to Meghan Cherry. Thanks.

* * *

GET MY LIFE BACK ON TRACK LIST

1. ~~Finalize Divorce~~
2. ~~Move back into condo~~
3. Cure my insomnia and acne
4. Figure out my finances
5. Lose 15 pounds / Work out ☹

Lying on her living room couch late into another sleepless night, Meghan cocooned herself in a blanket and flipped through stale re-runs and bad commercials. Moving back into the condo had been easy since she had only taken clothes and toiletries to her parent's house. Sleeping through the night was a different story.

Another Lunesta commercial made Meghan glance at the notebook on the coffee table open to her "Get My Life Back on Track" list. *That's the tenth Lunesta commercial I've seen tonight! How can it help you sleep well with all those potential side effects? My doctor wanted me to take Lunesta and Xanax when I first separated from Frank. I had just stopped taking the pill and she wanted me to add two more drugs. I know I get depressed and can't sleep, but I'm not taking those drugs. No thanks. But I wonder if I should try Proactiv. The products are expensive but they worked for Jessica Simpson and Diddy and they never endorse anything. Wait, that's not true. They endorse everything. I can't trust those stupid infomercials. But I gotta do something about this acne and I gotta get some sleep.*

Meghan flipped the channel to HGTV. A new show was just beginning. The pretty host smiled sweetly at the camera and said, "Feng shui is the ancient Chinese art of placement and aesthetics. The goal is to enhance the flow of good energy and create a harmonious, prosperous, and healthy environment. When we feng shui our home, we feng shui our life." The host accentuated her last sentence with an arm flourish.

Meghan rolled her eyes and reached for the remote. Before she could flip channels, the host continued, "Do you need to get a good night's sleep? Are you recently divorced? Does your sex life need a little pick-me-up? Then this show is for you. Grab a notebook and get ready to feng shui your bedroom right after this message from our sponsors."

How does she know all that about me? Meghan dropped the remote in her lap, cocked her head to the side and stared at the screen in disbelief. Picking up the notebook and a pencil from the table, she added Feng shui my life? as the sixth item on her list. The Lunesta and Restless Leg Syndrome commercials couldn't end fast enough.

When the show returned, the perky host was standing in the middle of a messy bedroom. "Decorating with feng shui principles can balance the energy flow of your home and ultimately your life. A bedroom should be a peaceful haven; a relaxing retreat for rest and romance. Look at this room." The host scrunched her nose in disapproval before continuing. "A messy room signals a messy mind. This bedroom needs a feng shui makeover pronto.

"The first thing we're going to do is clear the clutter. From a feng shui perspective, clutter symbolizes unfinished business and impedes forward progress in life. Since less is more, move out unnecessary furniture, throw away any stacks of paper, and clear off your messy bookshelf." Poof. With TV magic, the clutter and various pieces of furniture disappeared. She nodded her approval at the changes. "Items in the room that have negative memories and associations are also a form of clutter. That includes pictures and mementos from past relationships and furniture purchased with your ex." Poof. The pictures on the wall and more furniture disappeared. "Okay, it's looking much better in here. Come back after the break and we'll tackle the next feng shui phase."

Meghan sat up and looked around her condo. There was six months of unopened mail on the side table by the couch, wedding pictures on the wall, and all of the furniture represented a memory from the marriage. *I really need to feng shui*. Meghan changed the feng shui question mark to an exclamation point in her notebook, then flipped to a clean page and scribbled notes from the TV show.

"And we're back. The next thing we want to discuss is color. Paint is so important because wall color affects your mood. Feng shui your walls by painting them with rich earth colors like terra cotta, cream, tan and cocoa to create a warm, cozy feeling. Water colors like light blues and greens create a quiet, calming energy. Infuse red and pink accents to increase the romance and passion in the room." Poof. The stark white walls were transformed to a soft buttercream color and crimson bolster pillows appeared on the bed. "I like it. Now, let's move on to furniture placement. Since the bed is usually the biggest piece of furniture in the room, it must be placed with the upmost care and consideration. Feng shui experts recommend that the bed be placed as far away from the bedroom door as possible." Poof. The bed flipped to the opposite wall. "That looks great. We're making fantastic progress and now we need to make this bedroom a sanctuary; a place where you can shut out the outside world. Ringing phones, exercise gear, blaring televisions are all distractions from the rest and relaxation you desire. I recommend removing all these items from the room. Hey, don't look at me like that. I'm not crazy, just crazy for feng shui." The host laughed at her own joke. Meghan rolled her eyes again, but continued feverishly jotting down notes.

"If you just can't part with your distractions, then let's at least minimize them. Can you turn off the ringer at night, put your exercise bike behind a folding screen, and keep your TV in an armoire so you can *shut the door* on it while you sleep? I think you can. Feng shui isn't difficult and it doesn't have to be expensive. Even if you can't afford new furniture, you can rearrange your existing furniture and clean up for free. You'll thank me in your dreams." The host flashed her perfect smile then gave a few more tips for the bedroom and some brief recommendations on feng shui'ing the other rooms in your home. When the show ended, Meghan's notes filled up an entire page. And since she couldn't sleep, she decided to get to work.

Meghan walked from room to room, inventorying all of her ex's leave-behinds and contemplating how to increase the positive energy flow of her home. *Everything, every room, every piece of furniture reminds me of Frank. We decorated and painted this condo together. He may have moved out, but his presence is everywhere. It's no wonder I can't sleep.*

Meghan decided to start with the master bedroom. When Frank moved out, he took his clothes, his poker chips, and the flatscreen TV, which he feng shui'ed right out of the bedroom. On the dresser, there was a framed photo of them taken the first night they met. Meghan picked it up and stared at the young, happy couple.

Frank was a stockbroker. Meghan was an IT person by trade, but an artist and interior designer at heart. They met at an art gallery at a showing of one of her favorite abstract artists who was also one of Frank's clients. Meghan loved telling the story. *Our eyes met over a platter of brie and crackers and we spent the rest of the night talking and laughing.*

In many ways, Frank was Meghan's opposite. Meghan was a laid-back, artsy, and shy only child. Frank was a jovial, corporate, and gregarious middle child with five siblings. Meghan's ideal evening was a home-cooked meal, cuddling on the couch and watching a movie with Frank. Frank loved to take Meghan out for a night on the town. Meghan was a responsible straight arrow while Frank was a fly-by-the-seat-of-his-pants dreamer. Though they were very different, Meghan always thought they worked because they completed and balanced each other. Without Frank, Meghan would probably never leave the house. Without

Meghan, Frank would never eat a green vegetable.

They moved into the EastLake Condos three years ago and it took a full year, but Meghan transformed the stark white walls of their three-bedroom condo into wonderful works of art. Frank was there every step of the way, encouraging her and supporting her. Meghan poured all her artistic energy and vision into the design and Frank helped turn her dreams into reality.

After Meghan did such a fantastic job decorating their condo, Frank strongly encouraged her to quit her information technology job and go to interior design school full-time. Meghan was hesitant because they couldn't afford their condo and lifestyle on just one salary. She wanted to wait a couple of years. Frank said the time was now and to prove it to Meghan he upped his casual poker playing to high-stakes gaming. His goal was to double their savings, but the plan went astray. The more he gambled, the more he lost.

Each month, instead of helping Meghan achieve her dream, he squandered his paychecks, drained their savings, and lied to cover his gambling addiction. It took too long for Meghan to figure out something was wrong. She was great with technology and colors, but finances weren't her strong suit. For two years, he kept it all hidden until Meghan could no longer pretend that the declined credit cards, insistent collection calls, and bright-red disconnection notices weren't signs of a bigger problem. She was devastated, especially when Frank wouldn't stop gambling. He kept promising to get help, but never did. Meghan tried to make the marriage work, but after years of mounting debts, lies, and broken trust, she had finally had enough.

I can't afford new furniture or paint. Plus I love all the stuff I have so I guess I'll get started moving it all around. Meghan worked all night. Every piece of furniture was rearranged. Every bill and financial statement was collected in a box. When Meghan finally finished, the sun was rising on a new day. *The feng shui worked. It looks like a new place. The energy is so different. I wonder if Frank would like it. Stop it. Don't think about him. Think about all the bills he didn't pay. I should call in sick and figure out how much I owe and how I'm going to pay it back. Then I can go to the gym. It's time to get back on track.*

At her dining room table, it took hours to sort through all the bills and paperwork. The sight of those scarlet "payment past due" stamps made her sick to her stomach. Frank had promised to bring all the bills current before he moved out, but gamblers can only be counted on for two things: losing and lying. From Meghan's calculations, the outstanding bills exceeded $50,000. On one income, Meghan could barely afford the household bills. She didn't know how she was going to bring the mortgage, assessment, and credit cards current and still afford groceries. Frank had always handled the finances. Meghan hadn't looked at this stuff in six years. In hindsight, she wished she hadn't given up total control to Frank.

IDEAS TO SAVE MONEY

- Cancel the cable
- Disconnect the home phone
- No shopping
- Take the bus to work
- Clip coupons
- Brown bag lunches
- ~~No more Skinny Vanilla Lattes~~ Only three Skinny Vanilla Lattes a week

The ringing of her home phone interrupted her thoughts. Meghan left the financial disaster on her dining room table to find the phone on her sofa. Checking the caller ID, she recognized her mother's work number. *I really don't want to cancel my home phone. I hate talking on that cell phone too long*. She plopped on the sofa and answered the phone. "Hey, Mama."

"Hey, Baby. I called your job and got your out-of-office message. Are you okay? What are you doing at home?" Mama Cherry asked. Meghan could imagine the worry lines on Mama Cherry's forehead.

"I was up all night rearranging my furniture and figuring out how much debt Frank left me."

"Oh, Baby. How bad is it?" Mama Cherry groaned.

"Bad enough. I have to figure something out."

"If you need to borrow some money, your Papa and I can help."

"I don't want to do that. You guys have done enough. Mama, how could I make such a huge mistake marrying Frank?" Meghan's voice cracked.

"Life has no mistakes; just opportunities for growth. You're going to come out the other side of this smarter, stronger, and better. You had a starter marriage. Now you know what you want and don't want. You're my hero."

"Why? 'Cause I married the wrong man and got a divorce? I feel so stupid."

"You took a chance on love. It didn't work out. But you knew you were unhappy, and you left. All of that takes courage."

"When am I going to stop feeling like I'm going crazy? I'm sad, mad, lonely, and pissed all at the same time. Sometimes I want to call Frank and tell him what a jerk he is. Sometimes, I miss him so bad I think my heart's going to explode. But mostly, I want to crawl into my bed and cry myself to sleep." Meghan fought to hold back her tears.

"It'll get better, but it's going to take time. Papa and I are always here for you. And if you want to move back home, our door is always open."

"I know. But I've settled in here and I need to start piecing my life together. I can't hide at your house forever."

"I miss seeing you. At least come over for dinner tonight. I'm grilling grouper and serving it with a side of black beans and avocado," Mama Cherry said.

"Mama, one day you're going to turn into an avocado."

"Avocado adds a touch of decadence to everything. Like bacon, it makes everything better. Are you coming for dinner?"

"Yes, sounds delicious. Frank loved your grouper. I should call him and rub it in his face." Meghan snorted.

"I'm not sure if you're joking or not, but it's not a good idea to call Frank."

"I'm joking, kind of. Sometimes I really want to call him."

"Call me or Papa or one of your friends. Have you told any of them about the divorce yet?"

"No, it's too uncomfortable. I just can't right now," Meghan said.

"Keeping a secret this big is very stressful, and stress can make you gain weight and break out."

"I hear you, Mama. I'll think about it. Thanks for everything. I love you. You're my hero."

"I love you too. See you later."

"Okay. Bye."

Meghan hung up the phone. Usually her mother's pep talks helped, but this time she didn't feel any better. Surveying the financial mess in black, white, and red, her heart felt heavy with worry and contradictions. She hated Frank, but she missed her best friend. She wanted to call her friends and pour her heart out, but she felt too embarrassed by her divorce and debt. Since the finances were sorted, Meghan knew she should go to the gym, but her newly feng shui'ed bedroom and a box of tissues were calling her name and she didn't have the strength to refuse the invitation.

May

Chapter 7

Text Message to Button
Fr: Mike
Friday, May 1, 2009 8:10 PM
Cum over

Text Message to Mike
Fr: Button
Friday, May 1, 2009 8:13 PM
On my way

***

Button toweled off in the steamy warmth of the bathroom and massaged cocoa butter into her soft skin. She smiled to herself as she recalled Half's nickname for her, Cocoa Button. The aromatic scent was the only thing she wore as she strolled back into Mike's bedroom. It was the typical twenty-five-year-old jock's room. Cluttered, but clean, the walls and shelves were filled with sports memorabilia, trophies, and pictures. Mike sat up in his bed texting away on his phone, as usual.

Button stood in the doorway and admired him. The sight of his bulging pecs and biceps made her entire body shudder with pleasure. The sheets were soaked with perspiration and the air was filled with satisfaction. His body was absolute perfection, as it should be since he worked out six days a week and was a personal trainer at her gym. He was 205lbs, 6'1" and if he had any body fat, she'd yet to see it…and she'd seen everything. Every muscle was chiseled with definition. Button's favorite body part, his washboard abs, made her weak and he knew it. When he saw her at the gym, he always found a way to lift his shirt and give her a sneak peek. With his sexy gray eyes, full lips, and zigzag cornrows, Mike was sexy with a little thug thrown in. They eyed each other at the gym for a couple of months until he offered her a free personal training session. Button didn't need any help with her workouts, but she quickly accepted.

Her complimentary session was charged with sexual tension. His hands kept brushing her breasts and ass and she just smiled at him. The last ten minutes of the workout, he stretched her on the massage table. His hands were firm and experienced, and told her loud and clear that he was amazing in bed. With the session winding down, Button whispered in a sultry voice, "This feels so good. I don't want it to end."

"I could come over to your house later and really work out the knots in your neck," he offered, a devilish grin crossing his luscious lips. "Would you like that?"

"I would. What time?" Button inquired mischievously.

"I'll be there at ten."

"I'll be naked at quarter to." Button hopped off the massage table and felt his eyes follow her every step toward the locker room.

That first night, Mike sat at the island in Button's kitchen rolling a joint and telling stories about the quirky characters at the gym. He wasn't just a thug with a hot body, he was smart and entertaining. Button sat next to him and sipped a Hennessy and cranberry cocktail and watched his lips as he talked. She bet his tongue was as limber and powerful as his hands. Shifting in her stool, her silk robe brushed her nipple and she was overcome with desire.

"How old are you?" she interrupted his story.

"Old enough. Nice robe. What you got on under?" He winked.

"A knot, in my neck?"

"Lemme handle that." Mike slid off his stool and came up behind her. Massaging her neck and back through her thin robe, he stroked and kneaded Button's frenzy. His hands drove her crazy. Finally, he turned her around on the stool and his kiss confirmed Button's suspicion. Sensual and aggressive, their tongues danced and played with the emotion of an Argentinean tango. In a swift motion, he untied the robe and it floated to the floor. She pulled his t-shirt over his head and admired his six-pack abs. He kissed her again until she moaned in pleasure.

Mike asked, "Where's your bedroom?"

"Down the hallway, last door." Button's eyes lit up.

Mike carried her down the hall as if she were lighter than a feather. Button didn't know if it was the weed, Hennessy, or his sexual prowess, but sex with Mike was a sensory overload. It made good girls go bad and back again. Afterwards he took a shower and left; which Button also liked. With each encounter, Mike proved his consistent ability to please; three days of cardio and three days of weights every week did wonders for a man's endurance.

For the past year, Mike cemented himself in the role as "Quarter" on Button's team and of all the men that had filled the role, he was her favorite. The Quarter was responsible for two equally important functions: 1) providing no-strings-attached, amazing sex, which meant no dating and no excessive kissing and 2) providing physical interference to keep Button from getting too attached to whoever was her Half-boyfriend, a role currently filled by Henry.

Button smiled at Quarter in his bed, then sorted through the pile of clothes on the floor and put her bra on.

Quarter looked up from his phone and asked, "Whatcha doing?"

"Uhhhh, getting dressed," Button pointed out the obvious.

"B, it's late and you've worn a brother out. I'm too tired to walk you to your car. Stay." Quarter patted the empty space next to him. "I'll make you breakfast in the morning."

"I do love your eggs, but I want to sleep in my own bed. Plus when I stay here, I never make my Saturday spin class. Please walk me to my car," Button begged.

Quarter's face transformed to a sexy pout. "I'll wake up you up early. Stay, B. Sometimes a thug likes to cuddle too."

Button turned her head to look at Quarter incredulously, "Don't tell me you're getting soft?"

"It's not about being soft. It's about knowing what I like and doing it again in the morning. I know my role on the team. On the real, I'm tired as fuck. Get yo' fine azz over here and let Quarter get his spoon on. And take those clothes off. You know you gotta be naked to sleep in this bed."

Button reached for her shirt. Quarter made his pecs jump until she rolled her eyes, laughed and finally tossed her clothes back on the floor. He set his phone on the side table and scooted down in the bed until he was lying on his back. He reached for her and she curled her body into him; her stomach against his side, her leg wrapped around his, and her head nestled in the nook of his neck. Button inhaled his musky scent. "What's the name of your cologne? I love it."

"I want you." Quarter whispered and closed his arm around her.

"I thought you just wanted to spoon." Button glanced up at him.

"That's the name of my cologne and this feels nice. Why you always trying to leave?" Quarter kissed her forehead. His phone vibrated on the table with multiple text messages.

Button laughed. "Not like you'll be lonely."

"So, I like hanging out with you."

"Yeah, me too."

"I almost called you the other day. I wanted to see how your girlfriend mission was going. That shit is hilarious."

"Called me? I didn't think you knew how to make phone calls. All you do is text."

"That's why I didn't call. Knew it'd freak you out. You find a bestie yet?"

"No bestie yet. I don't think I'm the girlfriend kind of girl."

"That's bullshit. It's a good idea. You should do it. Just make sure I still get to see your brown azz at least twice a week." Mike smacked Button's butt. She giggled and thought about how lucky she was to have assembled such a good team. Silently, she said her goodnight prayer and asked God to look after her Mama, Half, and Quarter. Amen.

* * *

I knew Quarter wouldn't let me go to class this morning. Not that I minded the workout. He's such a Rock Star in bed. But next time I'm going to miss spin class, I should text Davis and let him know. Button was at the mailbox station in her condo building, thumbing through her mail.

"Davis missed you in class?" Button's thoughts were interrupted by a voice. She hadn't noticed the woman in the mailroom with her. Button turned the key to lock her box and looked at the woman, perplexed."Excuse me?"

"In spin class…this morning. He saved your bike in the front. That annoying lady who claps through the whole class wanted to use it, but he told her unless her name was Button Jackson she better not sit on that bike."

"What?" Button clipped.

"Spin class at the gym. You always take the bike in the front center. I like the back row."

"Are you kidding?" Button sized up the woman addressing her. She was petite with a slight thickness about her. Her straight, shoulder-length hair framed her caramel-colored, heart-shaped face. In a funky, tie-dyed fuschia top falling off one shoulder, denim leggings, and yellow Chuck Taylors, she reminded Button of *Flashdance*. "I get it." Button laughed hard. "Quarter put you up to this. Very funny."

"Quarter? No, I'm your neighbor...and I'm bothering you. Never mind," Meghan's cheeks burned as she slammed her mailbox door and hurried to the elevator.

Last night, Meghan spent another lonely Friday night drowning her sorrows in glasses of White Zinfandel. Still not ready to tell her old friends about the divorce and deciding that desperate times called for desperate measures, she added "Make a New Friend" to her get-back-on-track list. As the elevator ascended, Meghan thought about how she saw Button all the time. It was hard not to notice her. Button was tall, beautiful, and always dressed to the nines, even at the gym. She had a confident air about her that commanded attention when she walked into a room. Meghan knew Button was probably one of the popular girls in high school who only knew girls like Meghan existed when borrowing her homework or cheating off her test.

What the hell was I doing? I'm too old to make new friends. Women in their thirties don't make new friends. I'm supposed to be enjoying all the friends I made in my twenties. Striking up a conversation with Button was risky, but Meghan had decided to go for it anyway. What did she have to lose? *My dignity*. Meghan turned her key in the lock of her condo door.

Button's face was red with anger. *I can't believe he set me up*. She pulled her cell phone from her purse and called Quarter.

"B, I don't know what you're talking about," he said over the phone.

"You think I'm so pathetic that I can't make my own friends."

"What?"

"The thick, artsy chick from my spin class who just chatted me up in the mailroom. I don't know how you figured out we lived in the same building, but that was weird. I don't need you to set me up."

"Though I wouldn't mind seeing you in some girl-on-girl action, I didn't do anything, for real."

"So...she was just making small talk."

"Guess so. What'd you say to your new bestie?"

"No comment."

"Went that well?"

"Worse."

"Listen, this yo' shot. Go find her and make a friend. Start with something like 'Nice to meet you.' Call me back. Let me know how it goes."

"Call you back?"

"Yeah, this talking on the phone is awight. Good luck, B."

Button ended the call on her cell phone. She felt terrible. She couldn't believe she had laughed in that poor woman's face. Quarter was right. This was her shot. She went back to the mailbox station and looked at the woman's mailbox. Meghan Cherry lived in unit 805. Button made a quick stop to her penthouse, grabbed a bottle from her wine cooler, and then headed to the eighth floor.

Shocked at the sight of Button in her peephole, Meghan opened the door hesitantly. Before she could say a word, Button began, "I'm sorry for offending you. Really, sorry. I swear I wasn't laughing at you. I was...There was a miscommunication."

"Oh. It's fine. I caught you off guard. Don't worry about it." Meghan waved Button off and smiled unconvincingly as she started to shut her door.

"Wait, Meghan. It's nice to meet you," Button said robotically.

"Actually Button, we met last summer at the residents' barbecue. We sat next to each other."

She thought for a second and then remembered. "Right, I sat next to you and your husband. He wanted to organize a poker night fundraiser to keep assessments down. I thought it was a good idea. How is he?"

Meghan shifted her weight and her cheeks flushed. "I don't know. We're d-divorced," Meghan said stumbling over the word divorce. She hated that word. She hated saying it. And mostly she hated that now it applied to her.

"I'm sorry." Button held up a bottle of her favorite champagne, Veuve Cliquot. "I brought this for you." Button handed the chilled bottle to Meghan.

Meghan leaned in to Button and whispered conspiratorially, "Do you think it's mean to celebrate my divorce?"

"Celebrating a divorce is mean. Celebrating a new beginning is essential."

Meghan took a moment to consider Button's words. "I like that. Would you join me? If you pop the cork, I'll get the glasses," Meghan handed the bottle back to Button and opened her front door wide.

"My pleasure." Button followed Meghan through the living room and gasped, "I love your accent wall. It's hard to pull off red, but the sponge technique makes it work."

"When I first painted the red color, I didn't like it. It was too bright so I sponged a beige glaze on top to soften it. I love it now." Meghan beamed.

Meghan turned into the kitchen and Button gasped again.

"What?" Meghan turned around quickly.

"I've never seen a blue kitchen before. It's fabulous." Button stared admiringly.

"Thanks, decorating is my passion and I like to push the color envelope. I designed and painted every room."

"I'm impressed." Button walked over to the sink, peeled the foil from the bottle's nape, and popped the cork of the champagne in one fluid motion.

"How'd you that so fast?" Meghan set the flutes on the counter for Button to fill.

"I've spent years behind the bar. Have you ever been to Anand?" Button poured the glasses half full and waited for the liquid bubbles to subside.

"I've only been once, but my parents go every Sunday for brunch. Do you know the Cherrys?"

Button stopped pouring and stared at Megan. "Of course I know the Cherrys. I know all my regulars and they're so nice. I put a bacon, tomato, and avocado omelet on the menu just for your mom. Which makes you their techno-savvy daughter. You were supposed to be at brunch a couple of weeks ago. My computer was on the fritz and your parents said you would fix it, but you never showed up. We could have met last month." Button topped each glass and handed one to Meghan.

"Sorry, I couldn't get out of the bed that day. This is such a funny coincidence. We live in the same building, work out at the same gym, and you know my parents. Wow," Meghan marveled.

"I guess it was meant for us to meet."

"I guess so. What do you do at Anand?"

"I'm the proud owner and sommelier."

"So you pay yourself to drink wine. I'm jealous." Meghan sipped from her glass.

"Are you a wine connoisseur? What's your favorite bottle?"

"White Zinfandel."

Button laughed until she realized she was laughing alone. "Oh, you're serious."

"Yes, I'm serious and you're laughing at me again," Meghan shot back and cracked a smile. "I know it's not the most sophisticated bottle, but I love it."

"Bottle?!? White Zinfandel comes in a box."

"Box wine keeps longer than a bottle and it's easier to transport." Meghan opened her fridge to reveal a box of White Zinfandel, which sent Button into a fit of laughter. "What's wrong with White Zin?"

"It was discovered after a production mistake. White Zin is a bad accident that has continued to be manufactured for immediate consumption, rather than for aging, and thus it has no soul, no story, no character, and no complexity. The price is so low because it's made with low-quality fruit. It's like Kool-aid with a whole lot of sugar."

"I like Kool-aid. Reminds me of my youth," Meghan interjected. Button gave her a crazy look.

"It's a starter wine, barely one step up from Boone's and Mad Dog. No one over twenty-five should drink White Zinfandel and that includes you," Button squinted her eyes and pointed an accusatory finger at Meghan as she finished her diatribe.

"But I love the sweetness and the pretty color. And I'm not the only one who drinks it."

"You're right. Behind Chardonnay, White Zin is the number two best-selling wine in the US. It's very popular, but so are cigarettes and I don't like them either."

"Do you laugh at people when they order White Zin at Anand?"

"Whenever people order White Zin, I take that as my opportunity to expand their horizons. I offer them a complimentary wine tasting session and encourage them to try something new. Variety is the spice of life. I can get you color in a wonderful French Rosé. I can get you sweetness in a German Riesling or Gewürztraminer."

"But I want them *together* in my glass. White Zin is like me. Unpretentious, tasty, and easy-going. Because it is so reasonably priced, it's flexible. You can bring a bunch of bottles to a party, sip it, gulp it. There's plenty to go around. I add a little to everything I cook."

"You really need my help. You're not supposed to drink cooking wine," Button shook her head and sighed.

"Girl, that's where you're wrong. If you don't like the taste of it, then you shouldn't cook your food in it. I'm not saying you're pretentious, *but* when your overpriced bubbles run out, you'll be begging me to open that box," Meghan rolled her neck and laughed.

"I'm a purist. Real wine comes in a bottle, not a box; and don't even get me started on the cork-versus-twist-cap debate. But this is your celebration. If

I must, I'll take one for the team to keep the party going," Button struggled to maintain her straight face.

"Thank you for recognizing that. I'm glad you came over. The divorce blues were trying to get me again."

"I know about the divorce blues. My mom gets them a lot."

"Did she get divorced recently?"

"Over thirty years ago, but she won't let it go."

"That's what I'm afraid of. Letting go isn't easy."

"Are your family and friends supportive?" asked Button.

"My parents are great. I don't know how I would have gotten through this without them. But besides them and the people at the divorce hearing, you're the only other person who knows. I'm not ready to deal with people's reactions," Meghan's voice trailed off and she paused. "I just...I just want to move on with my life."

"My advice, not that you asked for it, is to move at your own pace. You'll figure it out. What you need is a distraction," Button suggested.

"Like what?" Meghan asked.

Button checked her watch. "It's getting late. I need to run, but what about a new decorating project?"

"I've decorated every room here and in my parents' house. There are no more blank canvases."

"I want to redecorate my home office. How much would you charge?"

"I'm not a professional decorator."

"I know, so I'm expecting a really good price."

"I could use the extra money," Meghan offered.

"Give me your number and we'll figure out a time for you to look at my place."

"Sure." Meghan's face lit up. She tore a piece of paper from her grocery list on the counter and scribbled her phone number as Button downed the rest of her champagne and hopped off the stool. Button took the phone number and followed Meghan to the front door.

"Thanks for the visit and the champagne," Meghan said as she opened the front door.

"No, thank you. I'll call you later." Walking down the hall to the elevator, Button gave herself a mental pat on the back for a job well done. Meghan seemed cool. Her taste in wine was sketchy, but Button could appreciate her funky creativity. Maybe Henry's idea wasn't so stupid after all.

Chapter 8

Text Message to Rick
Fr: Dawn
Sunday, May 10, 2009 4:09 PM
How did the move go?
Haven't heard from you all weekend.
Miss u already.

Text Message to Dawn
Fr: Rick
Monday, May 11, 2009 11:15 AM
Darling, move was exhausting.
Work is hectic.
Will call you later.
We still need to decide what we're doing.

⁂

Davis and Button huddled by the hostess stand watching Dawn pick at her lunch.

"Maybe she just lost a big case and an innocent man is going to the electric chair," Button guessed.

"Please stop watching those *Law & Order* marathons. She's not a crime lawyer anyway," Davis corrected.

"Maybe she couldn't get her bun perfectly round and tight this morning."

"No, no, no. Davis knows that look. Unrequited love. It's the worst fashion accessory."

"Yeah, it doesn't look on good anyone," Button agreed.

"Hold the Chardonnay, Davis just had a great idea. Go cheer her up. Add her to your friend posse. Ms. Martin needs a friend right now."

"I'm good with the one."

"Speaking of which, imagine the surprise when you asked Davis to save two bikes in the front of spin class. He may even have gotten a little jealous."
Button shot him a look of disbelief.

"Just kidding. Davis knows there's enough of his favorite Diva to go 'round. So, how's the neighbor friend?"

"It's been two weeks and she hasn't gotten on my nerves. She fixed a glitch on my computer and is going to re-decorate my home office. She wants to lose a few pounds so we're working out together. She's a great cook and invites me over for dinner. I love the food here, but it's nice to have another option so close to home."

"And don't forget she's the daughter of two of our favorite regulars. Ah, convenience and practicality; the foundations for a beautiful friendship. Now tell Davis what you don't like about her. He needs some fresh gossip."

"Davis, you're going to OD on gossip one day."

"Gossip is good for you. Carrots help you see. Gossip helps you hear."

Button shook her head disapprovingly. "There is one thing…"

"There's always one thing. Spill it, Sister." Davis smirked.

"Her favorite wine is…" Button paused for dramatic effect. "White Zin."

Davis made a gag face, which made Button laugh. "But she can drink a lot of it. Her choice of wine is tragic, but nothing gains my respect like a high tolerance."

"Mr. Henry must be happy with your progress."

"I didn't tell him and don't you tell either. She could still turn out to be crazy or even worse—annoying—and I'll have to cut her loose. I've only got two weeks until Henry's big Memorial Day party. I'm going to surprise him then."

"All the more reason to go chat up Ms. Lawyer. Why stop at one friend when you can make two? Prove Mr. Henry wrong *deux fois*." Davis pointed to Dawn.

"I don't want to go over there. That's an awful lot of female bonding for one month. I might OD on estrogen. Plus, we don't have anything in common."

"Did somebody OD on *Grey's Anatomy*?"

"Meg and I watched it last night. I love that show."

"You love TV. Listen, if you can befriend a White Zin drinker, you can find something in common with a woman who has faithfully eaten lunch here every Friday for the past two years. For instance, you and Dawn both love Veuve."

"Dawn's so conservative. Only a librarian should tuck her hair in a bun everyday. But I do love that scarlet Oriental tunic she's wearing even though she's not doing enough with it."

"Ms. Button, she's your inverse. You're brown and bold. She's high-yellow and reserved. You use designer labels and imaginative style to accentuate your shapely figure. Ms. Martin uses designer labels and smart choices to play down her lean physique and shift focus to her smarts."

"Davis, Dear, are you making a point?"

"Davis' point is that if you and Ms. Martin both wore the same vintage Coco Chanel little black dress, it would look completely different. Ms. Martin would sweep her long hair into a sophisticated chignon and pick a classic pair of Stuart Weitzman heels and a Paloma Picasso rose gold link necklace to complete her look. You'd trick your LBD out with a red corset cinch belt, outrageous red coral necklace, and Christian Louboutin satin platform peep-toes. Looking so good in that signature red sole, even Davis would have to watch you walk away." Davis glazed off into the distance.

Button snapped to bring him back. "Davis, though I love what ya' saying, why are ya' saying it?"

"Again, Davis' point is you both wear vintage Coco Chanel and love Veuve Clicquot. You're sisters from another mister. And when Mr. Henry was in here a week ago for dinner he made me promise to help you make some friends. You know Davis can't say no to that man's smile."

"Who was Half having dinner with?"

"We don't like when you call him that." Davis snapped back.

Button moaned with irritation but she knew sweetening her tone was the only way to get the information she wanted from Davis. "I'm sorry. My dearest Davis, who was Mr. Henry with?"

"Ms. Jackson, you sound a little jealous. Don't worry, Davis will give you the answers you seek, *after* you go talk to Ms. Lawyer."

"Fine."

"And you have to hang out with her this weekend." Davis added quickly.

"Are you my pimp now? Just tell me who Henry was with!" Button demanded.

"You are jealous. Jealousy can be a terrible accessory too, but it's cute on you. Now go. Davis said *after*." He winked and pointed again to Dawn.

"If you don't tell me now, I'm going to strangle you with your orange bowtie."

"It's tangerine and he was with his client who looks like the Hispanic version of Denzel. It was raining fine men that night. You didn't think Mr. Henry would be up in here with some skank or that Davis would allow any such foolishness? Now go work your magic while Davis watches." Davis leaned on the stand, satisfied with his deal. Button rolled her eyes, but dutifully walked towards Dawn's table.

* * *

I'm turning thirty in a few months and my life is falling apart. My five-year plan has me married at thirty, but Rick wants an open relationship. He said he isn't giving me an ultimatum, but that's what it feels like.

Dawn's cell phone vibrated. The display showed it was her sister calling again. By the alternating and routine frequency, she could tell that her sisters had worked out a "check on Dawn" call schedule. It was Caroline's turn and in two hours Carlisa would probably send her a text message.

If the twins tell me one more time about the great guy they can introduce me to or use the words piss or pot, I'm going to strangle them. And if I can't pull myself together at work I'm not going to make partner. I can't believe I had a panic attack during that big meeting yesterday. I need to impress the partners. I can't do that with my face in a paper bag.

Dawn dropped the phone in her purse and picked at her salad. She was too upset to eat. *Maybe I'll have another glass of wine. Is this my second or third?*

Button stopped at Dawn's table and smiled at her. "Ms. Martin, how is everything today?"

Dawn's eyes glazed over. "What do you mean? Don't I look okay? Don't I look like a woman with a five-year plan? A confident, smart lawyer who isn't bothered or jealous by her two younger sisters' happy marriages or adorable kids while my boyfriend just moved to Houston and wants an open relationship. Don't I look okay with that?"

Button froze, not sure how to respond. Her eyes darted around the room, looking for an escape, until Dawn continued, "Well, I'm not okay. I'm a grown woman having panic attacks every time her baby sisters mention the white

Grecian dress or pissing in a pot. I'm not okay dying single and alone." Dawn collapsed and hid her head in her folded arms on the table. Button looked over her shoulder at Davis. He mouthed "Get in there" and shooed her to move closer.

Button sighed and took a small step towards Dawn. "Are you dying?"

"No," Dawn mumbled into her arms.

Button moved a little closer. "What's the white Grecian?"

Dawn raised her head slightly. "The dress I wore the first time I thought Rick was proposing. My sisters are right. He doesn't want to marry me. Moving to Houston says that loud and clear. I hate being single. Single is depressing."

Button sat across from Dawn. "Single is sexy. How old are you?"

"Twenty-nine."

"The twenties are tough. They're confusing and they drag on forever. When's your birthday?"

Dawn sat up. "September."

"You'll see. Single in your thirties is fantastic."

"Single is depressing at every age."

"Being single in college was depressing. I'm from a small southern town and raised by a single mother. We barely made the tuition. When I didn't have a rich boyfriend, I was stuck in the dorm and depressed. Now, I've got a great life and spending money. I go where I want, eat what I want, buy what I want. I'm the queen. If I don't want to be bothered with some man, I'm not. Single with money is fabulous."

Dawn shook her head. "No, I want to be married to Rick."

"Now, what's depressing is chasing a man who doesn't want to be caught."

"But Rick Stallings is the love of my life," Dawn whined.

"Rick Stallings? Was he named one of the fifty most beautiful Chicagoans in *Chicago Magazine* last month?"

"Yes, that's my boyfriend. How'd you know that?"

"I was number eight. He was somewhere in the twenties. I don't know him, but his profile was cool."

"Rick Stallings is the total package and I wish I knew why doesn't he want to marry me." Dawn wiped a tear.

"Maybe he's not ready. Maybe he's not done playing the field."

Dawn's eyes got big. "You think he's cheating on me?"

"Asking to see other people is usually a rhetorical question."

Dawn's head fell again. "I hadn't even thought of that. Now I feel worse. I love him. Am I pathetic if I agree to an open relationship?"

"Can you learn to love it?"

"What does that mean?

"In every relationship, there's going to be some quirk about your mate that you don't like. But if you decide to be with that person, at some point you need to accept whatever that quirk is. No one's perfect. Sometimes the quirk is small like bad table etiquette or snoring. But sometimes, it's really big. Usually the better the guy, the bigger the quirk. In Rick's case, if you want to be with him, you have to accept that he's not ready to commit. Maybe somewhere down the line he'll change his mind, but there's no guarantee. That's his total package. Can you learn to love it?"

"What if I can't?"

"Then you need to cut him loose."

"Twenty-nine is too old to start over. Single at this age is so pathetic," Dawn exclaimed.

"Sweetie, I'm just two years older than you and I wear single like a tiara. There are so many fabulous single women that you could learn a lot from. Starting over is the stuff that legends are made of. Do you know what the French word 'veuve' means?"

"Four years of French says…it means widow."

"See, you're single and smart."

"Thanks, but how's the word 'veuve' going to help me?"

"I'm going to tell you a little story that began in France in 1798 when Mademoiselle Barbe-Nicole Ponsardin married Francois Clicquot, the head of the Clicquot business. This is a time when a woman's work was to be pretty, get married, and have babies. Mademoiselle Ponsardin probably thought she was doing pretty well for herself. She married a rich guy whose company was involved in banking, wool trading, and champagne production. She had access to money, beautiful clothes, and great liquor. So you know what he does? He dies after only seven years of marriage. What's the widow Clicquot to do?" Button paused dramatically.

"I don't know. Is learning to love it an option?"

"No. The widow Clicquot had a good cry, buried her husband, and then decided to run his company. She made an executive decision to focus all the firm's energy entirely on champagne, which had to be a hard choice. How do you decide between money, clothes, and liquor? But, I digress. Once she established her wine in royal courts throughout Europe as the noble drink of choice, champagne sales flourished. In recognition of her determination, her contemporaries gave her the name 'la grande dame' which meant that she delivered 'only one quality, the finest.'

"By the time she died in the late eighteen-hundreds, Veuve Clicquot had become both a substantial champagne house and a respected brand. That classic yellow label represents the amazing success achieved by a woman who had her single status unexpectedly thrust upon her. But with cunning, confidence, and business savvy, she turned a tragedy into a celebration. Veuve Clicquot, the woman and the wine, are expressions of independence and triumph."

"That's a nice story, but I don't know how it's going to help me. You got any other advice?"

"Yes. Talk less, drink more. I'm going to get us a bottle of Veuve. On the house."

"Veuve is for celebrations. There's nothing to celebrate here."

"Everyday's a celebration."

"Not today."

"Then every woman is a celebration."

"That's a nice thought, but I don't want champagne." Dawn shook her head. "When I feel like this, I want tequila. It dulls the pain. Can you bring that bottle?"

"Are you sure? Tequila's funny acting. He'll be your best friend today and worst enemy tomorrow."

"I'm sure. Nothing washes out a bad taste like salt, tequila, and lime."

Button stood up. "Are you going back to work?"

"No. I'll call my secretary and let her know I'm sick." While Dawn called the office, Button went to the bar to retrieve a bottle of tequila, limes, and a shot glass.

When she returned, she set the shot glass and limes in front of Dawn. "Let me get your address for the cab ride home before you start the dulling process."

After Dawn scribbled her address on a napkin, Button poured her a shot.

⁂

BRNNGT. BRNNGT. The shrill pitch of the phone ringer next to Dawn's ear jarred her awake. *Who is calling me? It's got to be like two in the morning. Maybe Rick wants to talk. Oww. My head is pounding*. Dawn tried to grab the phone quickly, but her body hurt. Her mouth felt like it was stuffed with cotton and she could barely push out the word hello.

"Hey, it's Button. From Anand."

She must be a night owl. She sounds wide awake. "What time is it?" Dawn croaked.

"A little after ten."

"Really. I don't feel good. What happened?"

"Tequila shots."

"Oh." The memories came flooding back to Dawn. "How'd you get my home number?"

"It's labeled 'home' in your cell phone, which you left at Anand."

"I left my dignity there too. Did you see that? I remember dancing with Davis and I think I groped him."

Button laughed so loudly that Dawn had to move the phone away from her ear. "Dawn, I'm as much to blame as you are. I knew tequila shots weren't a good idea, but I didn't stop you. Then I jokingly suggested you have a little fun with Davis. I didn't think you'd actually do it."

"He's going to tell everybody. I'm so embarrassed." Dawn sighed and rubbed her temple.

"Don't worry. I'll buy his silence with a bottle of Cabernet. Plus, I think he liked it." Button winked at Davis, who was listening nearby. "I'm almost done for the night. You're on my way home so I can drop off your phone."

"I don't think I can get out of bed right now. Can I pick it up from you tomorrow? I have to go in to work. Are you going to be downtown?"

"I'm having lunch at the Millennium Park Grill at noon with my neighbor. Why don't you meet us for lunch?"

"Okay."

"I'm calling from my cell phone. Do you have caller ID or do you need to take down my number?"

"I have caller ID." Dawn's head started to throb. "I need to go back to sleep. I don't feel good."

"You should get up, take some aspirin, and drink a big glass of water before you go back to sleep. It'll help flush the toxins and you'll feel better in the morning. I'll see you tomorrow." Button closed her cell phone and Davis applauded.

"That's my girl. See, that was easy," he cheered.

"I've never seen a pimp in an orange bowtie."

"It's tangerine and if Davis doesn't get a bottle of Cabernet, he's gon' have to smack a bitch." Button gave Davis a crazy look and they both fell out laughing.

Chapter 9

Fr: <Button>
To: <Meghan>
Saturday, May 16, 2009 10:13AM
Subject: I wonder who?

Did u leave that box of White Zinfandel on my doormat? You know it's my Kryptonite and I can't come near it. I almost couldn't get into my place last night. ☺ And why weren't you in spin class?

Fr: <Meghan>
To: <Button>
Saturday, May 16, 2009 10:24AM
Subject: RE: I wonder who?

Defeated by a bottle of blush. That's sad. The gym is my Kryptonite. I'm tired of working out. ☹
Still on for lunch and the Art Institute?

Fr: <Button>
To: <Meghan>
Saturday, May 16, 2009 10:32AM
Subject: RE: I wonder who?

Don't punk out already. Lunch is still a go. I'm driving, so meet me in the lobby at 11:30.

❖❖❖

Button and Meghan sipped ginger martinis at the Park Grill Restaurant's outdoor patio and waited for their appetizers. Sitting across from each other, Meghan faced the restaurant, which housed the "Cloud Gate" sculpture on its roof, while Button looked out at Michigan Avenue.

"This is perfect sit-outside weather. I've been waiting all winter for a day like today. I love summer!" Meghan exclaimed.

"You and everyone else. Millennium Park is packed. I love seeing all the tourist fashions; white gym shoes and fanny packs. The best are the inappropriate T-shirts. See *Horny in Texas* over there." Button nodded to a couple in matching cowboy hats.

"That's funny. We should go take a picture with The Bean. We can strike supermodel poses." Meghan puckered her lips and tossed her head back.

Button turned around to look at the sculpture. "Or we can blow kisses at our reflection like those girls over there." Button laughed.

"Who would have thought a gigantic piece of stainless steel shaped like a bean would amaze and delight so many? It's hours of free entertainment. Just let your imagination go."

"The Bean reminds me of when I was little and my mom took me to the County Fair every year. The Hall of Mirrors was my favorite. Thin me, fat me, short me, tall me, scary me, big-head me, squiggly me, funny me, multiple me. I couldn't get enough of me. Some things never change." Button winked at Meghan and then waved to a woman in a pink halter top with a ruffled collar, pinstripe grey tailored slacks, and pink slingbacks walking across the patio as her dark-green crocodile briefcase and cool strides alternated in rhythm.

"Hey, Button," Dawn greeted.

"Hey, Dawn." Button stood and extended her hand. After they shook hands, she continued, "I'm glad you made it. This is my neighbor, Meghan; Meghan, Dawn."

Meghan stood, walked around, and gave Dawn a hug. "Shaking hands is for strangers. Hugs are for friends." Button rolled her eyes and sat back down.

Dawn smiled at Meghan's warmth. Meghan continued, "Dawn, you can sit next to me and watch The Bean or sit next to Button and watch the fashion show."

"I'll sit next to you." Dawn sat next to Meghan and across from Button.

"How are you feeling? Better than yesterday?" Button reached into her Louis Vuitton handbag and passed Dawn her phone across the table.

"Thanks." Dawn picked up her phone and checked her email. "I took some aspirin and drank a huge glass of water like you suggested. I felt much better when I finally woke up,"

"What happened yesterday?" Meghan asked curiously.

"She was having lunch at Anand and got a little tipsy. 'It's the J.B.'s Monaurail' came on, Dawn grabbed Davis, and they started stepping in the middle of the restaurant. They looked like professional dancers. One thing led to another and Dawn goosed Davis. The look on his face was priceless." Button made a surprised face and laughed out loud.

Meghan joined Button's laughter. "Girl, I can't blame you. Davis has a great body. When he walks around our spin class in those little shorts referring to himself in the third person, Meghan has to hold back from grabbing his ass her damn self." Dawn set her phone down. She had the only serious face at the table.

"I'm so embarrassed. Did you talk to him? Are you sure he won't tell anyone?" Dawn implored.

"He's been sworn to silence, but he asked me for your phone number. He's going to ask you out. I told you he liked it," Button said with a straight face. She caught the attention of their busy waiter and held up three fingers, signaling for another round of drinks.

"Are you serious?" Dawn looked shocked. Her phone beeped and she checked it again, but kept looking back at Button.

"Really?" Dawn asked Button again.

"He said you have magic fingers. Maaaaagic." Button waved her fingers in the air.

"Oh no. What am I going to say to him?" Dawn asked worried.

Finally Button cracked a smile. "I'm kidding. You gotta lighten up. You need a drink."

"I don't want a drink. I'm going to the office after I leave here." Dawn typed a quick message into her phone and returned it to the table. "That was Rick following up. We talked this morning and he wants me to make a decision on what we're doing." Dawn turned to Meghan, "I don't want to take over your lunch, but yesterday Button gave me advice on my boyfriend situation and I was hoping to pick her brain some more. Is that okay?"

"Sure." Meghan responded, as the waiter arrived with three martinis and plates of appetizers. He set a drink in front of each woman and the food in the middle of the table.

"Do you ladies need anything else?" The waiter asked.

"What's in this drink? It looks like tequila. If it is, I can't drink it. Tequila and I broke up this morning," Dawn told the waiter.

"It's a ginger martini made with ginger-infused vodka, lemonade, and lime zest. And that's caramelized ginger on the rim. It's very refreshing," the waiter told her.

"Oh, it sounds good."

The waiter addressed the entire table, "Do you need anything else?"

"Thanks, we're good," Button answered, and the waiter dashed away.

"I don't think I should." Dawn pushed the drink away.

Button slid the martini back. "Drinks are a requirement for all relationship conversations. Alcohol makes you see and tell the truth."

"If you have one drink and eat some food, you'll be fine to go to work. The martinis and crab cakes are too good to pass up." Meghan sipped her new drink.

Dawn followed suit. "This is really good."

"And now that we have food and fresh martinis, the floor is all yours, Dawn," Meghan said, reaching for the sun-dried tomato hummus, pitas, and veggies.

Dawn took another sip and a deep breath. Her phone beeped again, but she ignored it. "I've been with my boyfriend, Rick Stallings, for three years. I love him and I'm ready to get married. He'll be a great husband and provider. He's smart, successful, and driven. Tall, good-looking, and has a great body. We have stimulating conversations about current events, politics, and economics. My family adores him. He's wonderful with my sisters' kids. He's the total package, right?" Dawn paused for confirmation.

"So far, so good." Meghan shrugged.

"I'm trying to make partner at my law firm this year. I work such long hours that I don't meet many new people and when I do, it's not often they're successful black men that I want to date. I swear most of the black men in Chicago are short. Tall is a commodity. And even though I may sound shallow, I'm just going to say it. I want a man who makes more money than me. I know modern women are independent, but I'm traditional. I don't want to be the primary breadwinner. When I have kids, I want the option to stay home and maintain my current lifestyle," Dawn said.

"You like what you like. You want what you want. Don't apologize. When you don't have standards, you'll put up with all sorts of foolishness," Button chimed in.

"Right, so here comes the foolishness. Two weeks ago, I was sure he was going to propose during a romantic dinner. Instead, he announced his latest business project was moving him to Houston for a year. He didn't ask me to go with him, and he wants to date other people while he's gone. I still can't believe he wants to go backwards, not forward. I feel so humiliated and disappointed, but I really love him and I can't imagine finding anyone better than Rick. I don't want to lose him, but I don't feel comfortable with an open relationship. My two younger sisters are both married. It's my turn."

"What advice did you give yesterday, Button?" Meghan asked.

"Never mind that. I didn't hear this full story yesterday. If I had, I would have told you that the next time a man tells you some bullshit like that, don't sit there speechless. Embarrass his ass good," Button demanded. "Start yelling 'you know you my baby daddy' or throw your drink in his face, something. You can't let them get away with that shit. When you do, men will keep testing you to see what else they can get away with."

"Girl, throw a drink in his face? They only do that on reality TV." Meghan repeated in disbelief.

"Every woman is entitled to a reality TV moment." Button told the table.

"That's a bit dramatic."

Button turned to Meghan. "Drama lets a man know you're serious. Dawn needs to let Rick know she means business." Button turned back to Dawn. "You've got to take a stand. If you want to get engaged, then tell him 'I want to get engaged.'"

Dawn was flustered. "I've tried, but whenever I bring it up, Rick asks me to be patient. I can't control when he proposes?"

"Yes you can. Tell Rick you wouldn't marry his tired, sorry ass if he had the last good dick on the planet. You'd rather go girl. Fuck him. That's how you exercise control." Dawn stared at Button wide-eyed while Meghan exploded with laughter.

"Are you serious?" Dawn asked.

"The way I see it, your options are to learn to love Rick and all his open relationship quirks or put your foot down and see what happens."

Meghan took a huge sip of her water and fanned her face. Regaining her composure, she cut in, "I'm sorry for laughing, but Button is crazy. Dawn, what's your heart telling you?"

"I'm turning thirty this year and I don't want to start over!" Dawn exclaimed.

"I'm thirty-two and I got divorced last month. I can say with absolute certainty that I would rather start over than spend fifty years in an unhappy marriage," Meghan said.

"Women in their twenties are so stressed. They feel pressure to have the perfect career, boyfriend, clothes, bank account, and life. They want to do it all and do it all now. When you get to your thirties, you've figured out nothing is perfect and that's okay. Just make some money and have some fun. This is a cliché but it's true; there are too many fish in the sea for you to be afraid to look for a better catch," Button said.

"You're exactly right. There are too many fish and it takes forever to wade through them all," Dawn argued.

"No it doesn't. It's called 'date and eliminate.' The twenties were for figuring out your likes and dislikes. At your age, you know what you want and you can figure out if a man is offering it in three dates. If he's got it, put him on your team. If he doesn't, eliminate him from the roster. Once you have a few on the team, weed them out until you figure out who's the star."

"What team?"

"The team of suitors that will either complement or replace Rick."

"You want me to date multiple men? I'll never get married dating like that."

"Dating is a numbers game. Stack the odds in your favor. I always keep a team and I've been proposed to six times."

"Six times?" Meghan repeated with wide eyes.

"Men need competition to keep them in line. Rick's problem is he knows he's got you. If you want a ring, accept his offer for an open relationship. Even if you don't actually do it, make him think you're dating other men. Once he realizes you aren't as available to him, he'll be motivated to propose," Button suggested.

"What happened to him proposing because he loves me?" Dawn asked.

"Unfortunately, love isn't enough to make a marriage work," Meghan offered. "I loved my ex-husband. He was my best friend and we did everything together. He was a great companion, but he wasn't a great husband. I finally had to recognize the situation for what it was: a great friendship, but a dysfunctional marriage. I decided that I deserve to be completely happy and I would rather be alone than badly accompanied. It hurts, but I'm thankful I found the strength to get out," Meghan said.

"What are you trying to say?" Dawn asked.

"I'm saying don't stay with Rick because you're afraid. Decisions based on fear usually leave us in worse situations," Meghan concluded.

"So, you think I should accept the open relationship or give Rick an ultimatum?"

"Girl, I think I want to hear more about Button's team." Meghan turned her full attention to Button.

"Right now, I've got an All-Star team; a player to fill any and every need. I've got my 'Half-boyfriend' who's all the fun and companionship of a boyfriend, but none of the responsibilities. I spend the most time with Half. I've got my 'Quarter-boyfriend' who I see once or twice a week and spend the most pleasurable time with, if you know what I mean. I only keep one Half and Quarter at a time. Everyone else plays the 'Sponsor' role. They're the benchwarmers waiting to get a call up to the big game. While they wait, they provide entertainment and filler when my star players are busy."

"Do you spend pleasurable time with the Sponsors?" Dawn asked.

"Unless they get promoted from the minor leagues, the Sponsors ain't never gonna get it."

"Why?"

"So many reasons. I'm not attracted to them, they're broke, something about them screams terrible in bed, no swagger, they're man-whores, or maybe they got it in the past but messed up so they're sniffing around trying to get it again. They all know getting it from me is a long shot, but they like to try. It's good for men to have goals. They like to chase and I like sponsored outings. It's the perfect arrangement." Button sat back and sipped her martini.

Meghan stared in fascination.

"Team dating. Button, again, are you serious?" Dawn asked.

"Why do women think they should only date one guy? Men do it all the time. Be honest and upfront. Tell the guy he's cool, but you want to keep your options open. Competition encourages men to bring their A-game," Button said as Meghan snickered. "What's so funny?" Button asked her.

"That I'm single and I can not only date again, but I can have a team." Meghan laughed out loud.

"Exactly. Where do you want to begin? Half, Quarter, or Sponsors?"

"Button, I haven't been on a date in so long. I wouldn't know what to do with one man, let alone a team. Do you get exhausted encouraging all this competition?"

"That's the beauty of it. If I don't want to be bothered, I'm not. All the fun and none of the responsibility. When I'm mean or ignore them, it makes them want me more. This is the only way to date. Monogamy is unnatural. No exclusivity, no expectations, no hurt feelings," Button stated matter-of-factly. "Meg, how long were you with your ex-husband?"

"Six years," Meghan answered.

"How long have you been separated?"

"Seven months."

"You're ready for a team. After being with the same man that long, you need a team."

"I don't think so." Meghan took a long sip from her drink.

"At least tell me the married sex was great."

"Can't say that it was," Meghan answered.

"Lame, married sex is equivalent to no sex. You're like a virgin. You need a Quarter." Button winked at Meghan.

"I'm not ready for any of that, but Dawn, you should think about it." Meghan shifted her attention back to Dawn.

"Dawn, can I help you put a team together?" Button asked eagerly.

"I don't want to date. I want to get married, have kids and not be the oldest mom at the park. I should wait for Rick to come around," Dawn said, defeated.

"That's your decision, but if you want to show him what's good for the goose is good for the gander, you know where to find me," Button leaned back in her chair and downed the rest of her martini. "Another round?" she asked the girls.

"Nah, that's all my wallet can handle. I'm on money conservation," Meghan answered.

"What's that?" Dawn asked.

"Money conservation is what needs to happen when you decide to keep the condo after the divorce. It's amazing how quickly you figure out one income doesn't pay for as much stuff as two incomes did," Meghan shook her head.

"What about alimony?" Dawn asked.

"Unless I want to get paid in plastic poker chips, there's no alimony. It was a simple divorce. I kept the condo. He kept his debts."

"Who handled your divorce?"

"I handled it *pro se*," Meghan emphasized the term. "Again, money conservation."

"What's *pro se*?" Button repeated.

"It's when a person represents himself or herself without a lawyer," Dawn answered.

"Meghan Cherry, computer whiz, interior decorator, chef, and legal eagle. You do it all," Button complimented.

"How'd you like working with the law? Any thoughts of going to law school? It pays well." Dawn asked.

"No, law isn't for me. If I went back to school it would be for interior design. That's my dream. But I have bills my ex-husband didn't pay, and a mortgage, so that dream's on hold."

"Sorry, Meg. You should have another martini and don't worry about the bill. It's my treat. My thanks for letting me crash and monopolize the conversation with my problems," Dawn offered.

"That's nice of you, but you don't have to. I didn't tell you about money conservation because I need you to pay for me. I have money to go out as long as I stay within my budget," Meghan said.

"If Dawn wants to pay, let Dawn pay," Button cut in.

"Neither of us is ready for team dating, so I'll be your Sponsor," Dawn said, and laughed for the first time.

"Wait, does that make me Button? Where's my champagne and my fractions?" Meghan mocked. She and Dawn laughed. Dawn's phone beeped again and she reached for it.

Button raised an eyebrow at them. "So now you two are making fun of me?"

"I gotta go. One of the partners needs a file. Thanks for listening. I enjoyed the adult female conversation. The only women I hang out with are my married sisters and their small children. I love my family, but it's nice to get through a lunch without any crying or food fights." Dawn dropped her phone in her purse, pulled out her credit card, and called the waiter over.

"Do you have to go to work? Button and I are going to the Art Institute after we leave here. I'm redecorating her home office and I need an inspiration piece. The Art Institute's featured collection is called *Artistic Inebriation: A Case for Wine Throughout the Ages*. It's a compilation of over four hundred pieces showcasing how wine has influenced and inspired artists from the Last Supper to the Harlem Renaissance. I get my best ideas from art and that's too perfect to pass up," Meghan said eagerly.

"Do I have to go?" Button whined. "I don't want to pay eighteen bucks to look at old stuff. My money is better spent on martinis. Dawn looks like she wants to go."

"Button, you're a flake, but if Dawn goes, you don't have to," Meghan compromised as the waiter approached the table.

"Can you bring two more martinis and charge everything to my card," Dawn told the waiter. She handed over her credit card and turned back to the table.

"I can't today, but I can go tomorrow. Plus my firm has free passes to all the museums so if you wait, I'll sponsor again."

"Yes, you two should go together tomorrow—without me." Button nodded.

Meghan shot Button a dirty look and wrote her phone number on a piece of paper, which she handed to Dawn. "Tomorrow works. I'm free all day so call me when you're ready to go. And thanks for lunch."

The waiter returned with two martinis and the bill. Dawn signed the receipt and reached over to hug Meghan. "My pleasure. I'm thinking one tomorrow. I'll call you later to finalize a time. Button, you ready for a hug?" Dawn stood and watched Button.

"Naw, I'm good. I'm glad you came. Don't work too hard and thanks for lunch." Button extended her hand, they shook goodbye, and Dawn walked away.

"Girl, you couldn't give her a hug?" Meghan asked.

"You're a hugger. I'm not," Button said.

"Yet. You're not a hugger *yet*." Meghan held up her martini glass to toast. "Here's to finding your inner hug."

Button raised her glass. "And here's to finding your reality TV moment. Cheers."

Chapter 10

Fr: <Rick>
To: <Dawn>
Sunday, May 17, 2009 9:47AM
Subject: Thanks

Thanks again for helping my mother file those papers. You know she loves you.

Fr: <Dawn>
To: <Rick>
Sunday, May 17, 2009 9:53AM
Subject: RE: Thanks

It's nice that someone loves me. Too bad you don't?

Fr: <Rick>
To: <Dawn>
Sunday, May 17, 2009 9:56AM
Subject: RE: Thanks

I didn't say I don't love you. I said I want to be sure.

⁂

Meghan stared wide-eyed at Archibald Motley Jr.'s "Nightlife" painting and said, "This picture makes me want to dance. The violets and reds. The lively strokes. I can hear the jazz. I love the men in their suits and the curvy ladies in their tight dresses. Not a care in the world. Just drinking and dancing at the nightclub. Jitterbugging till their legs fall off. This is perfect for Button."

Meghan wrote the name of the painting in her notebook, along with some design ideas for showcasing a replica in Button's home office. "If Button's restaurant had a live band and dancing, this is exactly how it would look. In fact, I think that's you and Davis dancing in the front of the bar. Isn't this perfect for Button's office?" Meghan bubbled with excitement. When Dawn didn't respond, she looked over her shoulder. Dawn was staring absentmindedly at the painting, but not really looking at it. Meghan waved her hand in front of Dawn's face. "Earth to Dawn. Come in Dawn."

"Huh?" Dawn flinched in surprise.

"I'm at the Art Institute. Where are you?"

"Um, I guess I'm still thinking about what you said yesterday. That love isn't enough to make a marriage work."

"I'm sorry, Dawn. Don't listen to me. Love wasn't enough for me, but it could be enough for you."

"Last night, I asked Rick what he thought and he agreed with you. Then he told me some crap about how he needs to make sure he's in love and seeing other people will help him figure that out. I thought we loved each other and were getting married. Now that's not enough." Dawn wiped a tear from her eye.

Meghan's excitement dissolved into concern. "Getting married is easy. Fall in love. Get a ring, tux, dress, church, say I do and it's done. Love and weddings are easy. Marriage is hard. A marriage is the joining of two people and their individual desires, goals, lifestyles, and experiences. And those two people have to constantly work at balancing their individuality into a harmonious union. You may be ready to get married, but Rick's not sure."

"How do I know if I should wait for him?" Dawn asked.

"Girl, let's go sit over there and talk." Meghan led Dawn to an isolated wooden bench tucked in the corner of the room. They sat close, their knees almost touching. "Before I left Frank, I thought long and hard about what I need to make a marriage work. I came up with ten essentials elements." Meghan flipped through the pages of her notebook until she found the list. "My list isn't going to be the same as yours. But looking at it may help you." Meghan handed her notebook to Dawn.

10 ESSENTIAL ELEMENTS OF MARRIAGE

1. Love (non-negotiable)
2. God is the head of our household (non-negotiable)
3. Companionship (non-negotiable)
4. Good communication on everyday-small things and big-picture-long-term goals. Words and actions must match. (non-negotiable)
5. Trust; our relationship has integrity and honesty. (non-negotiable)
6. We're committed to making the marriage work and will put in the work to make it succeed. (non-negotiable)
7. Physically satisfying
8. Good finances and good financial sense
9. Good family dynamic; We both want to have children and co-exist harmoniously in each other's existing families.
10. We work as a team. By being open and receptive to new ideas, we grow individually and together.

"How many of these elements did your marriage have?" Dawn asked.

"Two...of ten." Meghan laughed nervously. "My twenty-percent marriage had love and companionship, which is why I said for me love isn't enough to make a marriage work."

"Did you know before you got married that your relationship was missing a lot?" Dawn asked.

Meghan paused while she collected her thoughts. "Yes and no. Things and people change. I knew Frank didn't go to church before we got married and I thought it wouldn't bother me. But after we were married, I realized it's essential that my husband contribute to the spiritual nature of our relationship. I also knew Frank gambled occasionally, but I didn't know he would let it take over his life. People and relationships change, so you need a strong base to weather the changes. Our twenty percent wasn't enough."

"Does the next guy you date need to be a perfect one-hundred percent?"

Dawn asked.

"No one's perfect, which includes me, and no relationship is perfect. I may not get everything at a hundred percent, but I know we'll need to have a strong foundation and all my non-negotiables, which are the top six on my list."

Dawn looked back at the list. "How did you pick the non-negotiables?"

"Those are the relationship deal breakers; the things I absolutely have to have." Meghan looked at the list. "I won't compromise on love, spirituality, companionship, good communication, honesty, and commitment."

Dawn's forehead wrinkled. "I would think good finances would be non-negotiable for you?"

"I'm not great at finances and if my husband isn't either than that's okay, as long as we're communicating about it. I'm willing to forgive a lot as long as there is communication."

"Physical is negotiable?"

"Sex isn't everything," Meghan countered.

"It's not everything, but it's important. Fantastic, orgasmic, put-you-sound-to-sleep sex should be non-negotiable."

"Like I said, the list is personal. Your list is going to be different," Meghan responded.

"I don't know if ten is enough for a list. I'm thinking at least twenty-five essentials. Like tall. Can I put six feet as a non-negotiable?"

Meghan laughed. "I don't think a list should be that picky. Don't focus on a bunch of physical traits. Focus on the character and essence of the man you want to marry. What if you meet a great guy who gives you everything you want, but he's only five-ten?"

Dawn wrinkled her forehead again. "But I like tall. I like six feet."

"Would you rather have a tall jerk or a five-ten wonderful husband and father? As long as you're attracted to him, isn't that enough? And you're only, what, five-seven? Why does he have to be six feet?"

"I guess I need to figure out my own list. I definitely know trust is at the top. If I ever found out Rick cheated on me, I would never be able to trust him again," Dawn said.

"How do you feel about him asking for an open relationship?"

"Part of me respects that he's asking instead of cheating, but part of me feels like he's pulling away. I have panic attacks when I think about Rick not wanting to marry me."

Dawn gave the notebook back to Meghan. Then she looked Meghan straight in the eye. "Meg, how do you know? How do you know when you love someone enough to commit the rest of your life to him? How do you know if you should keep holding on or just let the relationship go?"

Meghan paused to collect her thoughts. "Girl, I don't have all the answers. I wish I did. All I can tell you is what I know as a women who fell in love with her best friend, got married, and then got divorced, which is that just because a man is a great companion, that doesn't mean he'll be a great husband. And just because a man has great finances, that doesn't mean he'll provide a happy home.

"My parents have been married thirty-six years and I want something like what they have. I want to be happy and I don't want to ever settle again. I wasn't happy in my marriage. I prayed and prayed on it until I realized that if my ex wouldn't put in the work necessary to make our marriage work, then I couldn't do it for him. As women, we try to do everything, but we can't. In a marriage, your partner has to meet you, help you, and be present. My ex wasn't doing any of those things, which is why even though I loved him then and I still love him now, I had to let him go and get out.

"I know Button has a very colorful way of saying things, but she made good points when she talked about taking control of your destiny. You can't force Rick into a commitment and you shouldn't wait too long for him to come around. Life is short, but it feels long if you're miserable. And marrying the wrong man will make you miserable."

"Meg, do you think I'm settling?"

"Dawn, do you think you're settling?"

Dawn was silent as she let the fullness of that question envelope her. She rolled it over in her mind then replied, "Sometimes I don't know the difference between settling and compromising. Every relationship requires some degree of compromise, right?"

Dawn looked at Meghan for a response. Meghan just returned her stare, not saying a word. After a long silence, Dawn continued, "At what point do you cross from compromising to settling? I don't know. I'm scared. What if I never find anyone as good as Rick?"

"Don't ask the woman who just got out of a twenty-percent marriage. Talking to me is the blind leading the blind. The best advice I can give you is to come up with your own list and see how much Rick is offering you. Only Dawn can decide what's best for Dawn," Meghan said, rubbing Dawn's arm in support.

"So you're not afraid to get married again?"

"Dawn, I loved being married. It's an experience and union unparallel to any other relationship. It's this one-of-a-kind connection of love and intimacy. Take the bond you have with your sisters and add physical, growth, commitment and whatever else you're looking for in a husband. It's holy and beautiful. The search for the right person isn't easy or simple. I'll have to kiss some frogs before I find my next husband. But with each frog, I learn more about myself, and more about what I do and don't want in a relationship. Those are the lesson I'm taking away from my divorce."

"Wow, that's amazing. I don't think I could survive a divorce."

"I'd rather be divorced than unhappily married. It's not always easy for me. I have days when I don't want to get out of bed. I've put on a freshman fifteen. I have acne from all the stress. And if one more person asks me 'How's married life,' I might strangle them. But I keep praying for strength. I'm not afraid and you shouldn't be afraid either. I'm not telling you what to do, but I encourage you to make an informed decision."

"Thanks for sharing with me. I feel much better. Now let's get back to business. We need to find an inspiration piece for Button's office." Dawn stood up from the bench and clapped her hands in determination.

"I was thinking about that painting over there." Meghan stood, tucked her notebook in her purse, and pointed to where they previously stood.

"Oooh, that's pretty. Good choice. Let's get a closer look." Dawn and Meghan linked arms and crossed the exhibit hall.

CHAPTER 11

Fr: <Meghan>
To: <undisclosed recipients>
Thursday, May 21, 2009 6:02PM
Subject: new email address

Hi. My new email address is just_meg@yahoo.com. Please update your contacts and delete the old address of MeghanCHenderson@yahoo.com. That account was getting too much spam. Thanks.

Fr: <Joy>
To: <Meghan>
Thursday, May 21, 2009 6:55PM
Subject: RE: new email address

Done. Long time...no hear. I miss you. How's married life? Ron and the kids are great. We have to do better about keeping in touch.

Fr: <Meghan>
To; <Joy>
Thursday, May 21, 2009 8:19PM
Subject: RE: new email address

Miss you too. Kiss the kids for me. Call you this weekend.

***

On their way to a red wine and chocolate tasting at Anand, Dawn and Meghan walked past the crowded Garrett's Popcorn shop on Michigan Avenue. As usual on a Friday evening, the long line spilled onto the sidewalk and down the street. The delicious aroma of warm butter, sweet caramel, and savory cheese popcorn wafted from the open door and was carried by the light evening breeze. The sweet scent of the caramel caught in Dawn's nostrils. She stopped near the beginning of the line and turned to Meghan. "Do you want to get some popcorn?"

"Do red wine, chocolate, and popcorn go together?" Meghan asked.

"Wine and chocolate goes with everything."

"Nah, I don't feel like waiting in line. Can we just go the tasting?" Meghan didn't sound like herself.

"Are you okay? You seem a little down." Dawn studied Meghan.

"Um, I'm fine."

"You sure? Did something happen at work?"

"I didn't go. I couldn't sleep at all last night. I was so tired that I called in sick."

"What did you do today?"

"Nothing. I didn't even leave the house. I didn't want to come to this, but Button said I had to since it was my idea that she have a money conservation event."

"Do you want to talk about it?"

"Nah, let's just go. Talk less, drink more."

As Dawn and Meghan passed the popcorn line, an older woman wearing an enormous hat over-accessorized with black feathers and sequins waved them over.

Meghan greeted the woman with a heavy smile, "Hello, Mrs. Campbell. How are you?"

Mrs. Campbell spoke with a strong southern accent. "Hello, Dear. I'm blessed by the Best. Praise the Lord. Just getting a bag of the cheese-caramel mix for my grandbabies."

"That's nice. My mom bringing home Garrett's popcorn is one of my favorite childhood memories," Meghan reminisced.

"How is yo mama? You know I had to stop going to that church. Can you believe they axe Mrs. Maybelline Campbell to remove her signature hat? I needs my hats when I pray. How else the Lord gon' know it's me? I gotta call yo mama to check on her. How you? How's married life?" Mrs. Campbell asked.

Dawn flinched and Meghan's face contorted like she had just been punched in the stomach. Her voice was high-pitched and sing-songy. "Oh, everything's great. Thanks, um, for asking,"

Mrs. Campbell didn't notice the discomfort and continued her interrogation. "When you gon' give yo mama some grandbabies? My Jackie's younger than you and she gave me two. How long you gon' make yo poor mama wait? It's almost a sin, I tell you. Now when are those babies coming?"

Mrs. Campbell waited for an answer, but Meghan looked like a deer in headlights. "Young lady, I'm waiting for an answer."

Meghan looked at Dawn. Her eyes pleaded for help. Dawn jumped into action. "You know Mrs. Campbell, if you ask that question, you're obligated by law to pay all daycare expenses."

"What the devil you talking 'bout, chile?" Mrs. Campbell squinted her eyes at Dawn.

"Yes, the new Pampers Oligatus law. Passed last month. Stipulates that anyone who inquires about future grandbabies is obligated to provide for said grandbabies," Dawn informed, while Meghan stifled a laugh and regained her composure.

"Mrs. Campbell, she's joking with you. Anyway, we have to go. Enjoy the popcorn." Meghan grabbed Dawn's arm and they walked away briskly, leaving Mrs. Campbell with her mouth open as the feathers on her hat quivered.

After they walked a couple of blocks, Dawn stopped and turned to Meghan. "Now I see what you meant about the 'how's married life' question."

Meghan threw her head back and yelled, "I hate that question!"

"That was really awkward," Dawn admitted.

"Awkward doesn't begin to describe it. It's excruciating. '*How's married life? Where are the grandbabies?*'" Meghan mocked Mrs. Campbell. "I wanted to strangle that old lady. Why do people keep asking me stupid crap like that?" Meghan shouted again.

"It's more of a rhetorical question, like 'How are you?'"

"If you don't already know the answer, don't ask. '*How's married life*' is a serious question that shouldn't be thrown around in public like that. It should only be asked sincerely by a good friend or close family member in a quiet, private space. Every time I'm asked that question, it's like a bullet barreling into my chest. Then I have to stand there bleeding with my guts exposed, pretending to enjoy another awkward moment," Meghan complained.

"It's like when people ask, 'When are you and Rick getting married?' It's so insensitive," Dawn sympathized.

"I never ask single people that question. And I now never ask married people, 'how's married life?' or 'when are you going to have kids?' I'm so tired of people asking me that crap. I've had it up to here." Meghan reached her arm as high as she could.

"Meg, I vow to never ask 'How's married life?' or 'When are you having kids?' ever again."

"On behalf of all married and divorced people everywhere, I thank you."

"Well, you know what goes great with awkward?"

"What?"

"Wine. Let's go get you a bottle."

"Are you sure I can't go home?"

"We're only a couple of blocks away. Just have one glass. If you don't feel better, then you can leave."

"Fine."

As they walked, Dawn tried to cheer Meghan up by pointing out quirky street vendors, but the puppet show on the corner and the band of kids bucket drumming only elicited a distracted "uh huh" from Meghan. "Smooth Criminal" blared from a stereo. The frozen Silver Man jumped to life and moonwalked right in front of them. His audience applauded wildly. Lost in a funk, Meghan didn't even notice.

Whirring through Anand's revolving doors, they were immediately greeted by Davis in the foyer.

"Ms. Martin and Ms. Cherry, don't you two just look like a lovely summer day." Davis nodded approvingly to Meghan's white and black polka dot dress and Dawn's gray linen suit.

"Thanks Davis. You look great in seersucker. The pink and white stripe is so chic," Dawn returned the compliment.

"Every year, this old thing debuts from Davis' closet the first warm day of May. It's his official start-of-summer suit. Come, Ms. Jackson has reserved a table for you." Linking arms with both Dawn and Meghan, he led them to the large baroque bar in the dining room. The bar area was packed and abuzz with activity. They quickly spotted Button at the far end of the bar, looking like an angel in a sleek and sleeveless white silkYvesSaintLaurent pantsuit, floating from group to group filling wide-rim glasses with a deep red wine and chatting with the patrons. She saw them enter and waved hello.

Davis removed a reserved sign from an empty table and held out the chairs for Dawn and Meghan.

"Davis will be back with appetizers and a delightful array of chocolate." Davis disappeared in the crowd. Meghan shifted uncomfortably in her chair and stared at the floor. Dawn watched her.

After a few minutes, Button arrived at the table holding a newly opened bottle of rose-colored wine. "Ladies, welcome to Anand's money conservation wine and chocolate tasting. The restaurant's doing so well, it's nice to give something back. Great idea, Meg."

Meghan didn't respond. Button looked at Dawn, who shrugged.

"Meg, what's wrong?" Button asked.

"Oh, I was in my own world. Nothing's wrong. Thanks for doing this. Did you take my other suggestion?" Meghan asked.

"Sorry, we still don't carry White Zin here, but I got this just for you." Button waved a pretty pink bottle at Meghan. "This is a Beaujolais Nouveau. It's a light, fruity wine with flavors of strawberry, raspberry, and fig. It's meant to be served chilled and the grapes must come from the Beaujolais region of France. It's released every year on the third Thursday of November, which in France is celebrated and heavily publicized 'Beaujolais Day.' In the United States, we promote this wine as a terrific Thanksgiving meal accompaniment. Enjoy." Button filled the three empty glasses on the table, put the bottle in the chiller on the table and sat down. Meghan downed her entire glass in one gulp.

Button looked at Meghan curiously. "I was going to add that it pairs nicely with dark chocolate, but you didn't wait for the chocolate to arrive."

"Sorry Girl, I'm having a rough day. Ask Dawn. She saw it," Meghan said.

"It was pretty bad." Dawn recounted the Garrett's Popcorn scene to Button.

"And I even got emailed a 'How's Married Life' grenade by my best friend last night. Can I have a refill?" Meghan held up her empty glass.

"Okay, but drink it slow this time." Button filled her glass. "When people drop those grenades on you, that's when you need to have a reality TV moment. Bring on the drama and tell them to leave you the hell alone."

"So I was supposed to throw a drink in that old lady's face? Or slap my best friend? I haven't even told her I'm divorced."

"You haven't told your best friend you're divorced?" Dawn was shocked.

"No. I haven't told anyone except you guys and my parents," Meghan admitted.

"Why not? What are you waiting for?" Dawn asked.

"My ex and I got along so well. Everyone will be so disappointed. Yesterday, I told my dry cleaner for practice. She just couldn't understand why I would leave a man who wasn't beating me or cheating on me. She looked at me like what's my problem," Meghan said.

"That's a stranger. Your friends will understand. They want you to be happy," Dawn redirected.

"I'm embarrassed. I let Frank gamble our marriage and money away. Then I gave up and got a divorce. I took the easy way out. You know, I was the only married woman most of my friend knew. They looked at me as their hope for the future that Black love and marriage are still possible. They'll be so disappointed."

"After what I just saw at the popcorn shop, I'm pretty sure you didn't take the easy way out. Meghan, you have nothing to be embarrassed about. You're not a disappointment. And the only way you're letting your friends down is by not telling them," Dawn interjected. "You're hurting and you need your friends. How are you keeping this a secret?"

"I just avoid everyone. I got tired of dodging questions about Frank."

"That's terrible. You need to tell them so they can be there for you and stop adding to your pain. If you were my best friend and I found out you went through a divorce without telling me, I'd be so mad at you."

"And you'd have every right. I hate this. I hate being divorced. I hate keeping it a secret. I hate my ex-husband. I hate my house. I hate my job. I hate that I can't sleep at night. I hate how I look. I hate this." Tears fell onto Meghan's cheek.

"Hey, hey, hey. What's going on?" Davis sat a chocolate sampler in front of Dawn and an appetizer platter in front of Meghan. Cupping Meghan's chin, he lifted her face to look her in the eyes. "You should be flirting with boys and working the room. This is the Single Girl Summer table. No crying allowed."

"I'm too old to be called a girl," Meghan told Davis as he wiped her tears with his handkerchief.

"You're a woman when you work but a girl when you play. And this girl needs to cheer up." Davis covered Meghan's hand with his and squeezed. Then he bounced away into the crowd.

"You're not too old. Thirty's the new twenty. Don't be so hard on yourself," Button added.

"I shouldn't be carrying on like this in public. Too many 'How's married life' encounters. If I had a dollar for each time somebody asked me that I wouldn't be on money conservation." Meghan blew her nose.

"I hate seeing you like this. Where's your positive attitude?" Dawn asked.

"Sorry, I've got the saddies," Meghan answered.

"The saddies?" Dawn asked.

"That's what my Mama calls it when you're feeling blue; the saddies," Meghan answered.

"What's wrong with your house and job?" Dawn asked.

"I love that condo, but I can't afford it on my one salary and I can't sell it in this recession because I owe more than it's worth. At work, there have always been two of us in the IT department for my section. Yesterday my counterpart gave his notice and my manager told me they aren't replacing him. They expect me to pick up all his work. I asked for a raise, which I really need and deserve. My manager said sales are down and there's no money. They want me to do the work of two people for the same money. I can't even begin to imagine how I'm going to get it all done. My head hurt thinking about it last night. That's one of the reasons I couldn't sleep and had to call in sick."

"Are you sure you can't get more money? I can help. I'm the queen of negotiating," Dawn offered.

"My manager said there isn't any money."

"If you're the only IT person, you have leverage. Threaten to quit. We'll squeeze a nice raise out of them." Dawn was fired up.

"I need a raise bad, but I need a job more than anything. What if I threaten to quit and they accept? I can't take that chance. I've got money stress, divorce stress, friend stress, work stress, acne and baby fat. People keep asking me about married life. Oh, and the bank sent me a nasty note demanding I get current on my mortgage. Not to mention that Frank has just moved on like I never existed. Some times I just want to crawl into a hole and…I don't know. I just don't know." Meghan's voice trailed off and her eyes watered again.

"Frank hasn't moved on and forgotten about you. You're too wonderful to forget about. You're every man's dream wife. Hell, you cook. I'm sure he's mad at himself for messing up a good thing. Plus, you did leave him. He's probably hurting too, but he's respecting your wishes," Button told Meghan.

"Do you think he'll ever call?"

"Do you really want him to? I was dating this guy who went crazy when I broke up with him. He was getting too attached. When he asked me to fly home with him to meet his parents on Valentine's Day, it was over. He didn't take the break-up well and started calling me all times of the day and night. When he started hanging around the building waiting for me; that was it. Fortunately, I was also dating this muscle head who beat the crap outta him. Never heard from him again. Ex-boyfriends, ex-husbands, ex-whatevers. We make them exes for good reasons and we don't want them keeping in touch."

"But Frank was my best friend. I lost my best friend," Meghan said softly.

"It would hurt even more to listen to your ex-husband talk about meeting new friends. You know what I mean. It's best not to talk. Make a clean break and heal uninterrupted. Talking to exes is like picking at an open wound."

"Sometimes I think I'll never be as happy as I once was or get caught up on my bills. Girl, that letter from the bank was scary."

"And you know what that was?"

"Yes, more crap I don't need," Meghan nibbled at a shrimp.

"No, that was a reminder of why you divorced Frank's ass. It's okay to have the saddies. Your divorce is fresh. You're doing great. Healing is a process and you're going to get through it. Frank's gone. You were right to get rid of him. Now move on to bigger and better."

"And you don't have to tell anybody about the divorce until you're ready. Button and I are here for you," Dawn added.

"I can't believe I'm crying in the middle of a crowded bar." Megan dabbed her eyes with a bar napkin.

"Been there, done that. Talk to me after you goose Davis." Dawn laughed and Meghan cracked a smile.

"The wine is free and everyone's at least four glasses in. They're too happy to notice you," Button refilled all the glasses.

"Yeah, no one's looking at you. They're all looking at Button. I can't believe you wore white silk to a red wine tasting. You're crazy." Dawn laughed.

"And I dare anybody to spill something on me. They'll never step foot in here again." Button proclaimed while Meghan and Dawn laughed.

"I'm going to wash my face. Be right back." Meghan excused herself from the table.

"I feel bad for making her come," Dawn confessed to Button.

"Don't. It's good for her to get out. Fresh air and free wine is a panacea."

"And friends. Fresh air, free wine, and friends—that's a panacea."

Button smiled and lifted her glass to toast Dawn.

CHAPTER 12

Fr: <Henry>
To: undisclosed recipients
Saturday, May 23, 2009 3:21PM
Subject: SUNDAY BACKYARD PARTY

Memorial Day party tomorrow. Four yards. One yard for food and drinks. Three for dancing. Party starts at noon and goes all night. No work MONDAY!!! Start your summer right.

Fr: <Button>
To: <Meghan>, <Dawn>
Saturday, May 23, 2009 3:52PM
Subject: Free Fun

Half's party is going to be bananas. (See the attached email). I'll be there early to set up the bar. Text me when you get there.

Fr: <Meghan>
To: <Button>, <Dawn>
Saturday, May 23, 2009 3:56PM
Subject: RE: Free Fun

Does he know you call him Half?

Fr: <Button>
To: <Meghan>, <Dawn>
Saturday, May 23, 2009 3:58PM
Subject: RE: Free Fun

Yes, but don't let HENRY know you know. Tnx.

***

Meghan and Dawn entered the yard that had enough food and drinks to feed and intoxicate the entire south side of Chicago. All four yards were packed and the party was in full swing. In the yard next to the food, the true house-heads spun in circles and jumped up and down. In the next yard, the smooth-steppers slid and bopped to the hottest R&B tracks. And in the furthest yard, everyone sang the verses of their favorite Old Skool raps and swayed in rhythm. The ladies were flaunting their cutest tank tops, shorts, skirts, and sundresses, and the men were thoroughly enjoying the summer fashions.

Meghan had to yell for Dawn to hear her. "This is awesome. I've never seen so many people at a house party."

Dawn nodded in agreement and bopped her head to the music. "There's no way we can find Button among all these people and I'm hungry. I'll send her a text to meet us by the food." Dawn sent a text on her phone and followed Meghan to the food table. They were loading their plates with barbecue ribs, hot links, chicken wings, pork and beans, macaroni and cheese, and potato salad when Button found them.

"Hey ladies," Button shouted over the music when she reached her friends. In her tight, yellow dress, the eyes of most of the men were glued to her shapely curves.

"Button, I love that dress. If you aren't careful, you're going to cause these men to get whiplash," Dawn greeted.

"When you walked across the yard, it reminded me of that old Climax song," Meghan added and then she began to sing the chorus of "The Men All Pause."

"I can't help that I'm cold as hell," Button said when Meghan finished singing.

Meghan laughed. "You're what?!"

"I'm Cold. As Hell. I was modest about it in my twenties, but now, in my thirties, I say fuck it. Let the world know. I'm cold as hell and so are you," Button said directly to Meghan.

"I love it on you, but I don't have it in me." Meghan laughed dismissively.

"Oh, you got it in you. You just need a little help bringing it out and that's what I'm here for," Button said.

"Does Half know you're cold as hell?" Dawn asked sarcastically.

"Not only does he know it, but if you ask, he'll tell you all about it. Speaking of *Henry*, I'll take you to meet him. I have drinks for us and a table in his house so you can eat in comfort," Button said.

They followed Button inside the house and were immediately greeted by a handsome, burly man with a southern drawl. Button stood by Henry's side while she made introductions.

Henry surveyed the food on Meghan's and Dawn's plates. "Welcome, ladies. I see y'all got some of those authentic Texas ribs. Made 'em myself. Tell me later whattcha think. I tried a new recipe for the rub. It's all about the rub."

"Thanks for having us. The food smells amazing," Dawn complimented.

"I made all the meat. Button's the wine expert. I'm the grill master." Henry patted Button on her butt and she laughed.

"Then you guys are the perfect couple," Dawn instigated and winked at Button.

"I keep telling her that, but you know how she is. It's great to meet you both. I told Button to find one friend and she one-upped me by finding two." Henry rubbed Button's back.

"Huh." Dawn and Meghan shot Button a look and then exchanged looks with each other.

"Don't listen to him," Button tried to change the subject.

Henry kept talking to Dawn and Meghan. "Seriously, I thought Button would find ugly friends so she wouldn't have any competition. Boy, was I wrong. My baby's growing up. I'ma call y'all the cold as hell crew," Henry kept talking until Button interrupted.

"Alright baby. You've scored enough points. Can they go eat now?" Button was uncharacteristically flustered.

"My house is your house. Eat, enjoy, and see y'all on the dance floor." Henry pecked Button on the lips and left out the back door. Button led Meghan and Dawn to a table in the den.

They sat down next to each other on the couch and put their plates on the snack trays in front on them. "Did Henry say he told you to find a friend?"

Meghan asked.

"That's a long story," Button replied quickly.

"You can tell it while we eat 'cause I want to hear it," Meghan picked at the food on her plate.

"It's really kind of funny. Henry suggested I make some female friends as a way of working on my attachment *issues*." Button made air quotes around the word issues.

"Making friends with me and Dawn was an assignment from Henry?" Meghan asked uneasily.

"Yes…and no," Button answered timidly.

"Is that why you don't hug?" Meghan asked.

"I'm just not a hugger."

"Is that why you didn't come to the Art Institute with us?" Dawn asked.

"You guys were getting along so well and I was feeling a little overwhelmed by all the female bonding." Button shuffled her feet.

"Is that why Davis called us Single Girl Summer? Is that how long your *assignment* lasts? Until the end of the summer?" Dawn rapid-fired the questions.

"It's not like that." Button shook her head and sat down in a chair across from them.

"What's it like, Girl? 'Cause I'm feeling like now's a good time for a reality TV moment." Meghan pushed her plate away. Dawn also waited for an answer.

"I'm trying to change so I don't end up like my mother," Button blurted out.

"What's wrong with your mother?" Meghan asked, in a softer tone.

"When my mother was seven months pregnant with me, she discovered her best friend and my father were having an affair when she found her friend's coat button and a hotel receipt in my father's pocket. She was so devastated that her water broke and she went into labor prematurely. She held on to that button the whole time during my birth. It was a miracle I survived. My father abandoned us that night and never looked back. I've never even seen him in person," Button admitted.

"How did your mother know it was her friend's button?"

"It was really distinct and she had noticed her friend's coat was missing a button. When she found it in my father's pants pocket, she put two and two together."

"Please tell me that's not why you're named Button," Meghan cut in.

"My mother didn't ever want to forget that lesson so she named me Button. Growing up, my mother talked non-stop about my good-for-nothing father and that husband-stealing whore. She said you can't trust men or women. If I talked about a girlfriend or brought one over, she lectured me on how sneaky women are. Eventually, I gave up on having girlfriends. I think the last female friend I had was in college and I could never really get close to her. And don't get me started on how she feels about dating and marriage. It was easier to detach from everyone. I've been doing it for so long, I don't know how to do anything else. But I'm trying to change. Please don't be mad and please eat your food," Button pleaded.

Meghan pulled her plate close and picked up her plastic fork. "Girl, that story is heavy. I assumed Button was a cute, quirky name."

"Beside Henry, I've never told anyone that story. I hope you can cut me some slack. Just like you and Dawn, I'm working through some stuff too. Henry's been pushing me to make friends for a while now. At first I thought he was crazy, but I'm glad I finally listened. I enjoy hanging out with both of you. Davis calls us Single Girl Summer." Button laughed.

"Do you think working on your issues will also apply to Henry? He really cares about you," Dawn said.

"Half is ready to settle down and he's getting sick of my shit. He's dating some new chick. I'm sure she'll be here. I really like him, but commitment isn't my thing. It is what it is. When he leaves, I'll be on to the next." Button shrugged nonchalantly.

"Are you sure? He seems like a good one. You should hold on to him," Dawn encouraged.

"Okay Dawn, for you, I'll think about it." Button winked at Meghan. "In the meantime, let me get your drinks. White Zinfandel, Veuve or something else?" Button asked.

"I'll have a glass of Veuve," Dawn answered.

"Whaaaat, you're going to serve me White Zinfandel? This must be a test, but I don't care and yes I want some," Meghan said excitedly.

"It was a test and you failed. Miserably. I'll be right back." Button shook her head at Meghan and left the room.

Meghan turned to Dawn. "Wow. That was a lesson in not making assumptions. I thought Button's life was picture perfect."

"Yeah, you never know what someone else is going through." Dawn nodded in agreement and picked up a chicken wing.

They sat in silence while they ate. After a couple of minutes, Button returned with glasses and open bottles of White Zinfandel and Veuve on a tray.

As she poured the drinks, Meghan commented, "I love that you drink Veuve on a random Sunday."

"It's not a random Sunday." Button handed Meghan and Dawn their glasses. "Today is the first official day of Single Girl Summer," Button raised her glass.

"You mean your friend experiment." Meghan snickered and raised her glass.

Dawn interrupted, "I'm not single."

"If you ain't married, you're single," Button said, lowering her glass.

"I'm in a relationship. A rocky relationship, but a relationship. I'm not single," Dawn insisted.

"Umm, you can't check *in a relationship* on your tax returns. The options are single, married, or widowed. Divorced isn't even an option. So I have to agree with Button. You're single." Meghan winked at Button. "What's going on with Rick anyway?"

"I put my foot down. I told him I don't want a Half or Quarter boyfriend. It's all or nothing. So the ball's in his court."

"I hope it works out, but right now you're single," Button told Dawn.

"I guess. And Rick's in Houston so I have lots of free time," Dawn admitted. "So what happens in Single Girl Summer?"

"Single Girl Summer is about keeping your mind off the men and issues that drive you crazy. We have to stay outside, conserve money, get in shape, plan activities for each other and have as much fun as possible. Today is the official start," Button declared.

"I love it. Especially the money conservation part. To Single Girl Summer." Meghan smiled wide and raised her glass in agreement.

"To Single Girl Summer," Dawn and Button repeated. They raised their glasses and drank, sealing the deal.

"Ooooh, can you hear that? The DJ's playing my song. We gotta hit the dance floor." Meghan rose from her chair.

"What song is this?" Dawn rose also.

"It's Natalie Cole's house version of 'Tell Me All About It.' It's the best dance song of all time and only ten minutes long so let's go." The three friends rushed out of the house and onto the dance floor in the next yard. Everyone around them was dancing frantically and singing along.

"Am I the only one who doesn't know this song?" Dawn yelled over the music.

"Yes, but that's okay. You'll know it after today." Meghan closed her eyes as she danced.

"This could be our official song," Button rocked with the music.

Meghan opened her eyes. "Yay, Single Girl Summer. I love it." The crowd began to jump up and down. Meghan grabbed Dawn's and Button's hands. They joined the crowd and let their hair dance in the wind.

June

Chapter 13

Fr: <Dawn>
To: <Meghan>, <Button>
Thursday, June 4, 2009 1:55PM
Subject: Dawn's Day Spa

Pamper yourself at home for a fraction of the cost. Manis, pedis, facials, and waxing begin at high noon on Saturday. Bring an old tank top.

Fr: <Meghan>
To: <Dawn>, <Button>
Thursday, June 4, 2009 2:25PM
Subject: RE: Dawn's Day Spa

I'm making a stir-fry for lunch. Looking forward to the waxing lesson.

Fr: <Button>
To: <Meghan>, <Dawn>
Thursday, June 4, 2009 2:42PM
Subject: RE: Dawn's Day Spa

I'm bringing sake.

⁂

Meghan was inspired by Dawn's home. *I always thought minimalism was boring and cold, but this is elegant and warm. It's calm and liberating. The lack of clutter really highlights her beautiful furniture and art. And this bathroom is almost as big as my spare bedroom. The stainless steel, maple, jeweled double sinks, and mosaic-tiled wall; I'm in decorator's heaven. I wonder where she got this vanity. It makes me feel like a princess.*

"Meg, your face is glowing." Dawn's voice reverberated off the tiles as she looked at Meghan's reflection.

"This green tea scrub is magic." Meghan stared at her face in the lighted vanity mirror.

"Use it every day for the next week. Afterwards, brew a cup of green tea. Let it cool and then use it as your toner. All your acne will be gone by the end of the week. Then use the scrub twice a week."

Button was across the room admiring her clean underarms in the full-length mirror. "Forget the tea. The waxing lesson will save me at least fifty bucks a month. Who knew I could wax my own underarms and legs?"

"How'd you learn all this stuff?" Meghan asked.

"Law school was all about money conservation. Most of the sisters were on a tight budget so we'd have monthly spa parties. My hand wasn't steady enough to help with manis and pedis, but I perfected that green tea scrub and waxing," Dawn informed.

"Is waxing really better than shaving?" Meghan asked skeptically.

"Shaving irritates my skin. Waxing doesn't. Plus the hair grows back thinner and finer each time." Dawn applied a moisturizer to Meghan's face.

"Waxing lasts longer." Button chimed in. "Dawn, I still can't believe how fast you waxed both your underarms. Wax on, Wax off."

"I've been doing it so long that it's easy. I can wax in the morning before I go to work. I only need ten minutes and I love how smooth it feels." Dawn smiled big. "And since waxing and facials are one of my favorite things, I'm giving you both your own waxing kits, a box of organic green tea, and a container of my homemade green tea facial scrub." Dawn opened the cabinet door under the sink, pulled out two adorably wrapped packages, and handed one to Meghan and one to Button.

"This is just like being on Oprah. Thanks." Button ripped open her gift.

"Thank you, thank you, thank you. Girl, you made this scrub?" Meghan gushed, wide-eyed.

"I read an article that said you shouldn't put anything on your skin that you wouldn't also put in your mouth. Ever since, I've made my own face and body scrubs."

"Speaking of eating, I'm starving. Meg's stir-fry is calling my name." Button left the bathroom and headed for the kitchen.

Meghan and Dawn followed behind her.

"Did you guys have a good time at Half's party?" Button asked over her shoulder.

"I did. The funny thing is I looked terrible that day, but at least four cute guys hit on me. Men are so strange." Meghan turned up the fire under the wok on the stove.

"And you turned every one of those strangers down and there was some fine stranger danger out there," Button pointed out. She and Dawn sat at the small glass kitchen table.

"It's weird being able to flirt and date again. I haven't done that in so many years. I was nervous. Girl, being single again ain't easy," Meghan answered. "And did you hear that one guy invite me to smoke weed with him in the alley? Really, that's your pick-up line? I've never smoked weed before and I'm not going in some alley to do it."

"*You've never smoked weed!*" Button stared at Meghan, who shrugged and continued to stir the contents of the wok.

"Have you?" Button asked Dawn.

"Not since law school. Those were the days." Dawn shook her head nostalgically.

"I'm planning that activity."

Meghan spooned rice and stir-fry into three bowls and passed them out. Button retrieved a bottle of sake from the freezer and poured it into three ceramic Japanese cups.

Dawn breathed in the fresh ginger and teriyaki sauce before taking a bite. "Meg, this stir-fry is wonderful. The last time my kitchen saw this much action was Christmas. My sisters and mom cooked for the family. I only use the microwave."

"I love to cook. That's another hard thing about not having Frank around. There's no one to cook for or to help me eat what I cook," Meghan complained before sipping her drink.

"I'm just an elevator ride away. And I always bring drinks." Button took a sip.

"I like the sake." Meghan said.

"I picked it just for you. It's the sweetest one I could find so I figured you'd like it." Button winked at Meghan. "I really can't believe Frank let you get away. You cook. Women our age who cook this good are not the norm. He's a fool," Button said in disbelief.

"Have you talked to him?" Dawn asked.

"No. It feels like he's dead, but there's no body or funeral," Meghan said.

"How are you doing?" Dawn asked.

"Most times I feel like I'm doing really well, but occasionally, like at the wine tasting, I'll start crying and I can't get a hold of myself. Some nights I feel like I'm drowning in my own tears. It's scary."

"Divorce can take a toll on the body. Have you gone to see your doctor?" Button asked.

"Your hormones are probably out of whack. Ask your doctor for a prescription of Valium or Prozac, or both." Dawn suggested.

"I don't want any drugs. I'm cleansing my body and mind naturally. I even came off the pill to give my body a break. It's the stress of the divorce and keeping it a secret so I finally started telling my friends."

"How are they taking the news?" Dawn asked.

"At first, they're shocked. Then they're concerned about me. Then they tell me they support me completely and are happy I had the courage to walk away. My best friend, Joy, who lives in Denver, is coming next month to visit."

"Really, that's great." Dawn said.

"I told her I was fine, but she insisted on coming. She said she has to see me with her own eyes and give me a hug. She's a hugger, like me." Meghan looked pointedly toward Button, who ignored her.

"I told you not to underestimate your friends."

"You were right, but making the calls isn't fun. I make a couple of calls a day."

"Can't you just change your Facebook status to single and let them figure it out?" Button asked.

"That's how everyone at my job found out. I just wanted to change my payroll check. But putting in that change triggered a bunch of other changes. When my coworkers noticed my email had gone back to my maiden name, I was the hot gossip of the week. But I don't want my family and friends to find out on the internet. If you came to the wedding, then you deserve a phone call."

"Do they deserve to get their wedding presents back too?" Dawn asked.

"Ummm, no!"

"Are you calling everyone who came to your wedding?" Button asked.

"Not everyone, but the important people—which is still a lot of calls, and every phone call is like reliving the break-up. But I'm not sure what's worse; family and friends phone calls or telling complete strangers when I call to change my name. That list is almost as long. But enough about me! How's Rick?" Meghan shifted the attention to Dawn.

"We haven't talked much this past week. He's busy settling in. He's coming to Chicago this weekend and we're going to spend some quality time together. He said he has something important to tell me."

"Any idea what that could be? His last big announcement was terrible," Button reminded.

"Hopefully, he's ready to drop this open relationship idea, but I don't know. I'm just hoping for a nice visit."

"Do you need to warm up your swinging arm?"

"I could never throw a drink in his face."

"Dawn, if he hits you with more bad news, don't sit there speechless this time. Do something. Call me. I'll help you get him good," Button advised.

"Yeah, I'm with Button on this one. If he has more bad news, then you need to pull a quote from the gospel of Beyoncé. I think the book of 'Irreplaceable' fits. So if Rick starts trippin' again, tell him…

'You must not know 'bout me
You must not know 'bout me
I could have another you in a minute
Matter fact, he'll be here in a minute, baby.'"

Button chimed in: "'*To the left / To the left.*'"

Meghan continued, "'*And keep talking that mess, that's fine*
Could you walk and talk, at the same time?
And it's my life that's on the move
Better off without you; this I'll prove.
You must not know 'bout Dawn.
You must not know 'bout Dawn.
Cause she can have another man by tomorrow.
So don't you ever for a second get to thinkin' Rick's irreplaceable.'"

Meghan and Button high-fived.

"You guys and Beyoncé give the best advice and I hear you loud and clear. But like I said, I'm hoping for good news this time and that's all I'm going to say about that. In fact it's time to put Button in the hot seat. I saw Henry at Anand two Fridays in a row," Dawn said.

Meghan's eyes got wide. "I've run into him every morning this week in the parking garage. You two are boo'ed up. Does this have anything to do with that woman who was following him around at the party?"

"You mean his number-two chick who's working hard for my number-one spot? Before the party, I could tell he was spending more time with her and I missed him a little. When I saw them together, that was a wake-up call. It really bothered me and it took me a few days to figure out why. But I finally had to admit to myself how truly great Half is and that I'd be sad to lose him. So I told him I'm considering the commitment thing." Button said.

"Whoa, that's huge. I'm so proud of you," Meghan said.

Dawn cut in. "Henry has a successful business, owns a home, and cooks. He's charming and attractive. What's there to consider?"

"Half's great, but..." Button began but was interrupted by Dawn.

"Button, I can't take you serious when you call him Half."

"What's wrong with Half?" Button asked, perplexed.

"Everything. How can you contemplate a committed relationship with a nickname? A Half will never make a whole," Dawn said.

Meghan jumped in. "Dawn has a point. Nicknames trivialize people and relationships. When you're dating someone seriously, nicknames aren't cool."

"*Henry* is serious about your relationship and would tell the world you're his cold-as-hell girlfriend. What about you?" Dawn asked point-blank.

Button thought for a minute. "Henry's great. But if I commit, I'll have to give up my mind-blowing sex with Quarter. The timing's terrible."

"How's sex with Half?" Meghan asked.

"Can you call that man by his Christian name?" Dawn corrected Meghan.

"What? I like Half. I think it's funny." Meghan chuckled and waved off Dawn's interruption. "Anyway, Button, Half's not blowing your mind?"

"He is. Our sex is mind-blowing too, but in a different way. It's wonderful and intense and passionate. He completely satisfies me too."

"So the bottom line is you have mind-blowing sex with two men and you're afraid to give one of them up. What about the Sponsors? Can you at least give them up?" Dawn's voice was laced with frustration.

"It's not that I'm afraid, it's just that I know me. I like new shit. I don't want to settle for the same ol', same ol' all the time. I like meeting new and interesting men who expose me to new restaurants, artwork, vacation spots, etcetera. I like new. I don't want to settle down and be bored," Button said.

"Well, Button, that's why women have girlfriends. Men aren't the only ones who can introduce you to new restaurants," Dawn said.

"Yeah, but girlfriends don't pay. Sponsors always pay. Not only that, I honestly don't want to get married. Half—I mean Henry—wants to get married and have a family. If he can find that with Number-Two Chick, I shouldn't stand in his way. I want him, but I don't want him the way he wants me to. He's a great guy and he deserves to be with someone who wants to be his wife and the mother of his children," Button admitted.

"Girl, how long have you and Henry been together?" Meghan asked.

"Two years," Button answered.

"I hate saying this, but it's time for you to piss or get off the pot," Dawn said.

"I told him I'll try moving toward a commitment. We'll see what happens. And I'm taking him to meet my mother."

"You mean the man-bashing-girlfriend-hating, bitter mother you told us about?" Meghan asked.

"The one and only," Button said.

"Where did this idea come from?"

"Not me. I don't think it's a good idea, but I need someone to fix the electrical problems with her house. It's an old house and her circuits keep blowing. Henry's an electrician so I asked him if he could find someone in Augusta to do the work right, but he offered to fly there with me to do it himself. He wants to meet my mother. He insists. We're going next weekend. Pray for me." Button laughed.

"You're both boo'ed up next weekend. What am I going to do?" Meghan whined.

"You can find someone to pop your single-girl cherry. Dawn's scrub, some good sex and a little weed would completely clear up that acne, help you lose a couple of pounds, and put a big smile on your face." Button suggested.

"Button, where do you propose I go to find a cherry-popper? Produce section at the grocery store, Craig's list, classifieds, church bulletin?" Meghan laughed.

"Anywhere there are men. Like the gym," Button said.

"But what if she doesn't want to be bothered seeing him afterwards?" Dawn asked.

"Our gym is a chain. Start working out at some other locations. The gym is perfect because you get to check out the package before you take it home." Button winked at Meghan.

"I hate working out with you, but I'm going and we've got a good routine. I don't want to mess with it." Meghan shot down that idea.

"The Apple Store. Every time I go, I spot at least three or four cute techno-savvy brothers." Button tried again.

"That's a good one, except when men are around electronics, they tune out. All the shiny buttons are hard to compete with."

"Excuses, excuses. Dawn and I are going to have to play matchmaker. I'll start scoping the restaurant and Dawn, can you scope out a hot lawyer or paralegal?"

"Ooh, I have the perfect guy." Dawn's eyes lit up.

"Who?" Button asked.

"There's this guy Brett, who works with Rick. He's a total playboy, very handsome, typical rich boy. Rick hates him, but Rick owes me. I can set up a double date for Saturday night. Just don't get attached to him. There's no long-term future in him," Dawn said.

"I don't know. Casual sex isn't for me," Meghan said.

"You don't have to sleep with him if you don't want to. Just get out and have a nice dinner. Knock the dust off your single girl shoes," Button said.

"Maybe. It'll depend on how my Saturday errands go. I'm getting my hair done and going straight to the DMV to change my driver's license to my maiden name. If I take a good picture, I'll be eager to show it off Saturday night. But if I don't, I probably won't be in the mood to leave the house," Meghan said.

"I thought you did that already. Don't you have to change your license before you can change anything else?" Dawn asked.

"My passport is still in my maiden name so I've been using that for photo ID."

"Why haven't you changed your license?"

"Ten years ago, the DMV took the ugliest picture of me and had the nerve to slap it on my license. I'm not a vain person. But when I showed people that license, they looked twice and laughed. Hard. It wasn't just an ugly license picture. It was literally the ugliest picture I've ever taken. I couldn't wait to get married so I could take a new one. I've vowed never to take another ugly license picture again. I even developed a list on how to take a good picture. The license I have now is really nice and my next picture will be even better," Meghan said confidently.

"What's on the list?" Dawn asked.

"Number one: Take your picture in the summer so you have a tan and can show some skin. Spaghetti straps and bare shoulders look great in a headshot. Number two: Though it goes without saying, hair and makeup must be flawless.

Red-toned makeup is preferred. Pale skin, split ends, and metallic lipstick are not photogenic; made all those mistakes before. Number three: Smile and show teeth. Number four: Be ready at all times. Number five: Be extra nice to the camera operator. Make it clear you want to take a nice picture so please tell you if anything doesn't look right. I'm going straight from the hairdresser to the DMV. With my fresh hair and summer tan, I'm taking a glamour shot."

"It's just a picture. Why don't you wait until you lose your fifteen pounds before you take it?" Button asked.

"I want to get it over with. It's the last thing on my name-change list. I know it sounds trivial, but it's important to me. If my picture comes out good and if Rick's okay with it, then I'm game," Meghan said.

"I hope the double date happens. Nothing makes you start forgetting an old love like a new fling." Button smiled at Meghan. "I'm back late on Sunday. We should have dinner Monday night for updates," Button suggested.

"Let's get together at my house. I'll cook lasagna," Meghan said.

"I'll bring garlic bread and tiramisu," Dawn said.

"I'll bring salad, Prosecco, and lots of crazy Momma stories." Button rolled her eyes and dug into her food.

"It's a date."

Chapter 14

Fr: <Mom>
To: <Button>
Thursday, June 11, 2009 1:57PM
Subject: VISIT HOME

WHY CAN'T YOU STAY HERE AND LET THAT MAN STAY IN A HOTEL? MAYBE THIS VISIT ISN'T A GOOD IDEA. LET'S DO IT ANOTHER TIME.

Fr: <Button>
To: <Mom>
Thursday, June 11, 2009 2:03PM
Subject: RE: VISIT HOME

His name is Henry and we're coming tomorrow. Please be on your best behavior. Remember, he's coming to do you a favor.

Fr: <Mom>
To: <Button>
Thursday, June 11, 2009 2:04PM
Subject: RE: VISIT HOME

HE AIN'T DOING ME NO FAVOR. HE'S DOING YOU A FAVOR. COME IF YOU WANT. I DON'T CARE.

⁂

"Nother round?" the words fell like molasses off the waitress' tongue. For the second night in a row, Henry and Button sat across from each other in the comfy chairs of the Augusta Inn. Henry calmed his nerves with whiskey and Button nursed a glass of wine.

"No, I'm good. Thanks," Button responded.

"Another Jack, light ice. Double this time," Henry ordered.

"Sure thang." The waitress departed for the bar.

"A double, huh?" Button asked gingerly.

"I need the whole bottle, but this is a small town. I don't want it getting back to Mommy Dearest that I was drunk in the hotel bar. Not that it would matter. Your mother's meaner than sin. Two days with her is enough to drive anybody crazy."

"You've done two days. I've done thirty-one years."

"Cocoa, meeting your mother explains a lot."

"I knew this was a bad idea. Listen, you stay here. I'll go over for dinner and tell her I asked you not to come so we could have some mother-daughter time."

"You don't have to give her a reason why I'm not there. She won't care."

"Henry, I really appreciate you working on her house and putting up with all her crap. Our plane leaves tomorrow morning and you never have to come back here ever again."

"I'd only put up with this amount of crap for you. And if you needed me to, I'd come back and put up with it again."

"I know." Button sighed and went to sit in Henry's lap. She kissed him passionately, longing to stay nestled against him all night, but her mother was waiting for her.

Henry watched Button as she crossed the room towards the exit. He leaned back in his chair, downed the last of his whiskey, and exhaled. *Man, I'm glad I don't have to back to that house for dinner. If I had to listen to Ms. Jackson talk about Button's no-good father one more time, I was gon' rewire that circuit box and electrocute myself. She just can't let it go. And it shows. She looks so old and bitter. I had to look real hard to find my baby's pretty features in Ms. Jackson's face. I don't want the same thing to happen to Cocoa. I love her, but I don't know if she can work through her issues. I don't know if she wants to. But I know Vivian's not gon' play second fiddle much longer. She's a great woman with a good head on her shoulders, but she ain't Button.*

"Excuse me." Henry's thoughts were interrupted. He snapped out of his daze to see an older gentleman around the age of his father holding a snifter and looking down at him. The man seemed familiar, but Henry couldn't place him.

"Yes, Sir," Henry answered.

"That woman who just left here, is her name Button?" The man asked, wide-eyed.

"Yeah, that's Button."

"She's beautiful. You're very lucky."

"I know. She has that affect on me too." Henry stood. "Henry James. How do you do, Sir?" The men shook hands.

"I'm much better now. Is Button coming back?"

"No, she's on her way to her mother's house."

"Oh, I'm not going over there," the man mumbled to himself.

"You look familiar. Have we met before?"

"I wish, but no. I'm Sonny, Button's father."

Henry looked like he'd just been sucker punched. "Seriously?"

"Can we sit?"

"Please." Henry gestured to the empty chair Button had previously occupied.

Sonny sat on the edge of the chair and placed his snifter filled with brown liquor on the table. Noticing Henry's empty glass, he asked, "Can I order you a drink?"

Henry mirrored Sonny's position, also sitting on his chair's edge. "I have a double Jack coming."

"Have you met Erica?"

"Yes. Hence the double Jack. What are you doing here?"

"Son, there's two sides to every story and it's time Button heard my side. Her mother has brainwashed her to hate me, but I want to know my daughter and have a relationship. I came down here to finally confront Erica. I wasn't expecting to see Button or you, but here we are. That's my Button. This has gone on too long." Sonny sounded heartbroken.

"What's gone on too long?"

"Erica's lies. I'm not perfect, but my ex-wife doesn't tell the whole story."

"I'd love to hear your side," Henry said as the waitress returned. She removed his old rocks glass and replaced it with the fresh drink.

"Y'all good?" she asked.

"Yeah, thanks." Henry and Sonny lifted their respective glasses and took a strong draw. Sonny settled back into his chair, using the armrest as a coaster.

Henry stayed on the edge of his chair, anxious for the story to begin.

Sonny took time to consider his words, as though he'd waited years for this opportunity. "I was fifteen when my parents died and I moved to Augusta to live with my grandmother. I met my current wife, Sandra, sophomore year of high school and we fell in love. I know love at first sight sounds old-fashioned, but it's true."

"I felt the same way when I saw your daughter." Henry smiled.

"Button's just as pretty as Erica used to be. Every boy and man in town would have done anything for her. But I didn't care. I loved Sandra."

"Erica's best friend?"

Sonny shook his head. "Sandra and Erica were never friends. Couldn't stand each other. I think that's why Erica kept trying to get with me. To piss Sandra off."

"Wait, so your ex-wife and your current wife weren't best friends?"

"No. Is that what she told Button? I ran off with her best friend? That's not true. Erica always had an active imagination and a forked tongue. Sandra and I were together through high school. After graduation, Sandra went to a nursing college in Florida, I got a job in town, and Erica went to the community college. Long distance was tough, but Sandra and I loved each other and tried to stay together. That summer before her senior year, we broke up. It was just too much distance. When Erica found out, she was all over me and I was happy for the distraction, but I missed Sandra.

"I don't remember who called who, but Sandra and I started talking again and I knew she was the only one for me. I could never love anyone the way I love her. I went to break up with Erica, but she told me she was pregnant. Back then when you got a girl pregnant, you married her. I apologized to Sandra for getting myself in this mess, but was determined to do right by my baby. I married Erica, but I didn't love her. I loved Sandra.

"Four months into the pregnancy, Erica said she lost baby. I was never sure she was pregnant. I never saw any tests or papers. I was miserable with her and I had this nagging feeling she tricked me. But she was a wreck. Doctor said she had depression. My grandmother, bless her soul, begged me to stay with Erica at least until she got better. After about a year, she was. Sandra had graduated and moved back to town. I told Erica I wanted a divorce and again she's pregnant. This time, I went with her to the doctor and it was true. The months dragged by and this time *I* had the depression. I'd see Sandra around town and my heart would break. I truly loved her but couldn't be with her. Erica wouldn't let me.

"When Erica was five months pregnant, Sandra told me she was moving to Atlanta. She couldn't take seeing us together. I begged her to stay. It was the worst situation, but at least we saw each other now and then. If she moved, I knew I'd never see her again. Sandra said I had to choose. I couldn't have both. I stayed, but I couldn't live that lie. We divorced a little after Button's first birthday and I moved to Atlanta. I've been with Sandra ever since."

"So you didn't leave when Ms. Jackson was seven months pregnant and almost dying in labor?"

"Hell no. I don't know if it's any better, but I didn't leave my pregnant wife and unborn child."

"Where'd the name Button come from?"

"Button is the name of my grandmother who raised me here in Augusta. She passed a couple of months before Button was born so I named her in the hospital as a tribute."

Henry shook his head. "Why didn't you keep in touch?"

"I tried, but Erica wouldn't allow it. I sent money and cards, but she'd send them back. I'd drive down to visit, but Erica wouldn't let me see Button. Finally, she threatened to tell the police I molested my baby. She scared me so bad. I just gave up. I know I shouldn't have, but I didn't see any other way. I sent letters to Button when she was in college, but like her mother, she just sent them back. I gotta make this right. I have a hole in my heart. A couple of months ago, I found Button's restaurant on the internet and sent her a card. I didn't hear anything back and I didn't want to just show up. I thought I'd start by making peace with Erica and then I see my baby. I saw my Button." Sonny choked up. "Sandra and I have two children. Even if she won't talk to me, at least she should know her sister and brother."

"Whoa, Button's not an only child."

"No, she's not."

Henry laughed. "That's crazy."

"What do you think I should do? Button needs to know I didn't abandon her. I only wanted to leave Erica, not her. Do you think I should go over to the house or try to catch Button here? I'm staying in the hotel too."

"Um, I don't think going to Ms. Jackson's house is a good idea and we're flying out in the morning. I hate to ask this, but how do I know you're telling the truth?"

"I have all the letters that were returned at home. And I have this." Sonny reached into his breast pocket and pulled out an old photograph. He admired it then passed it to Henry. Henry looked at the picture and smiled.

"Read the back," Sonny instructed.

Henry turned the photograph over and read the hand-written inscription on the back. Sonny was telling the truth. His eyes pleaded with Henry. "I hate to put you in the middle, but could you let Button know I'm here? Give her a heads up. Break the ice."

Henry took a shot of whiskey. *All these lies. All these years. How do you clean up this mess?* Henry looked at the hurt on Sonny's face. *You tell the truth*. "I'll call your room later. Can I hold on to this picture?"

Sonny picked up a hotel notepad and pen that was left on the table and began to scribble. "I love that picture, but I want Button to have it. This is my room number. Even if she doesn't want to see me, can you call me tonight? I appreciate it." Sonny passed the paper to Henry.

"Yes Sir."

Sonny stood and Henry rose to meet him. They shook hands. Sonny walked to the elevators and Henry went to the front desk to call a cab.

***

"Who the hell's ringing my doorbell this late at night?" Erica Jackson asked no one in particular as she shuffled across the living room in her sponge rollers, head scarf, and housecoat. She swung open the front door with fury. "Oh, it's you."

"It's nice to see you too, Ms. Jackson." Henry stepped around her to enter.

Button walked into the living room. She smiled when she saw Henry and hugged him hard.

"That's a nice hug. You okay?" Henry pulled back to look at Button's face.

"It's just nice to see a friendly face. Thanks for coming. Did you get lonely at the hotel?" Button looked sad. It was the look she always had after interaction with her mother. Ms. Jackson always made Button sad and that made Henry mad.

"Wasn't lonely at all. In fact, right after you left, I made a new friend," Henry said, loud enough for Button's mother to hear.

Ms. Jackson closed the front door and glared at him with scorn. "Bet ya did. You look like the friendly type. Sonny was real friendly too and you see how that turned out. Gotta watch the friendly ones."

"Mom, please. Who'd you meet, Baby?" Button asked.

"Sonny." Henry looked directly at Ms. Jackson. "We had a long conversation."

"Sonny who?" Button drew Henry's attention back.

"Your father, Sonny."

"Where? How?"

"He's in town to talk to your mother about you. He saw us in the hotel bar and came over after you left. He said you look just like your mother when she was younger so he knew it was you." Henry reached for Button. She looked like she might faint, so he rested his arm on her back for support.

Button's back stiffened at his touch. "Why would you talk to him?"

"He had a very different story of where the name Button came from. Very different." Henry's eyes pierced Button's mother.

Ms. Jackson turned pale and shuffled across the room to sit on the living room couch.

The words fell sharply and distinctly from Button's tongue. "Henry, *what are you talking about?*"

"Are you going to tell her the truth or do I have to do it? Tell her who named her Button and why," Henry said to Ms. Jackson, who looked like she was in shock.

"Henry, you know how I got my name." Button turned her mother. "Do you know what he's talking about?"

"Baby, I'm talking about the truth, which your mother hasn't been telling you." Button turned back to Henry. "You weren't named after some button in your father's pocket. Ms. Jackson, you always have so much to say. Jump in anytime."

Button's head volleyed back and forth from Henry to her mother, who refused to make eye contact. "Mom, say something."

Ms. Jackson lifted her head to face Button and began to cry. "I'm sorry," was all she whispered.

"Henry, what's going on? You're upsetting her and me." Button's face was bright red.

"Your father didn't abandon you. In fact, he named you Button on the night you were born. It's the name of his grandmother."

"My father ran off to Atlanta the night I was born. He's never even laid eyes on me."

"I got this from your father." Henry handed her a picture of a man, beaming with delight and holding a newborn baby. Button knew the man was her father. The resemblance was undeniable. The picture had been laminated to preserve it. Button flipped the picture over and recognized the distinct handwriting from the letters she always sent back. "Daddy's little Button."

"Okay, so he left after I was born. He still abandoned me."

"No he didn't. He left your mother, but he didn't want to leave you. He sent money and tried to stay in touch, but your mother wouldn't let him. She threatened to lie to the police and tell them he hurt you if he ever contacted you again. He felt like he didn't have any other choice but to let you go. But he didn't want to. You said it yourself that he sent you letters when you were in college."

"This isn't happening. How do you know he's telling the truth? You're just going to believe that stranger?"

"He said he has all the returned letters and he has that picture of you together. He can prove he was there when you were born and I believe he tried to be there for you after he left. Ask your mother if he's telling the truth."

Button looked at the picture again. She crossed the room to stand in front of her mother on the couch and held the picture in her face. Button spoke slowly, "What is this? What's going on? Did you lie about my father?"

Ms. Jackson's head hung low. "How dare you?" Her whispered words got lost in her lap. Her breath came quicker and deeper. Her chest rose and fell. She finally raised her head to growl at Henry. "How dare you? Coming to my house to poison my daughter against from me. You ain't nothing but the devil."

Henry opened his mouth to respond, but was cut off. Button moved slightly to the right, cutting off her mother's sight line to Henry.

"Mother, did you tell my father to stop contacting me?"

Ms. Jackson grabbed Button's hand. "It was for ya own good. He left us. He made his choice. He needed to live with it. He chose that woman."

Button snatched her hand away. "My entire life you've lied to me. You made me believe my father didn't give a shit about me, but he did. He didn't give a shit about you and you took it out on me. He left you. Not me. You used me to hurt him. You made up that ridiculous button story and made that my legacy, my, my handicap, my reason to not ever trust anyone. And you're the one I shouldn't trust. You're a bitter, crazy woman who wants me to be as unhappy and lonely as you are. I don't ever want to see you again. Let's go." Button grabbed her purse from a tattered chair and stormed out the front door as Henry held it open.

While Henry drove back to the hotel, he recounted all the details from his conversation with Sonny. Button sobbed softly in the passenger seat. In two years, he'd never seen her cry. He eased the rental car into a space in the hotel parking lot, shut down the engine, and turned to face her.

"Baby, I'm so sorry. I feel really bad about having to be the one to tell you."

"You don't have anything to be sorry about. I'm glad you told me. I'm glad to know that Button isn't a scarlet letter. It's my great-grandmother's name and my connection to my father."

"Do you want to see him tonight?"

"Will you go with me?"

"Of course. I wouldn't dream of letting you go through this without me."

"Henry, you're so good to me. I don't ever want to lose you."

"Anything for you, and that's why I keep telling you I want all of you."

"I know." Tears fell from her eyes.

Henry stroked her tear-stained face. Then he kissed her so tenderly that Button vowed to remember this moment forever, no matter what happened.

CHAPTER 15

Text Message to Andrea
Fr: Meghan
2:13pm 6/12/09 - Friday
Girl, can U get me n b4 9?
Getting a relaxer.
DMV closes at noon.
Got 2 b out by 1030.

Text Message to Meghan
Fr: Andrea
3:45pm 6/12/09 - Friday
U first n my chair. I got u.
In at 9. Out by 1030, on my mama.

⁂

Meghan's red Honda Accord barreled down the expressway, zooming past all the other cars. Meghan kept checking the speedometer and clock. They read 80 mph and 11:30 AM. *Crap, I need to slow down. If I get a ticket, the cops will take away my license and I won't be able to get a new one. But the DMV is about to close. I could kill Andrea. Out by 10:30 my ass. It was ten when she finally got to the shop. She's so unprofessional. I wish I could find another hairdresser, but nobody lays my hair like she does. And it looks good. My makeup is perfect, my skin is tanned, and my shoulders are out. I'm ready. If I can get there in time, this is going to be a great picture.*

The car screeched around the curve into the DMV parking lot. Meghan was surprised the lot was still packed at twenty minutes before closing time. Grabbing the first available space, she bolted from the car and ran to the building. Once inside, Meghan was immediately greeted by a cute, twenty-something year old woman who was stationed by the front door.

"Hi, welcome to the Illinois Secretary of State. How can we help you today?" Slightly out of breath, Meghan's words fell as fast as she'd been driving earlier. "I need to change my name on my driver's license. Is it too late? Can I still? Is it too late?"

The greeter smiled at Meghan. "Ma'am. Slow down. As long as you make it inside before noon, you're good. What's the reason for the name change?"

"Divorce."

"Ooooh, sorry." The greeter flinched. "Do you have your current license and Dissolution of Marriage Judgement?"

"Yes, right here."

"Okay, stand in line number three. Is there anything else I can help you with?"

"I just want to check that I can take a new picture. I called twice and they said I can. Is that right?"

"Of course you can take a new picture. And your hair looks really pretty so you should take a nice one. Anything else?"

"That's all, thanks." Satisfied with her answers, Meghan walked over to line number three.

It was quarter to noon and the sign on the wall said from this point the wait was fifteen minutes. Feeling relief settle in her soul, Meghan took her compact mirror out of her purse and touched up her hair and makeup while the line zig-zagged around. When she finished, she watched the clerks behind the service desks.

That's funny. I thought it was only old married couples that look alike, but these clerks are all carbon copies with the same bored expression and that annoying gum popping. I guess these people have worked here a long time.

"Next." Another cute twenty-something woman called Meghan up to her desk, but Meghan could already tell that she wasn't going to be anywhere as friendly as the front door greeter.

"Hi. How are you?" Meghan asked.

Pop. "Ready to go." Pop. "How can I help you?" The clerk answered stone-faced, punctuating each sentence with her chewing gum gymnastics.

"I'm changing the name on my license."

"Reason?" Pop.

"Divorce," Meghan whispered.

Lowering her voice had the opposite desired effect on the clerk, who raised her voice to a near scream. "Current license and divorce decree?" Pop. Pop. Pop.

Meghan looked around in shock before handing over the documents.

The clerk sighed. "Same address?" Pop.

"Yes."

"Same height, weight?" Pop.

"No changes. It's all the same. Can I take a new picture?"

Pop. "Yup. Take this to the cashier." Pop. "Around the corner. Pay ten dollars at the window. Follow signs to photo area. Next." Pop. The clerk gave Meghan her documents and looked past her to the next person in line. Pop.

"Thanks. Hope you get out of here soon." Meghan smiled sweetly at the clerk and then walked towards the cashier. *I don't care if she was short with me or had to tell everybody about my divorce. I'm getting rid of the name Henderson on my license and getting a pretty, new picture. This is my last name change and a new beginning.*

Meghan felt lighter with each step. After she paid the license renewal fee, Meghan was downright giddy. *I'm almost there.* Meghan walked over to the picture line and handed her paperwork to the photographer. The old man with kind eyes directed her to take a seat and listen for her name. Meghan took out her compact and fixed her hair and makeup again. She practiced her smile and didn't care if anyone was watching.

For the past two weeks, she'd been confessing divorce to family and friends and relived the pain with each exclamation of "what happened?" She was also calling perfect strangers to admit her failure when all she wanted to do was get a new credit card or change the name on her magazine subscription. She never wanted to see the name Meghan Henderson again. That name was like poison and she was erasing every trace of it from her life. And this was the big one. If she took a bad picture, it would be another slap in her face courtesy of her divorce. She just had to take a nice picture. Then she'd know for sure that bigger and better things were in store for Meghan Cherry.

Wait, something's wrong. Those people came after me. Meghan grabbed her purse and walked up to the photographer. "Excuse me. You haven't called my name yet, but you called two people who came after me."

"Did you turn in your paperwork? What's your name?" The photographer asked.

"I turned in my paperwork to you. My name's Meghan Cherry. Is it on your list?" He checked the computer screen. "Not yet. Sometimes these computers have no rhyme or reason. It'll pop up. Just give it a minute." He smiled at Meghan.

"No problem. And when my name does come up, can you please make sure I take a good picture. It's really important. So if I look funny, just let me know."

"I'll make sure your picture is so good, they'll hang it in the DMV hall of fame," he assured her. Meghan smiled big and walked back to the waiting area. Across the room, she saw where the finished licenses were spit out of a machine. A young male clerk scrutinized each one and then either nodded contently or smirked unmercifully. He seemed to really be enjoying his job and made no effort to cover his laughter when Meghan assumed he saw a bad picture. A new license slid out of the machine. The young man examined it, chuckled, then called "Silvia Ramirez." The woman came to the counter, looked at her license and grimaced. Meghan sympathized as she remembered having that same reaction ten years ago. Another license slid out of the machine. The young man inspected it a long time, longer than usual while he laughed, hard.

Meghan chuckled. *It must be worse than Silvia's. I know I shouldn't laugh, but I can't wait to see this person's reaction.* The young man looked up from the license and called "Meghan Cherry." Meghan didn't move an inch. *How could my license be finished when I haven't taken my picture?*

"Meghan Cherry," he called again. Meghan still didn't move.

"Ms. Cherry," The photographer called and waved at Meghan. "He's calling you. Your license is ready."

Meghan asked from her seat. "How's that possible?"

The elderly man shrugged. "Not sure, but you gotta go over there to pick it up."

The dingy linoleum was like quicksand. Meghan struggled to cross the room. She cautiously approached the counter as if the young man behind it might bite. Her heart beat loudly in her ears, but she tried to relax. *Maybe they pulled my last picture. I wanted a better picture, but the old one was cool.*

"I'm Meghan Cherry. You called my name?" It was supposed to be a statement, but it sounded more like a question.

"You look much better in person. Here you go." He handed the license to Meghan and she wanted to slap that silly grin off his face.

Meghan looked at the picture with disgust. "Um, excuse me. This isn't my license." She put the license back on the counter in front of the clerk.

"Ma'am, that's you in the picture."

"You take that back. That's not me. That's a hideous imitation of me."

The young man picked up the license, checked the picture, and then looked back at Meghan. "It's you. It's a bad picture of you, but it's you. Therefore, this is your new Illinois State Driver's License. Have a nice day."The young man placed the license back on the counter in front on Meghan.

"That picture is from ten years ago. It's not even my last license picture." Meghan wouldn't touch the license.

"Ma'am..." The young man was getting annoyed.

"Hey, I was told I could take a new picture, but they never called my name. How can you just reach back in time, find the ugliest picture of me ever taken, and slap it on my license again? I was told I could take a new picture." Meghan informed him with an escalating voice.

"I don't know what happened. But here's your license." The young man picked up the license and gave it to Meghan.

"Listen, if I can't take a new picture, that's fine. But I need you to use my last license picture. That was a nice picture. This...this is unacceptable." Meghan held up the license.

"I can't make you a new license."

"I'll pay for another renewal."

"Sorry, Ma'am. Once the license is generated, that's it. The machine associated this picture with your license. Even if you get another one, the same picture will come up again. Plus, it's after noon, so we're closed."

"You don't understand. I'm not walking around with this in my wallet. You know what...I need to talk to a supervisor."

"Great. Walk back into the first area, around the corner from the cashier. The supervisor is in the customer service line."

Meghan fumed as she stomped back to customer service line and struggled to keep her tears at bay. *Calm down, Meg. You'll catch more bees with honey so you need to calm down. Be rational and I'm sure they'll fix this mistake.* Meghan's composure was barely returning when she was called by a customer service agent who looked like an older version of the bored desk clerks, but with a definite no-nonsense demeanor and thankfully no chewing gum.

The agent's hands were folded calmly on the desk. "Hi, how can I help you?"

"Are you the supervisor? I need a supervisor." Meghan could feel her pulse quickening.

"Yes, I am. How can I help you?" The agent repeated.

Meghan placed the license on the counter and began to ramble, "I came in today to change my name on my license back to my maiden name. I called twice before coming and was told I could take a new picture. When I got here, I asked twice and again was told I could take a new license picture. I spent eighty-five dollars getting my hair done this morning. I got my outfit and makeup perfect so I could take a nice picture. But they never called my name. They pulled my picture from ten years ago, which is the ugliest picture I've ever taken. It's not even my last picture. I can't have this on my license. I need to take a new picture or at least use my last picture. I'll even pay again."

The supervisor looked down at the license but didn't pick it up. "Okay, let me get this straight. You changed from a married name back to your maiden name, correct?"

"Yes."

"Oh, I know what happened. The machine didn't pull your last picture because that picture is associated with your married name. The machine pulled the last picture taken under your maiden name." The supervisor smiled at Meghan like she had just solved the problem without having to even touch the license in front of her.

"Okay. So can I take a new picture?"

"No. Once the license is printed, I can't authorize a new one. That's your license."

"Why?"

"Security protocol."

Meghan's lip quivered. "There has to be something you can do. There's no way you can authorize a new license?"

The supervisor finally picked up the license. She analyzed the picture, then looked at Meghan. "The only way I can do that is if you look different than the picture and this picture looks like you."

"No, it doesn't. It's ug-gu-ly."

"It's not that bad. Look at it this way, ten years later and you still look the same. That's a good thing." The supervisor set the license in front of Meghan and smiled.

"That's not a good thing. This license is not a good thing. Who's your superior? I'm going over your head." Meghan's decibel level escalated with each exchange.

"I'm the final word on this matter. The picture looks like you so I can't authorize a new license. Furthermore, it's after noon and we're closed. I'm sorry you don't like your picture, but there's nothing I can do. You know in the grand scheme of things, it's just a picture." The supervisor shrugged her shoulders. The gesture enraged Meghan, who was sick of people delivering bad news to her and then shrugging their shoulders. It was the last insult she was going to put up with today.

"Look Lady, I know very well it's just a picture. It won't kill me to have an ugly license. I know there are starving children in Africa, homeless people, sick people, injured people, people at war and they would probably love to have their biggest problem be an ugly license picture. *But honestly, I don't give a crap.* All month, I've been calling my family, friends, and hell, even perfect strangers to tell them I'm divorced. My marriage failed and yes, I'd like to go back to my maiden name. All that I ask of you is to let me have a nice license picture so every time I look in my wallet, I don't have to see another failure. So, can you do your damn job and take my picture?"

"Ma'am, I sympathize with you, which is why I'm going to give you two minutes to leave on your own before I call security. Have a nice day. Oh, and don't forget your new license."

Meghan glared at the supervisor. Finally, she grabbed the ugly license and stomped towards the exit. She went five feet and stopped. Her face was red with fury. Tears gathered in the corners of her eyes and her breathing was hard and deep like a bull about to charge. As if in a slow motion, she pivoted on her heels and locked eyes with the dismissive woman again. Neither moved a muscle as they sized each other up. *I came here to take a nice picture and dammit that's what I'm going to do.*

"Ma'am. Ma'am." The overweight security guard in the wrinkled brown suit snapped his chunky fingers in Meghan's face. "We're closed. You need to proceed toward the exit, *now*."

Chapter 16

Fr: <Rick>
To: <Dawn>
Saturday, June 13, 2009 2:55PM
Subject: Can't wait to…

Darling, finishing up and then I'm coming back to you. I don't want to double date. I need you all to myself.

Fr: <Dawn>
To: <Rick>
Saturday, June 13, 2009 3:26PM
Subject: RE: Can't wait to…

Good news then. Meghan cancelled. I already let Brett know.
I like making up for lost time. Hurry back.

⁂

Lingering in the hallway outside Dawn's condo, Rick and Dawn looked like two high school kids making out under the bleachers. Dawn's back was pressed against the marbled tiled hallway and her neck tilted up to him. Rick's forearms, above either side of her head, supported most of his weight and allowed him to comfortably lean his brawn into her. Her hands explored his back and waist while their tongues explored each other's mouths. The teenaged son of one of Dawn's neighbors passed by and suggested they get a room. Dawn and Rick laughed and then peeled themselves away from the wall.

Dawn unlocked her front door. Rick held it open for her and said, "I don't know why you didn't take me stepping before. Darling, I'm a natural."

"Yeah, I don't know what my problem was. All these years I should've begged you to go." Dawn laughed and passed through the doorway.

Rick patted her on the butt and followed her into the living room. "I forgive you. I did pretty well for my first time. I couldn't do all the fancy footwork and spins like the guys in the bright suits, but I got the basics. Is there a correlation between loud suits and smooth moves?"

Dawn smirked. "Yes, the louder your suit, the smoother your moves. The night's young and I'm expecting to see more of your moves so you may want to run back over there to borrow a jacket. You look great in red."

Rick grabbed her, turned her around, and pulled her close. "I don't need a loud jacket to move you tonight." He kissed her with such intensity that Dawn felt light-headed. When they parted, Dawn spotted a tear falling from Rick's eye. He tried to speak, but the words caught in his throat.

"Baby, is everything okay?" Dawn watched him with worry as he went to sit on the couch. It was several moments before he finally spoke.

"Darling, I have to tell you something."

Dawn set her purse on the coffee table and sat next to him rubbing his back. "Baby, you're scaring me. What's wrong? You know you can tell me anything."

"You're so wonderful. I mean, you're perfect, and I didn't realize how wonderful you were so I moved and now you're going to leave me." Rick sobbed.

"The long-distance is hard, but we'll figure it out. I love you. I'm here for you. We'll make it work as long as it's just me and you…committed. I'm not mad about the open relationship discussion. We'll just move past it."

Rick mumbled something through his sobs, but Dawn couldn't understand him. "Rick, what's wrong? Please tell me. You're scaring me."

Rick tried to formulate words, but he couldn't pull it together.

"Baby, go to the bathroom and splash some water on your face." Dawn patted his knee. Rick left the room and Dawn went into the kitchen. She grabbed two glasses, a bottle of tequila from the freezer, and orange juice from the fridge. Her hands were shaking. *I've never seen him like this. Oh God, what could be wrong?* She built two tequila screwdrivers, took a big swallow from hers, and returned to the living room. *Maybe he has cancer. He's dying. He must be. What else could make him act like this way? I have to be strong for him.*

Dawn's eyes watered as she sat back on the couch and placed both tumblers on the coffee table. When she heard Rick in the hallway, she wiped her eyes with the back of her hand. He entered the living room, kneeled in front of her, and placed his head in her lap. She stroked his head and back. *Be strong. Be strong. You're his rock.* Finally, he raised his head and looked up at Dawn. "No matter what happens, know that I love you so much. I should have proposed and started building a life with you, but now it may be too late. I really hope it isn't, but I don't know."

Dawn covered Rick's lips with her index finger. "Rick, I love you. Whatever it is, we'll face it together. Me and you. Good and bad. Sickness and health. I'm your rock."

Rick smiled weakly. "Dawn, Darling, I really hope so." He kissed her knee. "Last week, this woman called and...she... um...said she's pregnant."

"Huh, I don't...I don't get it. Why would some woman call you?"

"Because...she thinks she's pregnant with my child. Dawn, I'm so sorry to do this to you—to us."

As comprehension settled in, Dawn's expression changed from worry to rage. She pushed Rick off her lap and stood up. She paced the living room, stopping occasionally to look at him. Rick sat on the floor and watched her like a wounded dog. Dawn finally stopped pacing, took a long swallow of her drink, and straightened her back. Clearing her throat, she began. "How does she know it's your baby?"

Dawn strained to hear Rick's answer. "Darling, it doesn't matter. I love you."

"Rick, answer the question. How. Does she know. It's. Your. Baby."

Rick shrugged. Dawn shot him her iciest glare.

Rick lowered his eyes and spoke to the floor. "She said she hasn't been with anyone else. Of course, we'll have a paternity test when the baby's born."

"Really? How far along is she?"

Rick began to sob again and mumbled, "I don't know."

"Come on now." Dawn slammed her palm on the side table. Rick jumped. "I think you do know. Let's have it. How far along she is? How many periods has she missed? You're the only man she's screwing, so I'm sure she told you the exact date you knocked her up."

Rick didn't respond.

"Hello. Is she showing? How far along is she?"

Rick wrung his hands, biding time. Finally, he covered his face with them.

"Three months."

"You moved two months ago, but you've been fucking her at least three months. Oh, that's why you were making all those business trips to Houston. Now she's having your baby. Well, I hope you, her, and the baby are very happy together."

Rick raised up on his knees. "Dawn, she means nothing to me. I got lonely in Houston. It only happened the one time. I love you. I want you. We can make this work. I can't lose you. I want to marry you." Rick pulled a ring box out of his pants pocket and assumed the pose Dawn had been waiting so long to see.

Dawn raised her right hand to stop him. "One time? Right. She means nothing? No. She and your unborn child sure as *hell* mean something to me. They mean that we can't make anything work. You disgust me. Get the hell out of my house. I don't ever want to see you again."

Rick crawled over to her, sobbing. He begged her to forgive him. Dawn glared at him and pulled away. She picked up her drink, walked across the room to the fireplace mantel, and watched him. *I can't believe this. And I can't believe how calm I am. This could be the part in the scary movie where the calm main character flips out and kills everybody. Rick should get away from me and I should call Button.*

Dawn finished her drink and set the glass on the mantel. Rick was sitting on the floor, crying and watching her. She crossed the room, grabbed Rick's drink, and retrieved her cell phone from her purse on the coffee table. She glared at him on the floor leaning on the sofa for support.

"Dawn, we, we, we need to talk." Rick hyperventilated.

"You need to calm down. Let me help," Dawn flung the contents of her glass in his face. "Get yourself together and get out of my house."

Rick was stunned as the liquid dripped down his face. He wiped the drink away with his shirt sleeve and retreated like a wounded, wet animal to the hallway powder room. *Button was right. That felt amazing. Speaking of which, I need to talk to her*. Dawn went to her bedroom and called Button. She recounted Rick's confession, laughed out loud at Button's suggestion, but agreed to think about it. When Dawn ended the call, she could hear Rick sobbing down the hallway. *What the hell is he crying about? I'm the one who should be upset. Button's right. I need to teach him a lesson*. Dawn made another phone call, then she packed Rick's suitcase and set it by the front door. As she crossed the living room, Rick came out of the bathroom and sat on the couch. "We need to talk," he repeated.

Dawn didn't look at him. She went into the master bathroom, took a long shower and applied her makeup flawlessly. Then she shimmied into her shortest and tightest dress. When she emerged from the bedroom again, Rick's long body was sprawled haphazardly on the couch with a wet washcloth over his eyes. He was spent. The scent of her sweet perfume wafted into the room and Rick sat up from the couch. His jaw dropped. Dawn looked amazing.

"Dawn?" Rick thought he was dreaming.

"Yes, Darling."

"What are you doing? We need to talk."

"There's nothing to say. I get it now. You're a liar and a womanizer. You're a spoiled, whorish stereotype, and I will no longer participate in your dysfunction." Dawn opened the front door, looked back at him, and pointed to his suitcase. "Take your time, but don't be here when I get back. And give my regards to Houston."

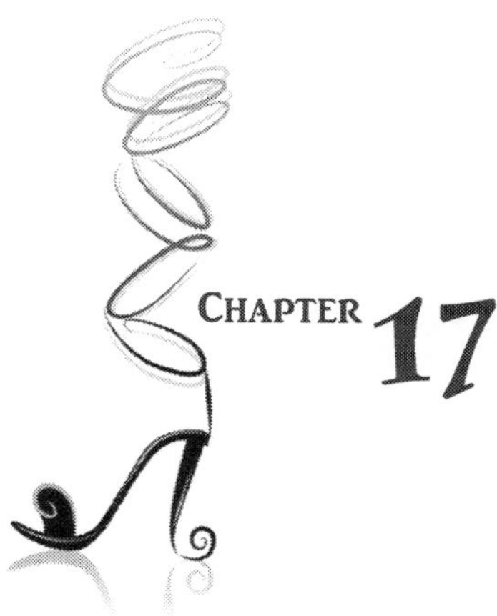

Chapter 17

Fr: <Meghan>
To: <Dawn>, <Button>
Monday, June 15, 2009 10:55AM
Subject: Dinner Tonite

Worst weekend EVER. The DMV COMPLETELY screwed me! I hope things went better for you. Just confirming dinner tonight at my house, 7pm. Italian theme. Me: lasagna. Button: salad and Prosecco. Dawn: garlic bread and tiramisu.

Fr: <Button>
To: <Meghan>, <Dawn>
Monday, June 15, 2009 11:23AM
Subject: RE: Dinner Tonite

Sorry. I extended my trip. Be back Wednesday afternoon. How about Wednesday night?

Fr: <Meghan>
To: <Dawn>, <Button>
Monday, June 15, 2009 11:25AM
Subject: RE: Dinner Tonite

Works for me.

Fr: <Dawn>
To: <Button>, <Meghan>
Monday, June 15, 2009 11:37AM
Subject: RE: Dinner Tonite

Me too. C U soon.

***

Meghan sat on her chaise, eating lasagna. Across from her, sitting on the couch, Button and Dawn passed her new driver's license back and forth. Their food sat untouched on the coffee table. "Can you believe they had security escort me out? Who gets thrown out of the DMV? It was the most humiliating experience of my life." She waited to be consoled and was shocked when her friends broke into laughter.

"It couldn't possibly be more humiliating than this picture." Button held her stomach as she doubled over with laughter.

"Hey, you're not supposed to laugh. Girl, gimme me back my license." Meghan reached across her mahogany coffee table and tried to snatch the license but Button out-maneuvered her.

"When you said this was the ugliest picture you've ever taken, you really meant that shit." Button gasped for air. "It's horrible."

"It's so bad, it's hilarious." Tears streamed down Dawn's face. "How did you get your eyes to roll back like that? What happened to your hair?"

"And what color lipstick is that? Solid gold? Meg, look at it again. You need a good laugh." Button tossed the license on the coffee table and Meghan snatched it up quickly.

"It's not funny! I can't believe you're carrying on like this. I had the worst weekend ever. You were both hanging out with your full and half boyfriends. I was humiliated. How can you think that's funny?" Meghan demanded.

"Calm down, Meg," Dawn managed through her laughter and tears.

Button sat up and tried to stop laughing. "Meg, it's a damn license picture. Nobody sees it but the clerk in the liquor section."

"I see it and I hate it." Tears welled in Meghan's eyes.

"Oh, no you don't. You're not going to cry over this," Button chastised.

"I can't help it. Lately, the smallest things make me cry. I feel like checking myself into a mental institution." Meghan covered her face.

"I think I know what your problem is," Button offered.

"I need to get high and get laid." Meghan rolled her eyes.

"Yes, you do. But you're also having a hormone imbalance."

"Huh?"

"Your divorce was taxing and you went off the pill. Your hormones are going crazy."

"I'm not going back on the pill," Meghan told Button.

"I'm not saying you should. I'm just saying that when you've been on birth control as long as we have, you forget how amazing those little pills are. They not only prevent pregnancy, but they also help with acne, weight, and PMS. You're not crazy, but your hormones are. When's your next period?"

"Um, sometime this week."

"See, you're not crazy. You're just PMSing. Well, check that. You're going a little crazy about this license foolishness, but I'm going to chalk it up to your hormones."

Meghan's face lit up. "That's why I've gained so much weight and I keep breaking out? I guess coming off the pill while I was getting a divorce was bad timing. Huh, good to know that I'm not losing my mind. I'm PMSing. So what should I do about my hormones?

"How long have you been off the pill?"

"Three months."

"It takes three to six months for your hormones to regulate, so you're past the worst part. Just know that if you start crying out of the blue, it's PMS and it'll get better."

Dawn turned to Button. "When did you turn into Button Jackson, MD?"

"My stepmother Sandra is a nurse and I was telling her about you. She figured it out."

"Sandra, the husband-stealing whore?" Meghan asked.

"Yes, which brings me to the story of my weekend, which I'm going to call, 'I wish the only shit I had to deal with was a bad DMV picture.'" Button recounted Henry's chance meeting and the fall-out with her mother. "Henry and I drove down to Atlanta on Sunday with Sonny so I could meet his kids. And overnight, I'm no longer an only child."

"Instant family weekend definitely trumps my DMV picture. What's your new family like?" Meghan asked.

"Sonny's so nice. I can see why he left my mother. His family is like the Cosbys. It was sweet and surreal. Wonderful and painful. I just keep thinking about all the time I've lost. I don't know if I can ever forgive my mother. But Henry's being so supportive. I'd be crazy to let him go."

"What's that mean? Are you going to cut your team?" Meghan's eyes widened.

"I'm working on it. And yes, my weekend trumped your weekend. But I have a feeling Dawn can trump us all."

"Button's cutting her team and Dawn can trump that. She has been awfully quiet." Meghan lowered her voice and turned toward Dawn. "What happened?"

"I'm calling it my 'Official Start of Single Girl Summer,'" Dawn smirked sheepishly.

"I want all the dirty details," Button clapped her hands in anticipation.

"Rick and I were having a perfect weekend. *Perfect*. He even took me stepping. I've begged him countless times to take me dancing and he never would. Yet on Saturday, he suggests going dancing. But it was all a set up for his big announcement," Dawn said.

"What?" Meghan whispered again.

"He got some hoochie in Houston pregnant three months ago. He's been cheating on me all along. But he's so sorry. Now, he realizes how wonderful I am and he just can't lose me. He even had an engagement ring. It was ridiculous. But I wasn't even mad at him. I was really mad at myself. How could I be so stupid to think he was being faithful on all those business trips to Houston? And then he moves down there without consulting me or asking me to go with him. Trust is not negotiable."

"That's right. Confessions like that are only acceptable from Usher singing with his shirt off," Meghan chimed in.

"As soon as the words came out of his mouth, I knew I was done. Those fantasies of Rick being so wonderful and irreplaceable were over and so were we. I told him to get out. I even threw my drink in his face."

"Good girl." Button slapped her knee and laughed.

"He still wouldn't leave. He kept bawling like a six-year-old who just got a whooping. He even starting that dry-heave hyperventilating. I called Button and she gave me some great advice."

"What did you tell her?" Meghan asked Button, wide-eyed.

"Good for the goose, good for the gander," Button answered smugly.

"And that's just what I did. I changed into my Beyoncé 'freakum' dress and went out for a night on the town with Brett," Dawn said.

"Brett! My playboy, cherry-popping Brett?" Meg asked in disbelief.

"Yeah, sorry. I had to hit Rick below the belt and Brett was the best guy for the job. Plus you didn't seem too interested in him. I hope you don't mind."

"Girl, I don't care. I see now why I got screwed at the DMV. It was all part of a master plan. I love it. Please go on," Meghan begged.

"We went to dinner and ended up at the W for drinks. Then, pardon my crassness, we fucked from dusk 'til dawn. I don't know if it was the Penthouse view, the tequila, or the revenge sex, but it was A-mazing. I've never done anything like that and I've certainly never felt like that. I was wrong when I said he's not a long-term guy. That brother could go all night," Dawn said, laughing.

"I'm so proud." Button high-fived Dawn.

"What happened to Rick?" Meghan asked.

"When I got back in the morning, he was waiting for me. He looked so pathetic. I almost felt sorry for him. Almost…then I remembered how he made me wait four hours to go to a romantic dinner so he could ask permission to screw around, which he was already doing. I got over that real quick. I wish I had a picture of the look on his face when I answered his 'Where have you been?' question."

"I love it. What did he say to that?" Button asked.

"He was pissed. Got his suitcase and left without a word," Dawn answered.

"That'll get rid of him," Button said.

"It got him out of my house, but I'm not rid of him. He's calling, texting, and emailing me non-stop saying he's not mad anymore. Now we're even and we can work things out. I'm going to give it a week. If he doesn't stop, I'm going to have to change my numbers. He's driving me crazy. I didn't think so before, but Meghan, you're lucky that Frank doesn't bother you."

"I didn't think so before either, but I guess I am lucky. Sometimes it's best not to talk after a break up. Did you look at the ring?" Meghan asked.

"No. I didn't care."

"I can't believe you didn't look at the ring."

"If he liked it, then he shoulda put a ring on it when he had the chance."

Meghan laughed, jumped up, and started singing like Beyoncé. Her back-up dancers, Dawn and Button, joined in at the chorus. All three women rolled their necks and hand-waved as they belted out the song.

CHAPTER 18

Fr: <Button>
To: <Meghan>, <Dawn>
Wednesday, June 24, 2009 1:58PM
Subject: Jazzin' at the Shedd

It's last minute, but a customer gave me tickets for Jazzin' at the Shedd tonight. Starts at six. Meg, I can pick you up from work and give you a ride home afterwards. Who's with me?

Fr: <Meghan>
To: <Button>, <Dawn>
Wednesday, June 24, 2009 2:05PM
Subject: RE: Jazzin' at the Shedd

It's too hot to go straight home. Shedd Aquarium sounds cool and free tix even better. I'm in.

Fr: <Dawn>
To: <Button>, <Meghan>
Wednesday, June 24, 2009 2:51PM
Subject: RE: Jazzin' at the Shedd

Earliest I can get there is 7 and I can't stay long. In the middle of a big deal.

* * *

The aquarium's terrace had been transformed into a jazz club and Button tapped the table in time with the music. Dawn spotted her and walked over. She sat in one of the empty chairs and put her purse in the other empty seat. "Button, this is amazing. I don't remember the last time I came to the aquarium. I definitely don't remember that three-sixty degree tank in the atrium with the string rays and sharks."

"There are giant sea turtles in there too. My favorite is the coral. I love the way it moves in the water."

"And this is breathtaking. Lakefront view, fantastic band, good-looking crowd. I wish I didn't have to work."

"I'm glad you could break away for a little bit. If you have time, go see the new dolphin exhibit. They're beautiful," Button suggested.

"I don't have time. I brought work home for later. Where's Meg?"

"See her, out on the dance floor with that attractive older gentleman?" Button pointed and Dawn followed her gaze. "Here, I got this drink for her, but it's going to waste." Button slid the untouched wine to Dawn.

"Don't mind if I do." Dawn took a sip. "They look really good out there. Who's the guy?"

"He looks familiar, but I can't place him. Meg left to go to the bathroom thirty minutes ago and she didn't come back. I thought she fell in the toilet until I spotted her a few minutes ago. Look at her smile. She's practically glowing. Anyway, how are you doing? Is Rick still calling everyday?"

"He stopped calling Sunday when I told him the next time he called I was going to three-way his mother and tell her about his Houston Baby Mama. I'm a little sad, but mostly I feel relieved. I didn't realize how much pressure I was putting on this whole getting-married mess."

"What about your sisters?"

"They've been trying to fix me up with some guy. My family is having a Fourth of July party and he's coming, so I'll meet him then."

"Sounds like you're regrouping nicely."

"Between you guys keeping my social calendar full, my sisters setting up blind dates, and this huge case at work, I'm keeping busy."

"How is work?"

"Great. It's been two weeks since the breakup, and I haven't had one panic attack. I've regained my focus and if I do well with this case, I'm definitely making partner this summer."

"Good for you. Have you talked to Brett? Are you going to see him again?"

"No. The bar was set too high that night. I don't want to go for seconds and find out he's not as good as I remember. I want to keep my revenge-night memory perfectly cemented in my mind."

"I hear ya. He served his purpose, now move on."

"Have you called your mom?"

"That's funny. She's my Rick; calling and emailing me all the time. I can't talk to her. I don't know what to say. What she did was so wrong, but I can't be mad forever. She's the only mother I have. I'll have to forgive her at some point, but not now."

"That's a lot to forgive." Dawn looked up to see Meghan approaching their table. She stood near Button and fanned her face with a postcard. "Hey, Meg. You can sit here." Dawn moved her purse from the empty chair.

Meghan took the napkin from under Button's drink and patted the perspiration on her forehead. "Hey, Girl. No, I'm going to stand for a minute to cool off."

"Somebody's got her dancing shoes on tonight. Who's the guy? Button said he looks familiar," Dawn said to Meghan.

"Phillip goes to our gym. He stopped me on the way back from the bathroom. He said he sees me at the gym all the time and I have the most beautiful smile. He's been wanting to talk to me, but hates when men hit on women at the gym. When he saw me here, he made his move." Meghan beamed.

"He's handsome. I may have to go ahead and join your gym since I'm officially single now," Dawn said.

"I'll get the scoop on him from the gym grapevine. What's his last name?" Button asked.

Meghan pulled his business card from the pocket of her tropical-print silk sheath dress. "'Phillip Buchanan. Owner, Windy City Flight School,'" she read. "He's fluent in Spanish *and* Italian." Meghan whispered the last part since she noticed Phillip walking towards their table carrying a glass of wine and a bottle of water.

"Hello, ladies." He handed both drinks to Meghan and then exchanged introductions with Button and Dawn. "Thanks for letting me borrow your beautiful friend and her gorgeous smile. Can I get you a drink?" He asked Button and Dawn.

"Thanks, but no. We just got these." Button nodded towards the glasses of wine on the table.

"Meghan, thank you for the dance. It was my pleasure. I'll call you later." Phillip's hand rested on Meghan's arm. He winked at her before walking away.

"I look forward to it." Meghan whispered as she watched Phillip disappear in the crowd. She sank into the empty chair with a sigh.

"He's handsome. How old do you think he is?" Meghan polled the table.

"My guess is forty-one. That's a good age for a man. He's got money and is still in his sexual peak," Button said.

"He's a great dancer," Meghan pointed out.

"Great on the dance floor, great in bed. Plus he brought drinks and was wearing an expensive suit. Tailored Brooks Brothers, this season. I say go for it. What do you think?" Button threw the conversation to Dawn.

"Definitely, Brooks Brothers and fashion forward. I like the way he matched the gray suit with the lavender shirt."

"I loved the tie. I'm a sucker for paisley. Plus, we had a really good conversation. He loves food, loves to cook, and goes to different restaurants. I hope he calls," Meghan giggled.

"He'll call. Brooks Brothers was feeling you." Button was matter-of-fact.

"I hope so. This feels so strange—being single again. But it's kind of exciting. Anyway, Dawn, did you take your leftovers for lunch?" Meghan changed the subject.

"Yes, and the fajitas tasted even better today. Thanks," Dawn said.

"What? Where are my fajitas?" Button asked.

"At Dawn's house, where we had dinner last night. I sent you a text letting you know. When I didn't hear back, I figured you were boo'ed up with your boyfriend, again," Meghan teased.

"No, I was hanging out with Mike," Button answered.

"Who's Mike?" Dawn asked.

"You know…Mike." Button gave them a knowing look.

"I have no idea who Mike is." Dawn shrugged.

"Mike…Quarter."

Dawn had to think a second to make the connection. "I've never heard you use his real name before. Wait…why are you using his name? I thought you cut your team and were exclusive with Henry."

"I'm working on it."

"Working on it? Mike's just a booty call and the rest of your team are just time and space fillers. Henry's the total package. You said it yourself." Dawn reminded Button.

"I like having my time and space filled. I also like having options. And Mike isn't just a booty call. I enjoy spending time with him. He's very sweet and supportive. Our relationship is light, carefree, and easy. When I thought about cutting him off, I realized we have an emotional attachment and I'm not ready to end it."

Meghan interrupted. "Button, I've got to meet this guy. He's a young, hot beefcake who's also supportive, sweet, and emotionally attached. What's he doing tonight? Tell him to come up here right now." Meghan pounded the table for emphasis.

"He's not emotionally attached. We have an emotional attachment. There's a difference. Believe me, he's getting it in with the ladies, but we have a nice groove. And he'd never come up here. He's probably getting high somewhere. Ooh, that reminds me of something we need to do." Button took out her phone and started texting.

"Button, are you serious about that?" Meghan asked sheepishly. Button's phone beeped with a text. She read it quickly and started typing again.

"Hell yeah, I'm serious. Call me Smokey, 'cause I'm getting you high tonight. Mike has a few people over and wants us to come through. Dawn, you in?"

Dawn shook her head. "As much as I would love to see Meg high, I can't. I have to work."

Button downed the rest of her wine. "We can walk out together. Let's roll."

They all exited the aquarium together. In the parking lot, Dawn hugged her friends good night, found her car, and headed home. Button and Meghan piled into Button's sporty, pearl-colored convertible. Button pulled a collection of silk scarves from her glove box. She and Meghan tied the scarves on their head and parked their sunglasses on top so they looked like Hollywood starlets. Button dropped the convertible top and sped out of the parking lot onto Lake Shore Drive. T.I.'s "Whatever You Like" blared from the car stereo as they sang loudly and enjoyed the warm summer breeze.

There was no traffic and they arrived at Mike's doorstop in thirty minutes. When he opened the door to let them in, a cloud of smoke billowed out. While Mike kissed Button on the doorstop, Meghan looked over his shoulder and couldn't believe her eyes. Mike's living room was full of mid-twenty-something, good looking, ripped hotties passing blunts, drinks, and video game controllers. Meghan followed Button and Mike into the kitchen, where Button mixed drinks while Mike entertained them with stories and flirted with Button.

"Ya'll never guess what happened today?" Mike said to them as he massaged Button's shoulders.

"What, Babe?" Button responded as she cut limes and poured vodka and cranberry juice into glasses.

"This guy at the gym was working out with a football. He ran on the treadmill holding a football. A football. He did the stairs with a football. He even did chin ups with a football."

Meghan laughed and shook her head in disbelief. "Mike, how'd he do chin ups with a football?"

"He held the football 'tween his legs. And you ain't seen nothing 'til you seen a grown man doing sit ups with a football."

Meghan was tickled watching them. Button and Mike kept exchanging lingering glances and copping feels of each other. Meghan knew if she wasn't there, they would have gone straight to his bedroom.

Eventually, the three of them settled at the spades table and Mike called over an attractive guy with a baby face, molasses complexion, and Popeye strong arms to be Meghan's partner. Meghan and her partner, Lee, vibed instantly and played spades like they'd been partners for life, winning the game after four rounds. Button and Mike excused themselves to go get some fresh air. Meghan and Lee sat at the table, talking and laughing for at least an hour until Mike returned and made two fresh drinks in the kitchen. Mike gave the drinks to Meghan and told her that Button wanted her and the drinks in the back. Meghan found Button lounging in a patio chair on the back balcony, grinning like a Cheshire cat. An unlit blunt rested on the table next to her chair.

"How's the fresh air?" Meghan grinned.

"Fucking fantastic. Isn't this a beautiful night? Look at those stars."

Meghan put the drinks on the table and sat in the empty chair. "Nights like these make me feel like anything is possible."

"Anything is possible. Are you ready for this?" Button held up the blunt.

"I think I already have a contact high."

"Then you're ready for the real thing." Button lit the blunt, took a hit, and passed it to Meghan. They lounged on the balcony enjoying the night air, cool drinks, and Mary Jane.

⁂ ⁂ ⁂

"Girl, I can't stop laughing." Meghan took a long drag and then examined the blunt. "I like this one better than the first one. It's sweeter."

"Mike wrapped it in a strawberry swisher."

"A what? I have no idea what you're talking about and I don't care. Mike's house is fun." Meghan laughed again. "I see what you mean about him. He's cool, but I'm still rooting for Henry."

"You got Mike thinking he's the headliner on Def Comedy Jam. He's funny, but not as funny as you're carrying on." Button ignored the Henry reference.

"Please. Those gym stories are hilarious. And then he told that joke about the guy and the other guy that go over to that place, you know…whatever he said… that was funny as hell." Meghan laughed at herself.

"Right, almost as funny as your license picture."

"Funny licenses." Meghan laughed even harder.

"What are you laughing at?"

"This night is crazy. I gave my phone number to two men and I'm smoking weed at midnight…on a school night."

"I know you gave your number to Brooks Brothers. Who else did you give your number to?" Button asked.

"My spades partner. Is that okay? Lee's a little young, but he's hot and really nice."

"Hell yeah. It's Single Girl Summer." Button winked at Meghan.

Meghan laughed again.

Button asked, "What's funny now?"

"In the near future I could be tucking one in or helping one out of bed. What's up with that?"

"You mean tucking one in *and* helping one out of bed. Phillip's not too old and Lee's not too young. Variety is the best foundation for a team. Work it, Girl."

Meghan took another hit. "Button, I'm so high and it's only Wednesday. Where the hell are we going to go this weekend to top this?"

"Sweetie, we can go wherever we like. Now stop hogging the blunt. It's puff, puff, pass. Not puff, puff, puff."

July

CHAPTER 19

Fr: <Meghan>
To: <Button>, <Dawn>
Wednesday, July 1, 2009 9:55AM
Subject: Work Out Barbie

Really Button, why did you have on a shrug at the gym yesterday? Who climbs the stairs for an hour in a color coordinated outfit and matching shrug? I can't take you seriously. LOL.

Fr: <Dawn>
To: <Button>, <Meghan>
Wednesday, July 1, 2009 10:05AM
Subject: RE: Work Out Barbie

Meg, say you took a picture of Black work-out Barbie and her big ego. ROFL.

Fr: <Button>
To: <Meghan>, <Dawn>
Wednesday, July 1, 2009 10:07AM
Subject: RE: Work Out Barbie

Ha Ha. I'm making tonight's workout extra hard. Hope you find that funny. C U both at the gym, 630 sharp.

Fr: <Dawn>
To: <Button>, <Meghan>
Wednesday, July 1, 2009 10:09AM
Subject: RE: Work Out Barbie

Button's going to kill us. So glad I joined your gym. Thanks, Meg ☹

Fr: <Meghan>
To: <Button>, <Dawn>
Wednesday, July 1, 2009 10:10AM
Subject: RE: Work Out Barbie

What? I love her huge ego. ROFL.

❊❊❊

Dawn winced as she crossed the wet tile floor and gingerly sat on the lowest level of three wooden benches in the gym's sauna. Meghan also sat on the lowest bench in her workout bra and shorts. Her head was tucked down and her eyes were closed as she concentrated on her breathing. Lying down on the top level, Button was wrapped in a towel with a wet towel covering her face.

"Sore tomorrow? Button, I'm sore right now," Dawn complained.

Button moved the towel so it just covered her eyes. "That's why we're here. The sauna will relax your muscles so you won't be too sore tomorrow. Plus it's great for your skin. Sweating is a natural way for your body to rid itself of toxins."

"That kind of torture was uncalled for. I'm afraid to move because I know it's going to hurt." Meghan sat like a statue.

"Meg, you said you like the definition you're starting to see and want more. If you aren't sore after your workout, then you haven't challenged your body enough. To get more, you have to do more. We have to keep pushing ourselves. You two are committed to having cold-as-hell bodies, right?" Button sat up on her elbows and removed the towel from her eyes so she could see her friends.

Both Meghan and Dawn murmured weak yeses.

"That was pathetic." Button flopped back down.

"Sorry, but it's hard to get excited when I'm imagining how sore I'm going to be tomorrow." Meghan complained.

"It's a beautiful burn," Button said.

"Whatever, Button. Meg, I forgot to tell you I saw Phillip from Jazzin' at the Shedd leaving the gym when I was coming in. What's going on with him?" Dawn asked.

"Ooh, I checked the gym grapevine. Word is Brooks Brothers is heterosexual, single, and loaded," Button said.

"That's nice, but nothing's up with him," Meghan answered.

"Don't tell me he didn't call. He was definitely into you." Button was shocked.

"He called the next day and we had a great conversation. We talked more about our favorite restaurants and foods. He suggested we go out for dinner over the weekend. I said I'd love to. Then he had to go into a meeting and never called back. I got here early to do my cardio since we were doing weights and saw him on the gym floor. He apologized for not calling me back and said he lost my number. He asked if I still had his card and I told him I did. Then he asked if I'd call him. I said sure. I let him walk away a little and then I called him back over to ask him what my name was."

"Meg, did you really?" Dawn asked laughing.

"Yes, Girl. It dawned on me that he didn't say my name so he probably didn't know it. He looked shocked." Meghan said.

"I bet he was. Call his ass out," Button encouraged.

"He admitted he didn't know my name. So I said 'You know I can't call you now.' He looked confused." Meghan shook her head.

Button and Dawn exploded in laughter. "He didn't call you back for whatever reason so the least he could do is remember your name," Button co-signed.

"Exactly. I remembered his name. I called him by his name. He couldn't remember my name or hold onto my number. That's foolishness. Clearly he's too busy to be bothered with."

"What happened next?" Button asked.

"He asked if he could find out my name and number would it be okay for him to call. I told him that would be fine. He said to expect his call because he's very resourceful. I wished him good luck and continued my workout."

"Did the cutie from Mike's house call?" Button asked.

"Lee called the next day too. He's cute, but he's so young."

"How young?"

"Twenty-three young. He's a drummer so his arms are amazing. I didn't know how much I liked arms until Lee let me feel his biceps."

"Biceps are my non-negotiable," Button added with a chuckle.

"Anyway, Friday night he took me to his gig at a jazz club. Then Saturday, he took me to his gig at a blues club. He's really talented. Watching him pound those drums was so hot! Then after that we went to this twenty-something club that I couldn't believe was still open. I remember going there ten years ago."

"When in Rome…So how was it?"

"Sooo much fun. He kept telling me how good I looked, which I loved. And I felt like I looked really good. We ended up being the couple making out in the club."

"The can-they-please-get-a-room couple?"

"That's the couple. And I didn't care. It wasn't like I was going to see anyone my own age there. It was fun to let loose. He brought me home at 4 a.m. We made out on my couch and watched the sun come up. Before you ask Button, no, I didn't let him pop my single-girl cherry and I'm not going to. He's sweet, but he's too young."

"Can he dance?"

"He's a drummer. He has great rhythm, but he doesn't have swagger like Phillip did."

"Lee's cute, but he's young and could have no idea what to do. You don't want to end up there. You want it to be so good that you say 'this is why I got divorced.' I'm glad you had a fun date. You broke the ice and got out there. You only made one mistake."

"What?" Meg turned to look at Button, who was propped up on her elbows again.

"You didn't tell anyone you were going out with a stranger?"

"Lee's not a stranger. He's Mike's friend and he works out here sometimes."

"Meg, this is dating in the new millennium. Nobody knew you were going out with Lee. If he stuffed you in the trunk of his car, we'd have no idea where to tell the police to start looking for you. Someone needs to know you're out and who you're out with, especially if he's picking you up from your house. Next time you go on a date, text me the name of your date, his phone number, home address, and license plate number."

"Who do you text?" Meghan asked Button.

"Davis. I just texted him last night about this guy I went out with," Button said.

"Wait, are you still adding to your team? I thought you were exclusive with Henry." Dawn turned painfully to face Button.

"Exclusivity is a process. I told you I'm working on the commitment thing, but I have to go at my own pace." Button sat up on her bench and rested her back on the wall so she could look down at Dawn and Meghan.

"When Rick and I decided to be exclusive—well, when I thought we were exclusive, I called up the other guy I was seeing and said 'You're great and it was fun, but I have a boyfriend now. I can't see you anymore.' It only took one conversation. It's been a month since you first talked about being exclusive with Henry. How long does your 'process' take?" Dawn challenged.

"You're starting to sound like Half. I've been single a long time and I enjoy my freedom. Giving that up isn't easy or fun, but I'm working on it. I'm doing my best to get there. Alright?"

"Good men like *Henry* who are genuinely ready to commit don't come around every day. Don't lose him by making him wait too long. Waiting for you can't be easy or fun for him," Dawn warned.

"Look Dawn, in addition to my relationship with Henry, I've got a lot going on with my mother, Sonny, and my new family. My mother's calling me all the time. Sonny wants me to visit again. It's all very stressful. Sorry, I can't give *Henry* my undivided attention. Like I said, I'm…getting…there."

"I worked seventy hours last week. I know all about stress. But I also know the value of a good man who wants to commit to you and only you. I wouldn't be your friend if I didn't point out the colossal mistake you're making. How does *Henry* feel about you *getting there?*" Dawn air-quoted the last part of her sentence.

"He's a little disappointed that I'm not there yet, but he's still seeing ol' girl so we're even."

"Henry would stop seeing her the instant you gave him a commitment. You wouldn't do the same for him so you and Henry aren't even. He's giving and you're taking. You can't have your cake and eat it too." Dawn's voice escalated.

"I hate that stupid expression. What's the point of having cake and not eating it? Yes, I want the cake and, yes, I want to eat it. Big fucking deal."

"How about this, Button? Pick one cake and eat that."

"Maybe I don't want just one cake. I like va-ri-e-ty." Button rolled her neck with emphasis.

"Then pick the damn seven-layer cake. What are you so afraid of, or are you really that selfish?"

"Dawn, keep it. I don't want any damn cake. I'm on a diet." Button laid back down.

Meghan cut in. "Hey, the Fourth of July's coming up. It's no time to be talking about a diet."

"Grow up, Button." Dawn ignored Meghan.

Meghan cut in again. "My best friend from college is coming in for the weekend. We're going to the Taste of Chicago on Saturday for the big Stevie Wonder concert. Do you guys want to come?"

"I can't. I have a family party," Dawn said dryly.

"Maybe. I'm supposed to hang out with Half. But he doesn't like crowds and I can *always* cancel him." Button shot Dawn a look.

"Humph." Dawn rolled her eyes.

"It's getting really hot and uncomfortable in here." Meghan reached for her water bottle and took a huge gulp.

"Yes it is. I'm out. Meg, let me know if Phillip calls you and I'll let you know about Saturday. Later." Button bounced down the stairs and exited the sauna.

"Girl, what was that?" Meghan asked.

"What?" Dawn shrugged her shoulders.

"Whatever that was you just did."

"I don't like the way she treats Henry. She doesn't appreciate him and she's playing with him like he's a toy. I'm her friend and as her friend I should tell her when she's messing up a good thing."

"I agree with you that friends should be honest with each other, but there's a way to do it and that was harsh."

"It wasn't harsh. It was honest."

"Button's not Rick. She's been honest with Henry and he chooses to wait for her."

"What are you talking about?"

"You and Rick. Button and Henry. The relationships are similar, but they're not the same. Rick didn't give you a choice. Henry has a choice. Plus, Button's been through a lot. I think she's doing the best she can. You should cut her some slack."

"I don't know what you're talking about."

"Think about it. I can't take this sauna anymore. Are you ready to go?"

"I'm going to stay a little longer."

"Alright. See ya." Meghan collected her water bottle and towel and waved good-bye to Dawn. She had a feeling this wasn't going to be the end of this discussion.

Fr: <Meghan>
To: <Button>
Thursday, July 2, 2009 6:43PM
Subject: RE: He found my number ☺

We're going to dinner tonight. Phillip Buchanan. 555-0100. 145 N. Michigan Avenue—Penthouse. License plate PBWCFS. He told me to tell you not to worry.

Do you have a quick sangria recipe?

Fr: <Button>
To: <Meghan>
Thursday, July 2, 2009 8:07PM
Subject: He found my number ☺

So happy for you. I hope you're having a fabulous time.

SINGLE GIRL SANGRIA
(recipe below fills a large punch bowl; takes ten minutes to make)

- Three bottles of dry white wine. (I prefer Rene Barbier Mediterranean White)
- One can of strawberry nectar
- Mix wine and nectar. Sweeten to taste with Splenda (it's low-cal ☺)
- Add chopped strawberries, pineapples, and oranges (if you want to make it really simple, buy a frozen bag of strawberries, pineapples in the

can, and already sliced apples in the produce section instead of oranges)

- Add ¾ can of lemon-lime soda
- Chill for a couple of hours. The longer the better, but if you don't have the time, that's okay. Serve and enjoy.

Meghan looked around the crowded lawn, smiled to herself, and reached for a barbecued turkey leg. Joy was lying on her stomach on their picnic blanket and using her Taste of Chicago information guide to shield her eyes from the sun.

"I can't believe this is my first time at the Taste. It's amazing. Chicago's such a great city. Look over there—those people have been line dancing for the past hour and I haven't seen any repeats. How many line dances are there? I thought it was just the Casper Slide and the Cupid Shuffle," Joy pointed at the dancers.

"There are hundreds of line dances and to every song you can think of. I need to go join them before I explode," Meghan said, but continued eating.

"Whatever, Meg. You look fantastic. Your arms look great. Your face is glowing and there's pep in your step. Summer agrees with you."

"There's nothing like summer in Chicago. We wait eight months for four months of summer. Four glorious months packed with festivals, music, people, and food! Girl, when summer finally gets here, you have to enjoy it and take every moment as it comes."

"I thought you were crazy when you woke me up for meditation on the lake this morning, but I'm glad you did. The sunrise was so peaceful. Then I thought you were crazy when you said we were getting here at two, even though the show didn't start until five-thirty, so we can buy food, but not eat it."

"There's method to my madness. Eating this gigantic turkey leg with extra sauce while walking through a crowd of three hundred thousand people is not even an option."

"This was a great idea. Buy all our food, pack it in the cart. Claim a patch of land with a great view of the stage and wait for Stevie while we eat and tan. I can't believe the show is free."

"Every year. I've seen New Edition, Patti LaBelle, and Frankie Beverly Maze. Frank called it doing the Taste right. There's going to be over a million people here for the concert so you gotta have a plan."

"And a list." Joy put down the Taste guide and reached into the pull cart to find Meghan's list. "Picnic blanket, pillows, playing cards, Tupperware, aluminum foil, ice, floss, fans, sunscreen, wet naps, hand towels, bottled waters, sangria, and red cups. You sure you don't need to add anything?" Joy squinted at her.

"Sunglasses and I may bring my own music next year. Add those to my list."

"I think you have enough on here." Joy smiled, tossed the list back in the cart and picked up the guide again.

"Did you have enough food?"

"Girl, yeah. I had sautéed goat meat with plantains, ox tails with red beans and rice, deep-dish spinach pizza, mustard-fried catfish, Italian beef, and roasted sweet corn on the cob. And we still have Eli's strawberry cheesecake, elephant ears and lots of delicious sangria."

"You also thought I was crazy when I told you the sangria only took ten minutes to make."

"I have to stop doubting you. It's so good. Are you sure it's okay to drink in the park?" Joy asked.

"As long as it's in a red cup, it's fine. The red cup is essential to the success of any outdoor activity. Not only does it save you from having to buy way overpriced beer, but it looks festive while concealing contraband."

"And what's this called?" Joy sipped from her red cup.

"Single Girl Sangria. For the single girl in you," Meghan smiled.

Joy sat up to face Meghan and a serious look replaced her smile. "Meg, I have to tell you, I was shocked when you told me you were divorced. I had no warning. You never said you were unhappy, thinking about separating, in marriage counseling, nothing. Just poof…you're divorced. I dropped my groceries when you told me."

"I heard the thud on the phone."

"I didn't even know you were having problems. I wish you'd told me sooner."

"I'm sorry. It was just so embarrassing. And I didn't want to burden you. I know you have your hands full with the kids. How are they?"

"Don't get me wrong, I love being a wife and a mother, but it's exhausting. I never have time for myself. I never come first anymore. I really needed this weekend away. It reminds me of all the fun we had in college. Those were such good times. Life before kids. Truth be told, I'm a little jealous of your new freedom."

"Freedom ain't free. I miss Frank. It hurts. I'm a little jealous of your family. Is everything okay at home?"

"I love my family, but I'm overwhelmed by their needs. Sometimes I dream about running away and joining the circus. Then I feel guilty and ungrateful because I have a great life," Joy sighed.

"You shouldn't feel guilty or ungrateful. I know being a wife is hard and I can only imagine how exhausting being a mother can be. It sounds like you need more Joy-time. Your kids don't have to be in every activity at school. And maybe you can ask their father or grandparents to keep them more so you can carve out some time for yourself. Don't let this weekend in Chicago be the last thing you do for yourself this year," Meghan suggested.

"You're right. I'm sorry for dumping on you. I'm supposed to be helping you," Joy said apologetically.

"I'm so glad you're here. Thank you." Meghan smiled at her old friend.

"I had to check on my girl. And don't thank me. I should be thanking you. I'm having such a good time. I just wish I could do more to help you."

"It helps to know I'm not the only one in the crazy boat. I should have told you earlier that Frank and I were having problems, but I didn't want to burden you and you were probably doing the same thing. We need to stop doing that. It's good therapy to talk about our problems."

"I completely agree. Don't ever again wait to tell me something like that. I'm still a little hurt that you only told me because you were making mass 'I'm divorced' calls."

"If it helps, you were the first phone call I made. I'm sorry it took me so long to tell you, but I was ashamed. Telling people I'm divorced is like confessing I failed at the sacrament of marriage over and over again. I've had to admit my failure to my family, friends, a courtroom full of people, coworkers, and way too many strangers. Some days I feel like pasting a scarlet D on my chest. It's overwhelming," Meghan admitted.

"You have nothing to be ashamed of. I'm proud of you. You're handling this so well. I don't think I could make those phone calls. How many have you made?" Joy asked.

"For the name-change stuff, I've made at least thirty calls in addition to the face-to-face visits for the DMV, Social Security, and my bank. The bane of my existence is wiping his last name out of my life. Every card in my wallet and every piece of mail that bore the name Henderson was a phone call that needed to be made. I've called my utilities, credit card companies, the library, Netflix, magazine subscriptions, mechanic, condo management, rewards cards, and practically every customer service operator from here to New Delhi to tell them 'I'm divorced and yes, I'd like to go back to my maiden name.'"

"That's horrible," Joy reached over to rub Meghan's arm.

"It is. When I changed to my married name, those phone calls were so fun. The customer service person would ask the reason for the name change. I'd practically sing 'I got married.' Then they'd offer congratulations, ask about the wedding, maybe throw in a story about their wedding or their child's upcoming wedding. Not nearly as much fun when the reason is 'I got divorced.' You'd be surprised at the responses," Meghan said.

"Why are people so rude?" Joy asked.

"I don't think it's because they're rude. The mention of divorce makes people uncomfortable and then they just blurt out without thinking."

"You know you don't have to tell them you're divorced," Joy said. Meghan gave her a blank stare. "You can simply state the reason is a change in marital status and leave it at that."

Meghan's jaw dropped. "Now you tell me! I didn't have to commit to one side or the other. I could have straddled the fence. Wish I had known that sooner. It's my own fault for not talking to you."

"Well, now you know. Are you done with the business calls?"

"I think so. I've done everything I could think of. But I'm sure I'll get a piece of mail addressed to Meghan Henderson to remind me of some random account I completely forgot about."

"How are you doing with the personal calls?"

"I'm about three-fourths done. The personal calls are exhausting. Every time I have to answer 'What happened?,' I relive the whole messy process."

"I've got a solution for that too. From now on, if someone asks 'What happened?,' tell them Frank's gay." Meghan exploded with laughter. "I'm serious!"

"Should I say I walked in on him with another man?"

"Down low, definitely. If you want, I'll do it for you. I'll knock out the rest of your divorce calls while I'm here." Joy picked up an imaginary phone and held it to her ear. "Hi, this is Joy, Meg's best friend. I'm just calling to let you know Meg's divorced now. She found Frank's extensive collection of man-on-man love magazines. Needless to say, she's gone back to her maiden name. Please update your address book. Have a good day." Joy mimed hanging up the phone and dialed a new number. "Hi, this is Joy. I'm calling to let you know Meg's divorced. Frank took his love of hamsters too far and they both ended up in the ER, pun intended. Needless to say, she's gone back to being Meghan Cherry. Please update your address book. Have a good day." Joy hung up her pretend phone and shrugged as Meghan rocked with laughter.

"Easy. Just give me your list."

"You're the best. Thanks for the offer, but I'll handle it. It's not fun, but it's something I need to do. These phone calls are necessary evils in this series of constant indignities called divorce. They're part of my cleansing process and they have taught me two very important lessons. Number one, if I can get through this, I can get through anything. Number two, if I get married again, I'm not changing my name until we have kids. With kids, your last names should be the same. No kids; I'm keeping my last name."

"You mean *when* you get married again. And after all you've been through, I'm sure Phillip will understand."

"That's funny. We've only been out twice and yesterday didn't count because you were there."

"The way he kept looking at you? Yesterday was a date. Your second date in two days. I love that you made him work to find your number. Calling all the unfamiliar numbers on his last cell phone bill was the least he could do."

"He's lucky I didn't answer the first time he called so he was able to get my name from my voicemail message. Otherwise that first conversation would have been awkward because I was not telling him my name again. I'm glad he figured it out though. We've only been out twice, but I really like him."

"I know it's Single Girl Summer and I probably don't fit in, but can I give you some advice?"

"What do you mean, you don't fit in? Joy, there'll always be a place for you wherever I am in my life."

"Yeah, right. Now that you're single, you're going to dump your old married friends like me. I'm too boring and settled. I cramp your style."

"Never! In fact, I'm appointing you as my Single Girl Summer Sidekick who gives the best advice, and I would love to hear more."

"My advice is don't date like a married woman. I've seen it before. When you're married, you're used to a certain level of intimacy and attachment so you have a tendency to rush in too quickly trying to replace what you had before. You were with Frank six years. You'll need to learn how to date again. Take things slow. Intimacy takes time to develop."

"Thank you, Single Girl Sidekick. Anything else?"

"Yes, pass me one of those pillows. My food coma is setting in. You can line dance if you want, but I need a nap before Stevie comes on." Meghan laughed and tossed Joy a pillow.

Chapter 21

Fr: <Meghan>
To: <Dawn>
Friday, July 17, 2009 1:58PM
Subject: Urban Mingling

Single Girl Summer is hanging on the South Side tonite. Happy Hour is on and popping at Reese's. The drinks are cheap, the DJ plays requests, and they step in the back. Button and I will be there at six. I haven't seen you in two weeks so you better meet us there.

Fr: <Dawn>
To: <Meghan>
Friday, July 17, 2009 2:28PM
Subject: RE: Urban Mingling

You know I never pass up a chance to get my step on. I had lunch at Anand and Button told me about Reese's. She also told me you're having a full-fledged romance with Phillip. Who's boo'ed up now? LOL. I have to work late. B there round eight.

Fr: <Meghan>
To: <Dawn>
Friday, July 17, 2009 2:30PM
Subject: RE: Urban Mingling

Great!!! I'm glad you guys are cool? Did you talk about what happened in the sauna?

Fr: <Dawn>
To: <Meghan>
Friday, July 17, 2009 2:33PM
Subject: RE: Urban Mingling

Nothing to talk about. C U soon.

***

A large bouncer buzzed the security door, allowing Dawn to enter with two men in transit authority coveralls. Friday night happy hour at Reese's started around 4 p.m. when the Chicago Public School teachers met at the bar to swap work stories. As the night progressed, faithful regulars—from lawyers to bus drivers—who either worked or lived near the watering hole packed the place.

The patrons sitting near the front greeted the two men by their names and nodded hello to Dawn, whose eyes greedily devoured all the details of the spot. She smiled at the bar top cluttered with an array of beer bottles, cocktail glasses, and baskets of fried chicken; the diverse attire of suits, jeans, city uniforms, and overalls; and especially the excited TGIF conversations and soulful music. *This is the black version of Cheers. Everyone's so friendly, but I feel a little overdressed. St. John would turn over in his grave if he knew this suit was in Reese's.*

Dawn spotted Button and Meghan seated at the far end of the bar laughing with the bartender. *Button didn't have on that dress when I saw her at lunch. And I know Meghan didn't wear that to work. But at least they're just as overdressed as I am.*

Dawn maneuvered through the crowd until she finally reached her friends. Since there were no empty bar stools, she stood behind them. "Hey, Ladies."

Button and Meghan swiveled on their bar stools to face Dawn. They all hugged.

Dawn continued, "Did you two change clothes after work?"

"Girl, yeah. It's sundress night." Button adjusted the strap of her emerald green, off-the-shoulder dress.

"I see Meg has the girls out. Nothing says party like a red dress and rhinestones." Dawn laughed.

"What? I added the rhinestones. I love the sweetheart neckline, but it was kind of boring. You don't like 'em?"

"I love them and there's nothing boring about you tonight. You and the girls are too hot."

Meghan shook her full bosom and laughed. "That's right."

"Why didn't I get the sundress memo?" Dawn directed to Button.

"That was Davis' call." Button flicked one of the gold buttons on Dawn's edged cardigan. "He said there's no good reason to ever change out of St. John or tangerine. Plus, you were already going to be late so no need to make you even later."

Dawn gave Button a face. "Well, besides the memo, did I miss anything else?"

"Yeaaaah, you missed two rounds of drinks and you need to catch up." Button called over her shoulder to the bartender, "Three lemon drop shots, please." The bartender nodded and hurried to find three shot glasses.

"Shots? What's the occasion?" Dawn asked.

"You also missed seeing my ex, and a Frank Henderson sighting calls for shots," Meghan explained.

"Really? What happened? Did you talk to him? Is he still here? Is this the first time you've seen him since the divorce? Did he see you in this hot little dress?" Dawn's eyes were wide as saucers as she bombarded Meghan with questions.

"I didn't see him at all. Button did. Girl, you tell the story," Meghan told Button.

"My pleasure," Button took over. "When we first got here, we were in the back room where the dance floor is. I was in the DJ booth hanging out and Meg hit the dance floor. I could see everything from the booth so I'm watching Meg get her step on with her red dress twirling all over the place and I notice this guy staring at her. I knew he looked familiar, but I couldn't place him right away. Finally, it dawned on me that it was Frank. I remember seeing him with Meg at some of our association meetings."

Meghan interrupted, "I'm so glad you declared sundress night. This dress shows off my five days a week at the gym." She flexed her guns.

"Frank wasn't ready for the fabulous. And aren't you glad you bought that dress now? No summer wardrobe is complete without a short, strapless sundress. It's classic," Button said.

"It was a little pricey, but tonight was worth every penny," Meghan chuckled.

"Meg looked at me crazy when I told her we should dress up tonight," Button told Dawn.

"Well, I think we're all a little over dressed for Reese's," Dawn said.

"Good. Single Girl Summer loves to overdress. Walk into a place, and be the baddest bitch in the room. I get so tired of people in casual clothes and comfortable shoes. Wear your good clothes and heels even if you aren't going downtown. Wear 'em to Reese's. You don't need a special occasion to dress like you're cold as hell."

"Duly noted. Now back to the story," Dawn interrupted.

"Right, Meg was dancing and she lit up the room. Frank's eyes almost popped out of his head and I'm watching the whole thing go down from the DJ booth. It was awesome. When she finally left the dance floor, she walked right past him but didn't notice. He reached out to speak, but changed his mind. He stood there for a while thinking it over, then he made a beeline for the exit. He even tripped over a chair. That was a great ex-encounter." Button hugged Meghan.

"Yay." Dawn applauded. "The worst thing after a break-up is running into an ex when you look tore up. That happened to me once in college and I vowed to never let it happen again. After a break-up you can cry at home, but if you leave the house, you must be flawless. Meg, how do you feel?"

"Mixed. On the one hand, I love that he was staring at me. But on the other hand, how dare he walk out and not say anything? No 'how ya doing?,' 'how's your family?,' 'here's some of the money I owe you.' Nothing. Do you know I had to disconnect my home phone to save money and because I couldn't take Frank's creditors and bookies calling anymore? I'm using my cell phone for everything."

"It's just money conservation," Button said, trying to put a positive spin on the situation.

"I wouldn't be in money conservation if Frank wasn't an asshole," Meghan declared. "I'm still behind on my mortgage and the bank isn't being nice about it. The least that jerk could do is say hello. It's amazing how I don't exist to him anymore. I want to punch him in the face," Meghan said.

"Have you thought about selling your engagement ring?" Dawn asked.

"It's on my list of fundraising options. I love that ring, but I don't know if I'll ever want to wear it again," Meghan answered.

"Don't sell your ring. Diamonds are an investment and they always hold their value. Just get the setting changed and wear it on your right hand. Make it your Single Girl Summer ring," Button suggested as the bartender returned and set three chilled shots in front of her. "Just in time. Thanks."

"Do you ladies want anything else?" he asked.

"Two white wines and a Zinfandel, please," Dawn ordered.

"The only wine we have is Zinfandel. Is that cool?" he asked Dawn.

"Yup, bring three of 'em. Gotta love the South Side." Meghan did a little dance in her seat, taunting Button.

"I'm not drinking that," Button declared.

"Yes, you are. It's a solidarity drink. I just saw my ex-husband and I need to know my friends have my back," Meghan demanded with a smile.

"I'm not drunk enough to drink White Zin," Button said.

"Well then, let's get you there. To flawless ex-counters." Dawn raised her shot in the air. Button and Meghan followed. They all clinked glasses, downed their shots, and slammed the glasses, rims down, on the bar.

"Enough about me. What's been up with you, Dawn? I haven't seen you in forever. Are they chaining you to your desk?" Meghan probed.

"I'm putting in the hours to make partner this year. And I'm dating a new guy," Dawn smirked. "He's not the typical guy I date, but I'm trying something new," Dawn admitted.

"He's white! Yes!" Button exclaimed. "That's great. I keep saying that sisters need to diversify their dating pool. Black men aren't settling down because they have so many options. They're picking from white, black, yellow, brown, red, and every color in between. Sisters need to realize that it's time we start sampling the rainbow too. I love it. When do we meet him?" Button shouted.

"He's not white. He's really nice, but I'm afraid you won't like him," Dawn countered.

"Why?"

"We'll see. You'll meet him tonight. He said he was sitting by the dance floor with his coworkers so I guess he's in the back room. He'll find us. And can you guys promise to keep an open mind and keep any negative comments to yourselves, especially you, Button?" Dawn asked sternly.

"Sure," Button and Meghan shrugged and exchanged perplexed looks.

"Seriously, because here he comes," Dawn announced. Button and Meghan turned their heads towards the back room and spotted an awkward, lanky man in glasses and blue scrubs walking toward them.

Button pursed her lips to keep her comments from slipping out. *He's definitely a fixer-upper and a far cry from Rick. He's not ugly, but he's not handsome. Not quite tall enough. Maybe she could do something with that frizzy hair. With the right products, it could be curly...maybe. With better hair and a pair of contacts, he could be a solid 6, but right now he's barely a 5. If he's Rick's replacement, he must have a great personality, thunder in his pants, or he's a doctor.*

When he reached Dawn, he planted a succession of sloppy kisses all over her face. Button flinched at the mauling. Meghan elbowed her in the ribs and mouthed "behave yourself."

"Pumpkin Pie, I've missed you. I'm starting to get jealous of that job of yours," he whined.

"Let me introduce you to my friends." Dawn pointed to Button and Meghan sitting on the bar stools behind him. "This is…"

"Let me guess," he cut Dawn off. "You're Meghan," he said to Button. "And you're Button," he said to Meghan, winking. "Benjamin Lawrence, at your service."

"Actually, I'm Meghan and she's Button." Meghan corrected.

"I knew that. I was making sure you were paying attention." Benjamin tweaked her nose. Meghan frowned instinctively and Button smirked in her seat. The bartender returned with three glasses of White Zinfandel and collected the shot glasses.

Benjamin eyed the empties. His voice dripped with condemnation. "Muffin Bottom, were you drinking shots?"

"We did a round," Dawn answered innocently. Benjamin shook his head in disgust.

Button asked, "Something wrong, Ben?"

"It's Benjamin. Not Ben. And no offense, but shots are so juvenile." He turned back to Dawn. "Blueberry Tart, you're too much of a lady to throw back shots at the bar. But that's okay. I'm sure it wasn't your idea." Benjamin planted more kisses on her.

Button rolled her eyes hard. "Benjamin, the shots were my idea."

Benjamin turned back around and wagged his finger at Button. "So, you're the one. I hope you aren't planning to get my Apple Crisp in any more trouble."

Button scooted back in her seat. *Why is Ben, sorry Benjamin, wagging his finger in my face? And why does he keep calling Dawn food names? Maybe he's hungry.*

"Benjamin, can I get you anything…a basket of wings or a drink?"

"Oh no. I'm not hungry and I've already had two virgin mojitos. That's enough for me."

Did he say virgin mojitos? He's in a bar drinking club soda, mint, and lime. And I'm pretty sure Reese's doesn't have any fresh mint, so he's drinking club soda and lime? Dawn can't be with this guy for his personality and this goofy having thunder in his pants is unlikely. He's a doctor. Maybe that's why he's not drinking. He's on his way to work. Okay

Button. Give him the benefit of the doubt.

"Are you on your way to work?" Meghan read Button's thoughts.

"No," Benjamin replied.

"Benjamin doesn't drink alcohol," Dawn explained.

Button shouted in her head, *Then why is he in a bar ordering virgin mojitoes? If you don't drink, order a Coke. Don't order a fake drink! What's the point?*

"Okay...so, um, Benjamin, what do you do for living?" Meghan asked.

"I work in the medical profession," Benjamin replied smugly and pushed his glasses up.

After waiting a couple of seconds and sneaking sideway glances at Button, Meghan tried again, "Doing what, exactly?"

"Helping people."

Button turned on her stool to face the bar and put her back to Dawn and Benjamin so they couldn't see the annoyed look on her face. *Benjamin Lawrence, medical mystery. What the hell is Dawn thinking? Benjamin may not drink, but he's giving me lots of reasons to. Desperate times call for desperate measures.* Having no other choice, she took a huge gulp from the glass of White Zinfindal the bartender left in front of her.

"Whoa there, Button. Save some water for the fishes. You're definitely the trouble maker in this group," Benjamin reprimanded and wagged his finger again. Button snorted dismissively.

"Anyway, I'm going to head out. I have an early start in the morrow." Benjamin plastered Dawn with more sloppy kisses. "Goodnight, ladies. Try not to get Sugar Plum in anymore trouble." Benjamin squeezed through the crowd toward the exit. Meghan and Button were speechless.

"Soooo, what do you think? He's nice, right?" Dawn asked hopefully. Meghan and Button were frozen.

"Right?"

"Cinnamon Bun, what do you think?" Button deflected to Meghan and chugged the rest of her White Zinfindel.

Meghan dropped her head to cover her laughter while she searched for the right words. "Umm, I think I want to know what he does for a living."

"He's a medical biller in a doctor's office. Isn't he nice?"

"Yeah, nice and definitely something new."

"He's shy," Dawn suggested.

"Benjamin Lawrence is not shy," Meghan said. "I know we talked about making a list of essential relationship elements, but...How do I say this? I thought

Rick had a lot of qualities you liked. Benjamin seems very different from Rick."

"In fact, he's the anti-Rick." Button added.

"Button, when I told you Rick was the total package, you told me to 'learn to love it.' No one's perfect. The better the man, the bigger the flaw. I re-evaluated my standards and decided I'm not dating men like Rick anymore. Men who are in such high demand that they cheat with no hesitation or consideration. I've decided to date someone more down-to-earth," Dawn told them.

"Dawn, *down-to-earth* men cheat too. A man's job or education isn't an indicator of fidelity. And I think you need to watch him. My mom always said never trust a man in a bar who doesn't drink," Button recalled.

"My mama always said never trust a man with two first names," Meghan added.

"So you got a double whammy with Benjamin, don't call me Ben, Lawrence," Button warned.

"Maybe you should re-evaluate the re-evaluation," Meghan looked at Button nervously.

Dawn pouted. "He can be a little extra, but he's growing on me. He's really nice."

"Gummy Bear, chicken pox grow on you too and they might be less annoying." Button reached for Dawn's glass.

"He's not annoying. He was nervous meeting you. You have to give him another chance," Dawn pleaded.

"Maybe, but please say you aren't bringing him to the Old Skool Picnic tomorrow. I don't want anybody sober around me until it's time to drive home," Button warned.

"He's not coming. Benjamin's from Chicago, but he doesn't like House music," Dawn said.

"He doesn't like House music? How can any black person in the city of Chicago not like House music?" Button lamented.

"I don't know, but I'm looking forward to tomorrow. I never heard of this event."

"Me either. Are you sure they have it every summer?" Meghan asked.

"I can't believe you two have never been. The Old Skool Picnic is the preeminent event of the summer. All of black Chicago will be there."

"I looked it up online. They have a webpage. They claim it's the largest House music event in the country. The music plays from ten in the morning until sunset. What happens at sunset? They kick you out of the park?"

"The music starts at ten, but people are there at the crack of dawn setting up. At sunset, they stop the music and everyone leaves in the same orderly fashion they arrived. After grilling, eating, drinking, dancing, and socializing all day, you're ready to go. It's so much fun."

"I can't wait. A house party on the lakefront!" Meghan danced in her chair.

"How many people will be there?"

"A lot. Maybe ten or fifteen thousand throughout the day."

"Is it safe? That's a lot of people."

"It's the Black Woodstock. Everybody's mama gives them the be-on-your-best-behavior and you-betta-not-embarrass-me speech before they come. When you have that many black folks conjugating, the police will take any excuse, large or small, to shut the whole thing down. But that doesn't even matter because everybody parties in peace."

"What time are you getting there, Button?" Dawn asked.

"Henry and I are on set-up duty. We'll be there at six AM to claim a spot, set up his tent, and drop off the grill, tables and supplies," Button answered.

"Six a.m.? It's that serious, huh?" Meghan questioned Button.

"Ladies, it's that serious. Henry and a few of his friends like to have an elaborate set up with a huge tent. Everyone chips in money for the food and we take shifts for the set up. Henry and I take the first shift since he has a van to transport all the supplies. We drop off early, set up for a couple of hours, then go back home to bed. There are shifts all morning to barbecue and hold down the fort. We like to have the food ready when the music starts."

"Do we need to chip in money for food?" Dawn asked.

"I signed you two up for drink duty. Meg's making sangria. Can you split the cost with her?" Button asked Dawn.

"Of course. I prefer to pay money and not do any work. Just let me know how much I owe you. Are you making the sangria tonight? What time are you getting there?" Dawn looked at her watch.

"I'm getting there at noon and I got up early this morning to make the sangria. I knew we'd be out late and I want the fruit and wine to marinate a whole day. Button, I filled both those containers you gave me so we have ten liters of sangria. Is that going to be enough?" Meghan asked.

"We'll set one pitcher out for everyone else and hide the other one just for us." Button and Meghan high-fived. "I'm telling you, it's the Black Woodstock. After Henry's Memorial Day party, the picnic is my second-favorite summer event. I'm going to be there with Henry, but I recommend you ladies come solo.

Don't bring sand to the beach." Button laughed.

Dawn said, "Well, my sand doesn't want to go. What about your sand, Meg? I need to have some one-on-one time with Philip. I want to find out what his intentions are."

"Phillip has to work tomorrow," Meghan answered.

"Well, when can I have a sit down with your new beau?"

"Hopefully tonight. Let me check my phone and see if he called." Meghan pulled her phone from her purse. "Perfect timing. He just texted me that he's fifteen minutes away. Are we ready to go or should he come in?"

"Where are we going?" Dawn asked.

"In addition to owning and running a flight school, he's also a pilot. I told him about our Single Girl Summer adventure and he wants to make a contribution by taking us all for a ride in his plane."

"I'm really out of the loop. Did you figure out how old he is?"

"He's forty-two, divorced eight years, and has one kid in high school. We have so much in common. Especially since we're both divorced, it's easy to talk to him about life after marriage. He gets it. I been trying to take it slow, but I don't think I am. He picks me up from work and takes me to lunch. He loves to cook so he comes over with exotic fruits and foods and we have so much fun making up recipes on the spot with whatever is in my kitchen. We talk and talk for hours. He's great."

"Total package?"

"Pretty much. The only quirk is he's super busy and doesn't give me a lot of notice when he wants to get together. I like to have my week planned in advance so that gets a little annoying. But the time we spend together is so wonderful that it's a small tradeoff."

"Has he landed your plane yet?" Dawn asked slyly.

"Huh?" Meghan looked at Dawn with confusion.

"He hasn't popped her cherry, if that's what you're asking. Meg's playing hard to get." Button cut in.

"I'm not playing. I am hard to get."

"Well, it's hard not to notice how happy you are talking about Phillip. I like that, but I think I'll pass on the flight. I'm not crazy about heights," Dawn said.

"You *have* to come. The aerial view of downtown Chicago at night is the most beautiful way to see the city. I really want us to do this together. I haven't seen you in two weeks. Please?" Meghan pouted and begged.

"How many times have you flown with him? Is it safe?"

"I've been up a few times. It's amazing and very safe." Meghan's phone vibrated with a text message. "Phillip's outside. Dawn, please come."

"Dawn, we're going up in our own private plane. This is taking Single Girl Summer to new heights. Do something daring! Face your fears." Button demanded.

Dawn thought for a few seconds, looking back and forth between her friends. "Alright, let's go!" Button and Meghan cheered. They left money on the bar, grabbed their purses, and ran outside.

CHAPTER 22

Text Message to Meghan
Fr: Dawn
1:55pm 7/18/09 - Saturday
OMG. This is amazing.
How can I find you?

Text Message to Dawn
Fr: Meghan
1:57pm 7/18/09 - Saturday
It's easier to come to you. Where RU?

Text Message to Meghan
Fr: Dawn
1:58pm 7/18/09 - Saturday
In front of the b-ball courts and near the motorcycles. Shirtless men to the right. Daredevils to the left. Enjoying the view. Take ur time. LOL

Yesterday, the soccer field in Jackson Park was spacious and quiet. Today, every inch was covered with tents, barbecue grills, and people. It was now hallowed ground for house heads, music lovers, dancers, and anyone who loved to have a good time. The temperature was in the high 70s but the wind off the lake made it feel like 73° F, which to Meghan was the ideal temperature to frolic outside all day.

Meghan carried two red cups as she zigzagged through a maze of tents and happy people and pondered the word perfect. In her opinion, that description should be used sparingly and with great consideration for it inferred a state of being so exact, flawless, and wonderful that it was rarely achieved. But as Soho's "Hot Music" created an invisible love bubble around the park, trapping the faint smell of marijuana in the air, she decreed the Old Skool Picnic was perfect.

Meghan found Dawn just where she said she would be, looking summer chic in a pink tank top and short denim wrap skirt in front of the basketball courts. She was happily munching on a hot dog and chatting with a tall stranger in a motorcycle vest.

"Girl, you made it! Fashionably late, but right on time." Meghan and Dawn hugged carefully so as not to spill the liquid in the two red cups Meghan carried.

"Hey, Meg. This is Dave. We went to high school together." Dawn swallowed the last of her hot dog and, with her hands free, relieved Meghan of one of her cups. "Thanks for the sangria. Good looking out."

"Where's my cup? I may ride a Harley, but I like sangria," Dave joked.

"Sorry, the contents of these cups are the last of the sangria," Meghan apologized.

"I thought you made two tons of the stuff. Henry's crew demolished it already?" Dawn asked.

"The sangria was the unfortunate sacrifice of a Button and Henry blow out. I'll tell you about it later."

"If you need a base camp, you can hang out with my guys. We've got plenty of food and drinks. I can ride Dawn on my bike and one of my boys can take you," Dave offered Meghan.

"Dawn! On a Harley! I'd like to see that. We flew in a small plane last night and she almost had a heart attack."

"When I think plane, I think United. I didn't think we'd be in a puddle jumper. I freaked out at first, but Meg's boyfriend was the pilot and he was great at calming me down. He must have to do that a lot. After I settled down, I enjoyed myself." Dawn laughed at herself.

"Life's the best adventure," David said. "You should keep it going and let me ride you around the park. I'll go slow. I promise you'll enjoy it."

"I don't know…maybe. Let me think about it," Dawn replied.

"Dave, she'll have to come back later. The DJ promised to play our Natalie

Cole song any minute now so we're meeting Button on the dance floor." Meghan pointed to the heart of the crowd.

"Duty calls. Bye, Dave. It was great to see you. I'll come back later." Dawn hugged Dave and followed Meghan into the wonderful chaos of tents and people. "Meg, I haven't seen him in forever. We dated two years in high school. He was sweet."

"Your Old Skool Picnic experience isn't complete until you run into at least three ex-boyfriends. I've seen two so I only have one more to go. And you just got here and you already saw one! He's tall, cute, and definitely was flirting with you," Meghan said as she and Dawn traversed the crowded walking path.

"Dave reminds me of Rick and I don't want to go down that pretty-boy path again. Plus, I want to see where things are going with Benjamin."

"Why don't you take Button's advice and date them both?"

"I'm done taking her advice. Speaking of Button, what happened with Henry and our sangria?"

"You remember Half's number-two chick who was following him around at his Memorial Day party?"

Dawn nodded, so Meghan continued, "She was hanging out in his tent and Button was pissed. She read him the riot act about disrespecting her, grabbed the half-empty sangria pitcher on the table, and stomped off. I completely forgot to get the full container we hid for ourselves. Now we're hanging out in my co-worker's tent and this is the last of it." Meghan nodded to their cups.

"Can we go back and get the other pitcher? I want more Single Girl Sangria. We shouldn't have to suffer because Button's crazy."

"The way Button snapped on Half...whew, you had to be there. She had one of those reality TV moments. Nevertheless, we ain't getting that sangria back. Charge that to the game. It's too bad Half didn't keep ol' girl hidden."

"Why should he hide her? Button belittles their relationship by calling him Half. Now she's got you doing it too. She's certainly seeing other people. What gives her the right to kick rocks? She always says 'good for the goose...'"

"Girl, I thought you were going to cut Button some slack?"

"You said to think about it. I thought about it and I don't agree. She needs some cold, hard truth. Henry has feelings and she treats him like an old shoe. People aren't disposable or interchangeable and I'm tired of walking on eggshells about it."

"Do I have to give you the be-on-your-best-behavior speech?" Meghan asked sarcastically. The numerous tents of every shape, size, and color formed a semicircle around the stage where Chicago's most notorious DJs spun magic. In front of the stage was a huge grassy area reserved for dancing which suddenly came into view.

Dawn stopped and grabbed Meghan's arm. "Oh. My. God. It's like a modern-day praise dance. This is beautiful."

Meghan smiled big. "I know. Look for Button."

The DJ changed the song to Stardust's "The Music Sounds Better with You" and the crowd went wild. Hands were thrown into the air and some women near Meghan shouted "*that's my song*." Dawn pointed to where Button looked like she was floating in the sea of dancers. Everyone was moving together like the colorful, live coral they saw at the aquarium. Meghan and Dawn soul-clapped through the crowd toward Button. The DJ changed the song again and Meghan instantly recognized the melodic beat and rhythmic shake of her song. Meghan gave her red cup to Dawn and began jumping up and down and shouting Button's name. Button heard her name and moved to where Meghan was still jumping up and down, yelling about the DJ playing her song. Dawn watched in amusement, still holding both cups. Button nudged Dawn and they both laughed at Meghan.

Meghan stopped jumping and asked, "Ladies, do you remember the first time we heard this song?"

"Yes, when we decreed the official start of Single Girl Summer at Half's house. Fucking Half. Fuck him," Button shouted.

Dawn rolled her eyes. "Whatever, Button."

"What the fuck is your problem?"

Meghan stepped in between the two women. "Button, what's up with all the F-bombs? I know you're upset, but don't let it ruin our good time."

"Meg, sometimes fuck is the only word strong enough to describe how I feel. And right now I feel like fuck Half and what the fuck is Dawn's problem?"

Dawn rolled her eyes again. "You're my problem. You have a great guy who's ready to commit and you keep pushing him off. Then you get mad when you see him with someone else. You've got some nerve. I can't believe how childish and selfish you are."

Meghan put her hand on Dawn's arm. "Do you have to do this here? It's Single Girl Summer. This is our song. We're supposed to be celebrating."

Dawn pushed both red cups to Meghan and squared off with Button. "I don't want to celebrate Single Girl Summer. I'd rather be in a loving relationship with a wonderful man who's happily offering to give me the total package. You have that, Button. You have that guy, and you treat him like shit. He's not a *Half* or a math equation. He's a great guy and *Henry* deserves more than you running around on him with every man in town. You're a hypocrite and whore."

Button snorted in disbelief. "Let me tell you a couple of things…"

Meghan interrupted. "Button…please don't say anything else that you're going to regret. Can we just drop it?"

"Hell no. Meg, stay out of this. She said her piece. Now it's my turn. Dawn, you're a spineless doormat. You let your sisters tell you how to live your life. You let Rick treat you like shit. You let Benjamin reduce you to dessert pet names. Now, you want to jump bad with me. You wanted to hurt Rick. You called me for advice. All I did was try to help. I never came at you foul about why it took so long for you to dump that loser Rick. I let you dump him in your own time. And, you're no angel either. If I'm a hypocrite and a whore, then birds of a feather. You happily got down with Brett to spite Rick."

"I did it listening to you. I don't know why I took relationship advice from the queen of dysfunction. You and your crazy mother."

"I may be dysfunctional, but at least I'm not a jealous, crazy control-freak. If you stopped looking so hard at Henry, maybe you could find your own man. My mother may be crazy, but she warned me about women like you. Jealous bitches who can't keep their own man happy so they come sniffing up under yours. I'm not ready to stop my life for Henry and especially not for you, so fuck you, Dawn." Button stormed away.

"Fuck you, too." Dawn yelled after Button and stomped off in the opposite direction, leaving Meghan alone. Her head volleyed back and forth, watching Dawn and Button shrink in the distance. She noticed a shirtless man nearby watching her with a concerned look on his face. His broad chest and tight abs were covered with sweat.

He came over to her. "Sister, you okay? That was pretty intense."

Like a deer in headlights, she asked him, "What should I do?"

"Carpe Diem."

"What?"

"Carpe Diem. Seize the day."

"I need to do something. My friends are fighting."

"Look, those sisters need to cool off. Even if you think one is right and one is wrong, keep out of that. Let 'em work it out. In the meantime, you're double fisted at the hottest party in the universe. Brush that shit off."

Meghan just stared at him.

"Sister, that's their fight, but this…this is your time. Take a big sip from one of those cups. You can give me the other one if you want. Close your eyes and let the music pull you through."

Meghan handed Dawn's cup to the stranger. "Am I really supposed to dance at a time like this?"

"Sister, sometimes you just gotta say fuck it and get your groove on. Do you know what I'm talking about?"

Meghan nodded her head. *Yes. Ex-husband, the saddies, and bills be damned. I look great and feel better about myself than I have all year. He's right. This is my time.*

The stranger swallowed from Dawn's cup and started dancing in front of Meghan. Swaying with the crowd, he reminded her of the palm trees that bend, but don't break. They're flexible, graceful, and even stronger after the storm. *I'm flourishing just like my mother said I would.*

Meghan smiled at the dancing stranger. "You're right. Fuck it."

The stranger swallowed from his red cup again. "Whacha say? *I can't hear you*," he shouted.

Meghan took a huge gulp from her own red cup. "*Fuck it*," Meghan shouted back. She joined the sweaty stranger and the rest of the crowd as they danced wildly to her song.

Chapter 23

Text Message to Meghan
Fr: Button
5:55pm 7/21/09 - Tuesday
Tonight's movie is Breakfast at Tiffany's.
Audrey Hepburn and her little black dresses.
One of my faves!
Meet me in front of the building in 15 minutes.
I got the sangria and red cups.

Text Message to Button
Fr: Meghan
5:58pm 7/21/09 - Tuesday
Had a delightful array of snacks, but I locked myself out the house. ☹
It's times like these I miss my ex.
He was my spare set of keys.
Now I have to go all the way over to my parents' house.

Text Message to Meghan
Fr: Button
5:59pm 7/21/09 - Tuesday
If that's the best reason you can come up with to be married, then it's a good thing you got divorced.
I'll keep your spare and I'll take u to ur folks.
Hope your mom cooked. ☺

***

The fragrant smell of tender meat, parsley, garlic, and cinnamon permeated the air. Button dropped her spoon, wiped her mouth with a napkin, let out a huge sigh, and slouched back in her seat. "Mama Cherry, that lamb stew was delicious."

Mama Cherry's face beamed with pride. "That's the least I can do since you drove my baby over here and missed your movie. I hope Meg and Papa Cherry can set up that new DVD player. It's taking them long enough. They missed dinner."

"And what a dinner it was. I thought Meg could throw down, but you… you put your foot in that. Whew, your lamb stew beats snacks in the park any day. I may have to buy the recipe from you and put it on my menu." Button used Hawaiian bread to slop up the remaining stew in her bowl.

"Thanks, Baby. One of the ladies from my church was talking about that 'Movies in the Park.' She made it seem like it was at her neighborhood park though. I know she doesn't go downtown."

"They show movies in the neighborhood parks and in Grant Park."

"Oh, she said it reminded her of the drive-in movies. She took her grandkids, a picnic basket, and a blanket and got to watch a movie outside in her own neighborhood."

"Close to home is nice, but I'm a downtown girl. Classic American movies on a big screen under the stars and the skyline; that's the best way to spend a Tuesday night if you aren't serving lamb stew."

Mama Cherry smiled. "Did you save room for dessert?"

"No, but maybe later. Whatcha got?"

"Avocado pie," Mama Cherry's eyes twinkled.

"I've never heard of that. What's in it?"

"The filling is the meat of two avocadoes, half a cup of lime juice, half a block of cream cheese, and five ounces of sweetened condensed milk. Blend it well with a hand mixer until smooth, pour into a graham cracker crust and let it chill overnight. Serve with real whipped cream and orange zest. So good."

Button eyed her suspiciously. "What's it taste like?"

"Subtle key lime pie with a hint of avocado. You know avocado is good fat and good for you. It's a magic food. Try it. You'll want the recipe for that too."

"When it comes to food, I believe whatever you say. You asked for that avocado omelet and now it's one of my most popular dishes. Give me a couple of minutes and I'll be ready for pie."

"If they can set up that DVD player, we can eat our pie while we watch *Breakfast at Tiffany's*. It's one of my favorites too."

"I don't know if I can stay awake for the movie. I feel a food coma coming. That lamb stew put it on me." Button rubbed her belly.

Mama Cherry laughed. "Your eyes look heavy. We don't have to watch the movie tonight. We can watch it this weekend and invite Dawn. I haven't met her yet."

Button scoffed and took her dirty dishes over to the sink.

"Did I say something wrong?" Mama Cherry looked worried.

"No. Actually, Mama Cherry, Dawn and I aren't speaking to each other. We had a big fight and I don't know if we're going to be friends anymore."

"Oh no. Meg said you three were having such fun together with your Single Girl Summer."

"We were and then Dawn went crazy on me. I..." Button's voice trailed off and her eyes watered. "Never mind, I don't want to bother you with my problems."

Mama Cherry sat on a stool at her kitchen island. She gestured for Button to have a seat next to her.

"I have always looked at Meg's girlfriends as my mini-daughters. If you want to talk, it's no bother."

"The truth is, Meg and Dawn are the first female friends I've had since college. My mother always discouraged female bonding because of a bad experience she had. I was beginning to think my mother was completely crazy, but now I'm not sure. Don't get me wrong, Meghan is wonderful, especially considering everything she's been through. But Dawn lost her mind."

"One thing I always try to remember," Mama Cherry said gently, "is that you never know what someone else is going through. If someone snaps at you unexpectedly, it could be because they're under tremendous stress, anger, or sadness. Those are the times that we have to blindly, unconditionally, and faithfully extend our love and understanding to that person.

"When Meghan told me about your Single Girl Summer and all the fun things you're doing, I thought 'what a wonderful therapy.' In my opinion, Single Girl Summer isn't just about getting out of the house and hanging out. Single Girl Summer is a healing experience. This is the time to figure out what negativity needs to be cleaned out of your life. Once you do that, you can eliminate it and replace it with things of your highest good. Do you think you should eliminate your relationship with Dawn?"

"Maybe? I don't know what I should eliminate," Button answered. "Lately, I don't know if I'm coming or going. Just last month, I found out my mother has fed me horrible lies about my father to keep me from having a relationship with him. The guy I've been non-exclusively dating for the past two years, Henry, started pulling away because he's tired of waiting for a commitment. He wants to get married and I care about him, but I don't know if marriage is for me. The same day I argued with Dawn, I went off on him because I saw him with another woman. Dawn's mad because she wants more than anything to get married and can't understand why I'm not jumping at the chance to marry Henry. She called me selfish and childish. With all this crap being dropped on me, I definitely need some therapy and healing. But I don't know where or how to start sorting it all out.

"Even though I want to, I know I can't eliminate my mother. I'm so mad at her, but she's my mother. She gave me everything growing up. I can't just cut her from my life, but I don't know how to deal with her right now. I'm happy to start getting to know my father, but I'm mad at him for letting this go on for so long. He should have done more. I'm mad at Henry for throwing that woman in my face. I'm mad at Dawn for sticking her nose in my business and judging me. Mama Cherry, I'm mad at four major people in my life. Lately, all I do is think about how mad I am. I know it's not healthy for me to carry around all this anger and hurt, but I don't know what else to do." Tears rolled down Button's cheeks.

Mama Cherry stood and wrapped her arms around Button. Button leaned into her embrace and they rocked slowly for a few minutes. "Baby, the key is forgiveness. There are a lot of hurt feelings and mistakes by all parties, and I'm sure that includes you. But if you truly love someone, you have to accept they're human and are going to make mistakes. And they need to accept the same about you. Love is the good, bad, and ugly. It's not easy to forgive, but it's truly divine. Forgiveness doesn't have to be instantaneous. Open your heart and allow yourself to gradually grow into your forgiveness. Pray to release the anger. Replace it with love. Baby, that's your therapy. That's your Single Girl Summer healing." Mama Cherry released Button, walked over to the refrigerator, and retrieved two bottles of water.

"Grow into forgiveness? How do I start?" Button took the bottle, opened it and took a sip.

"You could start with the easiest one and work your way up. Practice makes improvement."

"That would be Dawn. She's under a lot of pressure and I guess I can understand her frustration."

"It always helps to put yourself in someone else's shoes. What about Henry's shoes?"

"Mama Cherry, how did you know you were ready for a commitment? My parents' marriage ended horribly and I don't want the same thing to happen to me. Plus I don't think I'm the settling-down type, but how do I know?"

"I've been married thirty-six years so let me tell you this…true commitment, with the right person and in the right state of mind, is so beautiful and wonderful that you won't want to be without it. True commitment is a bond strengthened by intimacy, communication, common vision, respect, and loyalty. You know how you stand in front of a mirror and do a self-evaluation? You note all your positive attributes and areas for improvement?

"Well, when you have a partner in a true commitment, your partner is that mirror. He helps you see all the good and encourages you to improve. A true partner loves you the way you are, and also loves who you can become. And when you love him back, you gladly look at yourself through his eyes and want to be better. A true partner compliments your good and supplements any areas you lack. That type of relationship is rare and precious. So Button, you need to ask yourself, is Henry your mirror?"

Button thought for a long time before responding. "If it weren't for Henry encouraging me, I would never have met Meg and Dawn and had my first true girlfriends or my Single Girl Summer. And if it weren't for Henry, I may have never reunited with my father. So yes, Henry's my mirror. He loves me the way I am, but he loves who I can become. Lots of men buy me stuff, take me nice places, and entertain me. But no other man has ever given me a gift as precious as helping me grow and improve."

"Button, Henry sounds like a rare and precious man."

"He is. I guess you're telling me I owe Dawn and Henry a phone call."

"I'm telling you to follow your heart. If it tells you someone is worth keeping in your life, be it your mother, father, Dawn, or Henry, then you should listen and work on forgiving them. When you forgive someone, you aren't doing them a favor. You're doing yourself a favor. When you truly forgive someone, you release all the hurt and negative feelings you're holding onto. You're walking around looking like somebody kicked your dog and the person you're mad at has no idea or even cares that you're upset. When you let go of the pain, you're doing it for you. You're healing yourself."

"You sound just like this book Henry gave me. But I think I should wait for Dawn to call me. She went crazy on me." Button redirected.

"That's your choice. But what if Dawn doesn't call you right away? What if she doesn't call you until November? Are you okay spending the rest of Single Girl Summer without one of the founding members?"

"But she started the fight," Button whined. "She owes me an apology."

"'I'm sorry' is overrated. I would rather not lose someone important to me. In the grand scheme of things, are two little words of apology worth giving up a friend, a partner, or a family member? I always like to think, what if the person I'm mad at died tomorrow. How would I feel holding onto my anger and that person is gone? How would you feel, Button?"

"I feel like I've been holding on to anger for too long. It's time for me to forgive. And I'm going to start with you."

"Me, what did I do?" Mama Cherry was shocked.

"You didn't make enough lamb stew so I could take some to go, but I forgive you." Button laughed.

"Oh, really. I guess you have to start somewhere." Mama Cherry laughed too.

"I'm starting small and working my way up."

"Good, now let's go check on Papa Cherry and Meg. I want to see that movie."

"I'm right behind you."

CHAPTER 24

Fr: <Button>
To: <Meghan>, <Dawn>
Wednesday, July 22, 2009 10:56AM
Subject: VENETIAN NIGHT

Picture it: Gorgeous boats, amazing fireworks & a lakefront view. It could only be Venetian Night. I'm organizing a get together for Saturday. I've got the snacks and champagne. All you need to bring is yourself and a chair. Unless Phillip has a boat we can hang out on. ☺

The boat parade begins at 8pm and the fireworks are at 9. I'm setting up camp at 6 to get a good spot. I hope we can all make it. Let me know.

Fr: <Meghan>
To: <Button>, <Dawn>
Wednesday, July 22, 2009 10:59AM
Subject: RE: VENETIAN NIGHT

Sorry ladies. Phillip and I already have plans. He doesn't have a boat, but he has the best view of Lake Michigan from his place. I hope you two get together without me.

Fr: <Dawn>
To: <Button>
Wednesday, July 22, 2009 3:23PM
Subject: RE: VENETIAN NIGHT

Sure Button. I'll meet you there around 730. How will I find you?

Fr: <Button>
To: <Dawn>
Wednesday, July 22, 2009 3:49PM
Subject: RE: VENETIAN NIGHT

Cross Lakeshore at Balbo street.
Look for the white balloons.

* * *

Dawn crossed Lake Shore Drive with a diverse crowd of young, old, families, friends, singles, and couples; all carrying travel chairs and chatting excitedly about their favorite boats and decorations from last year's show. Admiring the stars twinkling in the sky, she noticed the huge banner announcing this year's theme as "Hollywood on the Lake" and spotted the white balloons bobbing in the pleasant breeze. Nervous butterflies flittered in Dawn's stomach.

I hope this isn't too awkward. I wish I had gone to lunch at Anand yesterday, but I had to finish that brief. Hell, I didn't even leave my desk to go to the bathroom. I should have called. Does it count that I picked up the phone to call like five times, but I didn't know what to say? She needed to hear the truth. She needs to consider how Henry feels. I don't owe her an apology—I don't think. I wish Meg would have given me her opinion, but all she would say is she hopes we work it out. Me too. But I don't owe her an apology.

Dawn found Button lounging in a chaise with her feet propped on a large picnic basket atop a colorful, patchwork blanket. Button looked like a 1950s movie star, sipping from a crystal champagne flute with two fluffy white boas around her neck. Her head was tilted back and the night breeze played in her short hair. "Hey, Button. The balloon was a good idea and the boa is classic."

Button looked up and smiled. She set her flute down on the basket and stood. "Hey, Dawn." They hugged awkwardly. "I got the balloon idea from the Old Skool Picnic. I'm glad you came." She removed one of the boas from her neck and handed it to Dawn. "It's 'Hollywood on the Lake' so we have to glam it up."

Dawn set her travel chair down and flung the boa dramatically over her shoulders. "I feel like a movie star."

"You should have been with me at Buckingham Fountain earlier. Everyone thought I was famous and kept asking to take pictures with me. It was great." Button laughed.

"Did you sign autographs too?" Dawn teased as she set up her chair next to Button's.

"Of course. I've got a bunch of snacks in the basket and Veuve. Do you want a glass?"

"I'd love a glass, but aren't you supposed to put that in a red cup? Please don't get us arrested for having open alcohol in the park," Dawn lectured as Button poured.

"It's Hollywood night. I can't drink champagne out of a cup. That's uncivilized." Button handed Dawn a flute and they sat down in their chairs facing the lakefront.

"I'd love to see you sign autographs in jail." Dawn snickered.

"Between me and you, I've got a good friend who's a hot shot lawyer. I hope she'd help me out if I was in the clink. Well, that is if she's still my friend. We had a big fight and she's mad at me."

"Button, I'm not mad at you."

"Dawn, you went off on me in the sauna, gave me the business in the middle of the Old Skool Picnic, haven't talked to me all week, and didn't come to lunch yesterday. It's clear you're mad."

"I'm not mad at you. I'm mad at the situation and I'm taking it out on you. Maybe I was a little out of line and I'm sorry about that. I don't want to fight. Can we just move on and forget about it?"

"The old Button would say fine, pretend to forget it, and then stop talking to you in a couple of weeks. The new Button doesn't want that to happen. I think you're a great person and I want to be your friend, but I need you to accept me the way I am. I'm not perfect and I'm working on some things. I know I have issues and relationship dysfunction. I can't wave a magic wand to fix myself and neither can you. I'm sorry about Rick, but truth be told, it's good you found out what a jerk he was so you could move on. Rick lied to you. I've never lied to Henry and he accepts me the way I am. If you're going to be my friend, I need you to do the same."

Dawn shook her head. "But I just don't understand why you can't commit to Henry. He's so great. I don't want you to miss out on your Mister Wonderful."

"Dawn, I know your heart's in the right place and you want the best for me.

Henry told me he wanted me to have girlfriends because they call you on your shit and I really need to be called on some of my shit. I heard what you were saying. I got it. You can't be mad at me until I do what you want me to. You can't control everything and I need you to stop trying. I'm human. I'm going to make mistakes. As my girlfriend, you should call me on my shit, but you also have to stand by me even if I'm making the biggest mistake ever."

Dawn nodded slowly. "You're right. I'm a crazy control freak. But I'm also your friend and I need to start acting like it. I support you and I'm there for you. And the next time I need to call you on your shit, because I'm sure there'll be a next time, I'll find a more diplomatic way to do it."

"Diplomatic and private. I don't like to be on that side of the reality TV moment. I like to dish the drama and not have it dumped on me." Button and Dawn laughed.

"I'm sorry about that. We really clowned out there. Poor Meg was mortified."

Button stopped laughing. "I'm sorry too for the mean things I said. You're a crazy control-freak, but that's who you are and I love you for it."

"And you're wonderfully crazy and I love you for it. Let's toast," Dawn said, holding up her flute. "To girlfriends—good, crazy, and cold-as-hell. Who else can you wear a boa on the lakefront with?"

"I'll drink to that." Button clinked her flute with Dawn's.

"I love that sound. Red cups make no sound." Button smiled at her crystal flute.

"Look—the boat parade's starting. I can see everything. These are great seats. I wonder if Meg's view is as good as this."

"Boo'ed up as she is, I bet her view is fantastic," Button said. "I can't wait for the fireworks to start."

"I bet Meg's saying the same thing." Dawn and Button fell out laughing.

***

"Meg, Meg," Phillip whispered as he nudged Meghan, "Wake up, Baby. The fireworks are starting."

Meghan rubbed her eyes. "You got me fireworks, too?" She rolled over in bed to face him. "You fly me to Lake Geneva for a couple's massage and a wine tasting festival. Then you fly us back and make the most incredible dinner."

"Yeah, but you missed the boat parade," Phillip whispered into her ear.

"Oh, those two orgasms were worth so much more than some stupid boats. You better watch out. You're spoiling me." Meghan smiled wide.

"You deserve to be spoiled. I have a feeling your Single Girl Summer isn't going to last much longer." Phillip winked at her.

"Is that right?" Meghan replied sarcastically.

"There you go, being stubborn again. It's that same stubbornness that almost kept us apart. I still can't believe you wouldn't give me your number when I didn't know your name."

"It's not that I'm stubborn. It's that I'm special. Since you didn't remember my name or keep my number, then you obviously didn't recognize how special I am. And I don't have time to waste with someone who doesn't recognize my special."

Phillip kissed Meghan's lips softly. "I not only recognize, but I appreciate how special you are, which is why I plan on spoiling all the single out of your special. I also recognize that your ex-husband must be crazy because I can now officially say everything, and I mean everything, about you is wonderful."

"Everything, like what?"

Phillip straddled Meghan. "Your full lips, your delicate earlobes, your beautiful breasts, the happy trail down the middle of your stomach that leads to the promised land, and especially the way you squeeze me between your thighs. Everything about you is won-der-ful. I want to make love to you all night long, again and again."

"You really better watch out...you're spoiling me."

"Baby, do you know why I'm so successful in my business?"

"Please tell me."

"Because I over-serve my clients. I want them to be completely and thoroughly satisfied, and I don't stop until they are."

A provocative smile crossed Meghan's lips. "Umm, I hear you talking, but I don't know if I believe you."

"Is that right? Baby, I'm not even close to being done with you. Tonight, I'm going to make you believe." Phillip kissed Meghan from head to toe.

Meghan smiled at the fireworks exploding right outside their window. *This is perfect. This is why I got a divorce.*

August & September

CHAPTER 25

Fr: <Mama Cherry>
To: <Meghan>
Wednesday, August 5, 2009 7:15AM
Subject: Your vision

Sweetie, I'm so glad I got to see the room you designed for Button last night. It's vibrant, elegant, and wonderful. You truly captured her essence. It's amazing how much you've accomplished in a short period of time. You've always had excellent taste and designer-inspired ideas, but someone was purposely blocking your vision and creativity. Roadblocks are an impediment to finding your inner spirit and soul's growth. We wish the roadblocks good luck, but they cannot remain in our path.

Best of luck on the job interview. If they offer you the job, make sure you get more money. Keep me posted. ☺Love, Mom.

⁂

Meghan shouted into the phone. "Girl, where have you been?"

"I was in a meeting. My secretary said you've been blowing up my phone all morning. What's going on?" Dawn asked.

"Yesterday, out of the blue, I got a call from the IT manager at another firm. I had heard through the grapevine they were hiring, but I didn't think anything about it. He said he's heard a lot of good things about me, they are fast-tracking the hiring process, and he asked me to interview for the position today. I interviewed at eight this morning and he called me an hour ago to offer me the job. The salary is fifteen thousand more than I'm making here."

"Girl, that's awesome. Did you accept or do you want to play for a counter offer?"

"I didn't accept yet, but they want an answer today. I like my job here. I really like everyone I work with and I have this job down to a science. Plus, I've had so many changes this year with the divorce that I don't have the energy to adapt to a new work environment. Oh, and I've decided to enroll part-time in interior design school in the fall so it's probably best I stick with the devil I know."

"Interior design school is fantastic, but how are you going to find the time? Are you still doing the work of two people?"

"Thankfully, no. I was overwhelmed. Anyone would have been. It was too much for one person and my manager knew it. He found a way to split the work between me and an IT person from another department so I'm doing the work of one and a half people. I've adjusted to the new role and it's fine now, but I want, need, and deserve more money. How do I play for the counter offer?"

"The one caveat about the counter offer is you have to be prepared for the chance they won't negotiate. Will you be okay taking the other job?"

"I'm okay taking a job that pays more money, but I would prefer to stay here and get a raise."

"Okay, this is how you play it. First, you lay the foundation. Walk into your manager's office with a resignation letter in your hand. At no point do you ever give him the resignation letter or resign, but it's a prop to let him know you're serious."

"Okay. Then what?"

"The tone you're going for is serious but conflicted. Remind him how long you've worked there, mention any major accomplishments, and point out that you've taken on half the responsibility of another job without financial compensation. After you've laid the foundation, you start the negotiation. Tell him you've received an offer from a competitor with a substantial salary increase and you're considering it. But you enjoy working for the company so you'd like to give him an opportunity to present a counter offer. Then you wait." There was a long pause.

Meghan finally broke the silence. "What if he doesn't say anything?"

"*Wait*! I repeat, wait. The next word has to come from him. You lay out the situation and wait for his response. If you heard through the grapevine a competitor was hiring, then he has too and management has already decided if they'll present counter offers. The only question is how much of a raise can you negotiate. You want him to show his hand."

"Lay out the situation and wait? I hate uncomfortable silences," Meghan lamented.

Dawn pounded on her desk and shouted. "Get. Over. It. You're negotiating. This is your power play. You have to be strong here. The silence lets him know you'll walk if he doesn't make it worth your while."

"Okay, okay. Lawyer Dawn is a little feisty. I'll wait. Then what?" Meghan asked.

"One of three things. Option one, he says nice knowing you. Game over. You accept the other offer. Option two, he says the company values you, but doesn't have any money to increase your compensation. At that point, you have to decide if fifteen thousand is enough motivation to change jobs. If you decide to stay, then negotiate for an extra week of vacation or some other perk like working from home one day a week. Option three, and the option we want, is that he'll present a counter offer. When he asks what they offered, tell him thirty-thousand more than your current salary. He'll have to get approval from whoever's above him and that's when the dance begins. Are you wearing your dancing shoes?"

"No, but I'll channel my inner Alvin Ailey. Alright, I'm going to type up a resignation letter and ask my manager to dance. Wish me luck."

"Good luck. Call me back as soon as you're done talking to him. I'll wait by the phone."

"Thanks. Bye."

Dawn hung up the phone and checked her email. Minutes later, her secretary sauntered into her office with a brochure in her hand. Nicole had worked for Dawn for several years. Since they were close in age, they occasionally hung out after work to girl- and shop-talk. One of Nicole's greatest assets was her ability to work the secretary pool and gather important intel on the firm's inner-workings, which she then passed on to Dawn.

"This is where I did my tandem skydive and I highly recommend it. It's a couple of hours away in Wisconsin." Nicole handed Dawn the brochure. "I don't believe you're going to jump out of a plane. This is very uncharacteristic of you."

"I'm exploring my inner daredevil and I want to do something big to celebrate my thirtieth birthday in September."

"By next month you'll have come to your senses and your inner daredevil will be banished to the land of 'what the hell was I thinking?' You need to go this weekend," Nicole demanded.

"But I don't have anything big to celebrate."

"Word in the secretary pool is the partnership announcement is coming in the next couple of weeks. We're on the top of the list. I think we'll be celebrating very soon."

"We?" Dawn laughed.

"We're a team. When you get promoted, I get promoted. Meg's not the only one who needs a raise. I had to talk your girl off the ledge this morning."

"How many times did she call?"

"Every ten minutes, even though I assured her I'd give you the message as soon as you got out of your meeting. It's the same speech I give Benjamin Lawrence at least five times a day. Why does he tell me his full name every time he calls? Like I don't know who he is by now."

Dawn shrugged her shoulders but didn't answer, so Nicole continued, "Anyway, Meg was calling so much, I gave up the idea of getting any work done and tried to calm her down while she waited for you. I hope it works out for her. I told her about a skydiving trip as the perfect way to celebrate our promotion—hers and yours—and she agreed."

Dawn rolled her eyes at Nicole. "Aren't you helpful?"

"I sure am. I get the ball rolling. Only one of many reasons we deserve a raise."

"Did I have any other calls?"

"Yes, your daily nine-thirty AM Muffin Bottom check-in call. Why does Benjamin Lawrence address you as dessert and how much do I have to pay him to stop?"

"I'm not sure, but I'll go half with you." Dawn's phone rang. The caller ID showed Meg's work number.

"It's Meg," Dawn said excitedly. Nicole crossed her fingers in luck and ducked out of the office.

Dawn grabbed the phone. "What happened?"

"I did my dance and was prepared to wait for a response. But I didn't have to. My manager immediately said he expected this because he knew that company is poaching his best people. He said the company really values me and would like to present a counter offer."

"Yes!" Dawn drummed her desk.

"I told him the offer was for forty thousand more. He said he knows he can't match that amount, but he would try to get me something. I think he knew I was bluffing. He's calling corporate in New York right now. That would be so incredible if I get a raise and get to keep this job. It all happened so quickly. I was in and out of his office in ten minutes. Now I wait again?"

"That's the dance, Meg. Let's see what he can shake loose from corporate."

"Negotiating is stressful. I almost threw up walking down to my manager's office."

"Men do this all the time. That's one reason they make more than women. Some men ask for a raise every year."

"If you don't ask, you won't receive. I'm glad I asked. I hope the offer is good. I really need this. I'm going to get off this phone and pray. I need to thank God in advance because I know this is already done."

"Get your mind right, Girl. Call me back as soon as you get the offer."

Dawn hung up the phone again and turned back to her computer. After a few minutes, there was a soft knock on the door.

"So?" Nicole peeped her head in Dawn's office.

"She's still negotiating, but it looks good."

"Let me know when to start booking your skydiving trip. I recommend taking a limo up, skydiving in the morning, and then relaxing at the spa in the afternoon. The executive secretaries book these corporate trips all the time. I have all the details and phone numbers. I can book your trip in ten minutes. Just let me know the date, how many people, and what spa services you want."

"Do you get a referral fee if I go?" Dawn asked suspiciously.

"No, I get the satisfaction of doing a good deed for my boss. I know how stressed out you were a few months ago. I really like working for you so I vowed to take better care of you. I think you need to do this. You'll love the free fall. It's so relaxing and serene. You'll feel like a bird."

"That's sweet. Thanks for looking out for me. I guess a limo and spa would round out the trip nicely. Alright, if Meg gets the raise, the skydive celebration is on. Now let me get back to work." A huge smile crossed Nicole's face and she turned to leave.

Dawn tried to do some research, but she couldn't concentrate. *When is she going to call? It's been like an hour. Oh, no. It's only been twenty minutes. It feels like an hour. Please let Meghan get a big raise. Please, please, please!* The phone rang and Meg's number showed on the caller ID again.

"What happened?" Dawn demanded.

"The counter offer was a thirty-thousand dollar raise. I accepted!" Meghan shouted.

Dawn fist-pumped the air. "Congratulations. You deserve it."

"Yes I do. I'm so happy. Nicole suggested skydiving and a spa day to celebrate. If you're game, I'm in."

"Let's go this Saturday," Dawn suggested.

"I can't. The Bud Biliken parade is Saturday."

"You do know that parade is for going back to elementary school. I'm excited about you going to design school too, but I don't think they'll let you be in the parade for that," Dawn laughed.

"You do know that parade is the oldest and largest African-American parade in the country and a family tradition. My aunt has an apartment overlooking the parade route. All the family comes. We bring gifts for the kids. We barbecue and watch the parade from the comfort of her balcony. No crowds and no Porta-Potties. Plus, Button's going to Atlanta this weekend to visit her father," Meghan said.

"Did she and Henry ever make up?" Dawn asked.

"I don't think so. I think she has the saddies over it. Skydiving would really cheer her up. How about next Saturday?"

"I'm free next Saturday. I'll check with Button and hopefully we can book it today."

"Dawn, thanks for all your help. I couldn't have done this without you."

"Yes, you could have. You're one of the strongest, smartest, and most wonderful women I know. You and your faith never cease to amaze me. I'm so glad you're my friend."

"You're a great friend, too! And you're equally amazing."

"Tell Button about my raise when you call her. I gotta go call my parents and then I need to get back to work. Talk to you later."

Chapter 26

Text Message to Button
Fr: Henry
8:34pm 8/11/09 - Tuesday
I need to see you.

Text Message to Henry
Fr: Button
8:36pm 8/11/09 - Tuesday
Driving home from airport.
Went to see my father.
20 minutes away.
Can I come now?

Text Message to Button
Fr: Henry
8:37pm 8/11/09 - Tuesday
Yes.

***

After the big fight at the Old Skool Picnic, Henry and Button decided over text messages to give each other some space. They had never gone this long without any communication. Button sat on the oversized leather couch while

Henry went to the kitchen to get her a glass of water. Henry's house was a cozy bungalow that Button nicknamed "The Jack Daniels" because, like his favorite liquor, all the rooms were smooth, comfortable shades of brown.

I've had some good times on this couch. Just watching a movie, reading, or fooling around, which is funny because I usually don't allow couch dates. I think the last few times we stayed in, it was even my idea. With anyone else, I'm strictly a go-out girl. But it's different with Henry. I missed this couch. I wonder if Henry missed me or if he already gave my seat away. A lot can happen in a month, but he still looks good. When he opened that front door, whew, I got a little woozy.

Henry returned and handed Button a glass of water. Then he sat on the edge of a chair across the room, facing her, and watched as she drank. "How was your trip?"

"It was good. I hung out with my brother and sister. Got to know them a little better. And my Dad and I really got a chance to talk. I was nervous about it at first, but I needed to ask him some questions."

"Like what?"

"If he thought it had been worth it to sacrifice our relationship for his current family."

"What did he say?"

Button took another sip and sat the glass on the coffee table coaster. "He said it was complicated. Not a day went by that he didn't regret my absence. But also not a day went by that he didn't feel blessed for being with Sandra. He wishes he would've tried harder to keep me in his life and hopes we can make up for lost time. That's really all we can do at this point." Button shrugged.

"That's tough. I feel for your dad. He seems like a nice guy who got a raw deal."

"He had to decide between staying in an unhappy marriage and making a huge sacrifice to be with his true love. He said he knows more about regret than any person should know in one lifetime. He encouraged me to go see my mother 'cause he would hate if something happened to her and I never set things right. Regret is a heavy cross to bear."

"Your Dad's a saint."

"He is, especially since he drove down to Augusta with me."

"How'd your Mom act?"

"She apologized a lot. She even apologized to him once. She admitted it was wrong to use me as a weapon. She was just so mad and once she started the lie, it took on a life of its own. She could never find a way to stop it and tell the truth

Plus, she hated him for leaving and she hates not getting her way." Button rolled her eyes.

"How are you feeling about your Mom and Dad?"

"It's terrible that she sabotaged my relationship with him, but I have to accept my part too. My Dad reached out to me a few times and I never gave him a chance. He could have tried harder, but he did try. I never tried at all. I can only blame so much on my Mom. Button has to start taking responsibility for Button. I forgave my mother and we're going to rebuild our relationship. She's even going to get a little counseling."

"Really? Wow. I didn't expect you to hand out forgiveness like Pez. Did you bring me any?"

"No."

"No? Did you run out?"

"You don't need to be forgiven by me. You need to forgive me. I had no right going off on you at the picnic. This half relationship was my idea and you're well within your rights to have anyone you like in your tent."

"Forgive you? Hell, I was happy you got so upset. In every relationship, one person is going to be further in than the other. In our relationship, that person is me and most of the time I'm fine with that. But sometimes, it doesn't feel good to love someone who doesn't love you back. It was nice to see you get worked up over me. It gave me hope that one day you'll care for me the way I care for you. Button, I don't want anyone else in my tent. I want you completely and whole-heartedly. I don't want to play this half game with you anymore."

"Henry, I feel whole when I'm with you, but I'm scared."

Henry rose and walked toward the couch. Button rose to meet him. He took her face in his hands and stared into her eyes.

"I love you. I'll never leave you. Let me make you whole." Henry's eyes searched hers.

"Seeing my dad and Sandra…" Her eyes watered and the words caught in her throat. "They're committed to each other and so happy. I know it's possible and I want that. I want that with you…and only you."

The corners of Henry's eyes crinkled with his smile. He stared at Button like he was seeing her for the first time. Henry hugged her so hard she could barely breathe, but she didn't care. She held onto him and squeezed with all her might. She felt his heart racing and body heat rising. Finally, he pulled back. They locked eyes and held each other in their stares. It had been a month since they'd last seen each other. Button smiled seductively and pulled his lips to hers. They'd kissed a million times, but he'd never tasted so good. There was something different… better. Button couldn't put her finger on what that difference was, but she didn't care. She was so happy.

She melted to the floor and pulled him down to the thick carpet. Henry made love to her like he'd never done before. She always thought their sex was fantastic and couldn't get any better, but now it was. He kept whispering in her ear, "I love you. Cocoa, I love you."

Then it dawned on Button. Something was different, but it wasn't him. She was different. She felt closer to him and happier than she could ever remember. Overwhelmed with emotion, she said, "I love you, too." He squeezed her even tighter. She clung to him. Her pulse raced and tears welled in her eyes. The tears turned to sobs and Button couldn't control herself.

"What's wrong with me?" She asked through her sobs. This was the second time she'd cried in front of Henry. He kissed her tears and blew air on her chest and neck to cool her down.

"You're in love. And it looks so good on you."

Chapter 27

Fr: <Button>
To: <Meghan>, <Dawn>
Friday, August 14, 2009 9:18AM
Subject: Skydiving

Did I really agree to hurl my delicate body out of a moving airplane tomorrow? I must really love you girls.

Fr: <Dawn>
To: <Button>, <Meghan>
Friday, August 14, 2009 10:05AM
Subject: RE: Skydiving

You're really going to love the spa day I booked for us after. Olive oil mani/pedi, essential mint facial, hot stone massage, full body wax, and gourmet spa lunch. Someone else will wax our underarms and I'm picking up the tab! Being friends with a PARTNER at law firm has its rewards. ☺ Limo will be at your building at 8am. We fly at 11. BE THERE!!!!

Fr: <Button>
To: <Meghan>, <Dawn>
Friday, August 14, 2009 10:23AM
Subject: RE: Skydiving

CONGRATS GIRL. Did you just find out? I can't wait to hear the story at lunch. And you know I'd never turn down a spa day. I'm bringing two bottles of Veuve for tomorrow.

***

Swaddled in cashmere robes, Dawn and Meghan relaxed on plush velvet chaises with cucumber slices covering their eyes. Soft violins played in the background and the tranquil scent of roses and almonds floated in the air. There was a soft knock at the door and the spa attendant slipped quietly into the private lounge.

"Ladies, are you ready for lunch? The chef has prepared warm crab cake salad, lemon and herb salmon, and grilled asparagus sprinkled with sea salt. We've chilled your bottle of champagne and will serve it with lunch when you're ready," she whispered.

"That all sounds delicious and I'm starving. Who knew all this pampering could make me so hungry?" Meghan said drowsily to Dawn.

"Can you please bring the champagne now, but hold lunch until my other friend returns? Do you know where she is?" Dawn asked the spa attendant.

"She's in the front lounge. It's the only place you can use a cell phone. I can let her know her presence is requested for lunch."

"Yes, that would be great. Thanks." Dawn said.

"My pleasure." The attendant smiled and exited.

Dawn removed the cucumbers from her eyes. "This is the good life. I love this room. I need something like this in my place. Meg, how I do get this spa into my house?"

"Your bathroom is already like a spa," Meghan said.

"I want a place to do yoga. I can't do yoga in my bathroom."

"We can turn your office into a meditation space," Meg answered.

"I can't give up my whole office," Dawn objected.

Meghan removed her cucumbers and looked around the room. "I can use Japanese shoji screens like those and lots of pillows to create a serenity corner in your office where you can practice yoga."

"Now you're talking. I like it. Can we work on it now or do I have to wait for you to go to design school?"

"Let's do it now. Girl, when I enroll, I'm not going to have any free time."

"When's enrollment?"

"January. I should hear back next month if I got in."

"You're getting in. There's no doubt in my mind so we need to start working on my serenity corner asap. Do we have to go back to the Art Institute?"

"No, this spa is my inspiration piece. I can come over tonight. I'll take some measurements and pictures of the space then get back to you with the plans."

"I love having talented friends." Dawn looked over her shoulder as the lounge door flung open.

Button wheeled in a beverage cart. "Which one of you sent Helga to get me off the phone?" She parked the cart, lifted the frosted champagne bottle from the chiller, and filled three champagne flutes.

"I did. I want us all to eat lunch together and I'm hungry," Dawn admitted.

"Sorry, I had to call Henry." Button distributed the flutes and sat next to Dawn. "He made me promise to call when we landed safely. I should have called on the way to the spa, but the adrenaline rush made me forget. That was awesome. I thought Phillip's plane took Single Girl Summer to new heights, but no; skydiving, that's what's up, literally."

"After jumping out of a moving airplane, I truly feel like I can do anything. Jumping was the hardest part. Once we got out there, the instructor did everything. All I had to do was relax and enjoy the ride. I'm glad I didn't back out," Meghan said.

"I saw you and Button exchanging furtive glances." Dawn laughed.

"Waiting in that airplane was scary. When the door opened, the air kicked up, and my guy started scooting us up to the front, my stomach cartwheeled and my heart jumped out of my chest. I looked at Meghan and her face was a putrid shade of green. But then I looked at you and you were so calm. Were you scared at all?" Button asked.

"Terrified, but this was my idea, so I had to set the example. It was obvious you two were looking for an easy out and I wasn't going to give it to you. I put on my brave face and jumped. It was scary at first with the wind smacking me in the face. But after we pulled the parachute and started floating, my terror melted into a Zen tranquility. I was a bird soaring through the air, peaceful and liberated," Dawn said.

"You should have said all the bird shit before I talked to Henry. I couldn't find the right words to describe skydiving. Liberated would have helped five minutes ago."

"That's your second Henry reference in two minutes. Is it safe to say you and Henry made up?" Dawn asked.

"After my outburst at the Old Skool Picnic, Henry and I decided to give each other some space. My dad asked me to come back to Atlanta so we could talk and I needed a change of scenery. Talking to my dad, I realized the importance of having a consistent and dependable male perspective in my life. He and I really talked about everything. We even went to visit my mother. To borrow your descriptions Dawn, I found peace in my relationships with each of them and liberated myself of some old baggage. Our relationships aren't perfect, but we're working on them. And being apart from Henry made me realize how he adds so much to my life. I depend on him and I trust him. Our time apart made me realize that I'm ready to be exclusive with Henry."

"No more Half?" Dawn asked.

"No more Half," Button confirmed.

"And how do you feel about that?" Dawn asked.

"I feel fantastic. Henry's amazing," Button declared and then she reached over and hugged Dawn.

"When did you become a hugger?" Dawn laughed. "I'm so happy for you."

"Thanks, Dawn."

"What about you, Meg? Do you need to call Phillip now too?" Dawn asked.

"I don't need to, but I want to. He's so wonderful," Meghan smiled wide.

"Smiling like that, he must be wonderful."

"We have so much in common and have such a good time together. He makes me so happy. I keep pinching myself because this has to be a dream. He's too good to be true."

"Don't say that. You deserve a whirlwind romance. He's too good not to be true."

"I said the same thing about Henry to my dad. He told me everyone has rocky relationships in their past. If you use those experiences to learn about yourself and make better decisions in the future, eventually life will give you double for your trouble. Henry and Phillip are our doubles," Button said.

"And Benjamin too," Dawn added.

"Are you sure about Benjamin? He seems like more trouble than double."

"He was nervous. You need to give him another chance," Dawn implored.

"I don't want to. I want you to date. I want to live vicariously through you. I want lots of dating stories and Benjamin doesn't seem like a fun date."

"What happened with the cute motorcycle guy from the Old Skool Picnic?" Meghan asked.

"He's been calling me, but I don't think he's for me. He's such a pretty boy and he reminds me of Rick too much. I really think Benjamin is more my speed," Dawn said.

"Girl, if you like him, I love him. I'll give him another chance," Meghan offered.

"Fine, whatever. I'm in too good a mood to argue. I'll give him another chance too," Button agreed.

"So when are we going to triple date?" Dawn asked.

"Henry's organizing a coed paint ball scrimmage for Labor Day weekend. Bring your guys and we'll see what happens," Button said.

"Count us in. Where's Helga with our lunch? I'm about to die from starvation." Dawn pretended to pass out while Button and Meg shook their heads and laughed.

Fr: <Henry>
To: undisclosed recipients
Thursday, August 27, 2009 10:18AM
Subject: Paintball scrimmage

It's Labor Day weekend and I still got open slots. Details below. Let's get it in.

What: Paintball scrimmage
Who: Everyone...teams are co-ed
When: Saturday, August 29, high noon
Where: Extreme Challenge Park; meet in the south parking lot and the trolley will drive us to Bedlam Field
How much: $75 includes paintballs, gun, mask, paintball suit, lunch, and drinks
Rules: Since it's co-ed, guns will be set at low power. NO HEAD SHOTS.

Note to the ladies:
My girlfriend has played a few times and loves it. Dress for war. The paintball suit gets hot. The face mask gets hot. You'll be running and getting hit. Think camouflage and combat; not cute and cold-as-hell.

***

Button looked out the back window of the trolley just as Benjamin Lawrence took a paintball to the head. Button laughed out loud.

"What?" Dawn asked.

"Benjamin just got one to the dome," Button told her.

Meghan scrambled to the back of the trolley to see his orange-paint head wound. She laughed hard. "I heard Henry's friends plotting to shoot him in the head."

Dawn looked at the back window. "I thought Henry said no head shots."

Button wiped her forehead. "For real, for real, Dawn. What's up with him? You're way out of his league. He's an annoying nerd. Does he know scientists got together and came up with an amazing invention so he doesn't have to wear glasses anymore? You're cold-as-hell and need a man with some swagger who doesn't refer to you as dessert and can afford some contacts."

"Button, don't you know those aren't regular glasses," Meghan pointed out. "Those are Dawn Martin tracking glasses. He doesn't let you out of his sight."

"You're being too hard on Benjamin. He's nice," Dawn objected.

"He's obnoxious. I don't like him," Meghan told Dawn. "Did you see him get in my face and threaten to take me down? Hello, I'm a girl. Why was he picking on me?"

"Sometimes he's socially awkward, but it's not malicious."

Button gave Dawn a look. "You saw his skinny butt yelling in Meg's face? Henry wanted to kick his ass."

"Instead, the boys decided to shoot him in the head." Meghan winked at Button.

"Is that why you made me come with you, so Henry and his boys could gang up on Benjamin? That's mean," Dawn chastised. "But I am happy for breathing room. He can be like white on rice."

"I have to call you on this. When are you going to cut that lame and start recruiting some decent talent?" Button asked.

"He's nice and really likes me. He's just a little needy."

"Needy how?"

"It's only been a month and he's complaining that I spend too much time at work and don't have enough time for him. We haven't even had sex yet and when he looks at me, I feel like he's planning our wedding. He's all in. I'm still undecided, but it's nice to be adored like that," Dawn admitted.

"Did he ask you to go steady yet?" Button asked.

"No, but I'm sure that's coming. I kind of wish I hadn't brought him today. Henry's friends are tall and cute," Dawn said.

"You brought sand to the beach, but don't worry about it. Let me know who you like and I can hook up a double date," Button fanned herself with her hand.

"Let me think about it. Anyway, I'm exhausted. This is fun, but this paint suit is hot. It's a good thing the weather's cool. I couldn't imagine running around out here on a warm day." Dawn closed her eyes and rested her head on the headrest behind her.

"The trolley is a good idea. After all that running and ducking, I'm glad we don't have to walk back to the picnic area," Button said.

"What's for lunch?" Dawn asked.

"Pizza, wings, and salad. There's also a container of Camouflage Punch and one of Single Girl Sangria. Meg, have you heard from Phillip?" Button asked. Meghan shook her head.

"Maybe something happened to him." Dawn said.

"Why do women say that? There's a less than one percent chance that a tragic accident has occurred and he's lying comatose in a hospital bed. In all the years I dated before I was married, no disaster ever occurred right before my date was supposed to pick me up. If the guy was late or didn't show up, I used to worry that something happened to him until I realized that nothing happened. He was just late, inconsiderate, or an asshole," Meghan said bitterly.

"Whoa, Meg. What's going on here?" Button asked.

"No, Meg's right. Men don't want to disappoint you with bad news so they avoid you. If you aren't coming, just tell me. You add insult to injury when you don't say anything. Men are so childish," Dawn agreed.

"So childish…no matter how old they are. And I'm starting to think that's Phillip's story. He's been weird lately," Meghan said.

"What happened, Meg? At the spa, everything was going so well. Don't tell me it went from sugar to shit in two weeks." Button looked at Meghan with concern.

"Remember Lee, the guy I went out with that I met at Quarter's house?" Meghan asked.

"The talented drummer." Button smiled.

"Yeah. Last week, I was at the gym and Lee was working out with Quarter. He catches me as I'm leaving and starts flirting with me. Telling me how good I look, that I should let him take me out again, and stuff like that. Granted, I was flattered. He's young and attractive so I let him go on a little. It was very innocent, though. I had already told him I was with Phillip and told him again. I didn't know Phillip saw the whole thing. That night he sent me a text that he was having second thoughts dating someone as young as me. I was caught completely off guard. I dropped my phone," Meghan said.

"He texted that to you!" Dawn was shocked.

"That's a text bomb," Button said.

"Yes, he text-bombed me. I called him to find out what he was talking about, but he didn't answer the phone. He didn't call me until the next day to explain himself. He's been flakey ever since. Okay, that's not true. He was a little flakey before. But now, he's extra flakey and distant. And I think he's standing me up as we speak."

"I'm sorry, Sweetie. But if he is an insecure flake, it's best to find out now," Button reasoned.

"I know. I wish he were here so I could shoot him, but he's not. And like my grandmother always said, one monkey don't stop no show. I'm still having a really good time without him," Meghan said.

"Well, if you're ready to replace him, you got plenty of options with Henry's friends," Button said.

"I'm not ready to replace him. I hope this is a temporary hitch and things will smooth out. Nevertheless, what's up for the rest of the weekend? Labor Day isn't the official end of summer, but it's definitely when the party starts to wind down. I don't want to sit in the house waiting for Phillip to grow up," Meghan said.

"If Dawn can peel herself away from Benjamin Lawrence and his glasses, we can hit the Jazz Fest in Grant Park tomorrow and the African Fest in Washington Park on Monday. Plus, there are fireworks at Navy Pier."

"Sounds like a plan. I want to keep our Single Girl Summer party going as long as possible," Meghan said.

CHAPTER 29

Text Message to Meghan
Fr: Button
3:51pm 9/12/09 - Saturday
Carpool leaves at 6:30.
Dinner and salsa.
Muy Caliente.

Text Message to Button
Fr: Meghan
3:55pm 9/12/09 - Saturday
Not n the mood to go outside.
Phillip gave me the saddies again. ☹

Text Message to Meghan
Fr: Button
4:30pm 9/12/09 - Saturday
New plan: Movie night at ur place.
Me, u, Dawn and Nemo at 6:30.

***

Meghan set the popcorn bowl down and sat up on the couch. "That was so good. I even cried a little. I was skeptical when you brought in 'Finding

Nemo' for movie night, but it was great," Meghan said.

"My niece let me borrow it,' Dawn said from the other couch.

Meghan's phone beeped, indicating a new text message. She checked the screen and sighed.

"That better not be Phillip with another text bomb," Button sat up from her pillow pallet on the floor and set her glass of sangria on the coffee table.

"No, I explained to him about text bombs and asked him to refrain from using his phone as a nuclear device in the future. He texted that he misses me. I hate when he does that almost as much as his text bombs. He puts space between us, then whines that he misses me. I'm here. Where's he?" Meghan rolled her eyes and tossed the phone back on the coffee table.

"Is he still upset over Lee?" Button asked.

"He got over that and our relationship was getting back on track. Then I told him I got into my Interior Design program and was starting in January," Meghan began. "I thought he'd be happy for me. I'm finally pursing my big dream, but he just got real quiet. I had to keep asking what's wrong. Finally, he asked me 'Who's for me?' He said his ex-wife got too busy for him. His kid is too busy for him. He thought I was different. He said going back to school will take time away from our relationship. He pretty much gave me an ultimatum."

"You're kidding," Dawn said. "What'd you tell him?"

"I hope you said screw you," Button said.

"I know I should, but I don't want to lose him. I left my ex because he was terrible with money and drowning in his gambling addiction. Then I meet Phillip, who has a lucrative and successful business. He's driven and has long-term goals. He has everything my ex lacked. No relationship is perfect. And I really don't feel like going through another break-up." Meghan buried her face in her hands.

"Meg, it's okay," Dawn went to sit next to Meghan on the couch and rubbed her back. "I know how you feel. I still haven't broken up with Benjamin for the same reason. Break-ups take a toll on your emotions." A quiet sadness settled over Dawn and Meghan. Button cocked her head to the side, watched her two friends, and considered their situations.

"No." Button stood up. "This is not okay. Meghan and Dawn, I won't let you two settle. Remember in the movie when all the fish were trying to get out the fisherman's net and Nemo told them to 'keep swimming, keep swimming, don't give up, just keep swimming.' That's what you need to do." Button paused, then asked, "Meghan, what are the non-negotiables on your list of essential elements?"

"Love, spirituality, companionship, good communication, trust, and commitment," Meghan answered.

"Is text-bombing, flakey Phillip giving you your non-negotiables? Is he a good communicator?"

"No," Meghan said softly.

"And Dawn, don't get me started on your anti-Rick. I know you had a hard break-up, but don't make the mistake of settling for the first guy that likes you. I can't be quiet and watch you two settle anymore," Button said.

"Button, it's easy for you to tell us not to settle. You have the total package, but Henry's the exception," Dawn countered.

"The three of us are beautiful, smart, and wonderful. We bring a lot to the table. Men who lie, cheat, flake, annoy, and issue ultimatums are ordinary. We're looking for extraordinary. Do. Not. Settle. Meg, you upgraded from your ex-husband to Phillip. You attracted someone better because you deserve someone better. Just think how great the next guy will be. Damn it ladies, you need to raise your expectations. Step your game up." Button folded her arms across her chest and stared at her friends on the couch. No one said anything. Meghan and Dawn just stared back at her.

Button continued, "I was looking at the calendar today and the autumn equinox is in two weeks. That means it's almost the end of Single Girl Summer. I'm not letting you go out like this."

Finally, Dawn broke the silence from the couch. "Button's right. I'm two weeks away from fall and my thirtieth birthday and I'm acting like I haven't learned anything from Single Girl Summer. Meg, if it weren't for seeing how positive you were after your divorce, I wouldn't have been able to handle the break-up with Rick. You survived your divorce and we can survive another break-up. Single Girl Summer is about healing ourselves and reclaiming our joy. We need to get ourselves together."

"Yeah, I guess it's unrealistic to think I was going to marry the first guy I dated after my divorce. Maybe I should kiss a few more frogs," Meghan acknowledged.

"That's right. I love Henry, but if he starts acting ordinary, I won't hesitate to bounce."

Dawn looked at Meghan. "Did she say..." Dawn said.

"What I think she said?" Meghan finished the sentence.

"What... What did I say? I'm cold-as-hell. I'll bounce in a heartbeat," Button said.

"Girl, no—you said you love Henry," Meghan said excitedly.

"Oh, oh, I guess I did. I guess I do. Humph. Or it might be the sangria talking," Button said.

Meghan started singing, "*Button and Henry sitting in a tree. K-I-S-S-I-N-G.*"

"Real mature, Nemo," Button taunted.

Dawn joined in, "*First comes love, then comes marriage. Then comes Button with a baby carriage.*"

"Oh, hell no. You can stop right there." Button grabbed pillows from the floor and threw them, one by one, at Meghan and Dawn, who just keep repeating their taunts and laughing.

Fr: <Button>
To: <Meghan>, <Dawn>
Friday, September 25, 2009 7:11AM
Subject: HAPPY BIRTHDAY

Welcome to the dirty thirties, Dawn. Reservations are set at Anand for seven. We're dining in the private back room so we have plenty of room for our SGS gift exchange. Personally, I've never heard of a woman giving gifts on her own birthday, but that's our Dawn—she's one of a kind.

Fr: <Meghan>
To: <Dawn>, <Button>
Friday, September 25, 2009 8:46AM
Subject: RE: HAPPY BIRTHDAY

Happy Birthday to ya. Happy Birthday to ya. Happy Birthday. I don't know if I can wait until tonight. I'm about to burst. Can I give you a clue?

Fr: <Dawn>
To: <Button>, <Meghan>
Friday, September 25, 2009 8:52AM
Subject: RE: HAPPY BIRTHDAY

Thanks, ladies. No clues, Meg. I'm spending the day at the spa. Seaweed wrap here I come. C U soon.

Fr: <Meghan>
To: <Dawn>, <Button>
Friday, September 25, 2009 8:59AM
Subject: RE: HAPPY BIRTHDAY

Alright. I HEAR you. wink, wink. LOL

***

"Can we open gifts now?" Meghan asked for the second time.

"I thought we'd open gifts after dinner," Dawn told her.

"*After dinner*! I can't wait that long. Plus, there was a lull in the conversation and the gift exchange would fill the empty space," Meghan suggested.

"There's no lull. Don't be so impatient. I was just about to ask Dawn about her hot date last Friday with Henry's friend," Button said.

"It was fun. My date on Saturday night was fun too," Dawn said.

"You went out with him two nights in a row?" Button asked.

"No, I went out with David from the Old Skool Picnic on Saturday. My team is coming together nicely."

"I know Henry's friend is just under six feet. How tall is your other guy?" Button asked.

"Six-five, but that doesn't matter. I was thinking about this all day at the spa and I decided that none of that really matters," Dawn said.

"None of what matters?" Button questioned.

The look on Dawn's face was stoic. "Height, looks…It's all so superficial. At the end of the day, it doesn't matter if he's tall, short, svelte, fat, on a team, my husband or my boyfriend because none of that will make me happy. Nobody else, no outside thing, no label can make me happy. I have to find happiness within. Unless I have that, I'll never be satisfied with any guy I meet."

"Um, how tight were you wrapped in seaweed? Henry's friend is tall, cute, never been married, no kids, and owns a successful business. Don't give me that enlightened crap. I want to see a happy dance," Button said.

Dawn's face cracked in a smile. "Sorry, the day at the spa and turning another year older has put me in an existential mood. I did happy dances after both of my dates. They were tall and I like it." Dawn laughed and pounded on the table.

"That's more like it," Button said.

"I'm serious, though, about finding happiness within. That's the most important thing I learned this summer," Dawn added.

"Speaking of summer and now that that's settled, can we open gifts?" Meghan asked again.

"Fine. Button you go first," Dawn said.

"But, I want to..." Meghan stopped short when Dawn started wagging her finger.

"Don't be a troublemaker," Dawn scolded.

"Or a Muffin Button." Button stuck out her tongue at Meghan.

"Even though we're all getting gifts, today is my birthday so you have to play by my rules. Button, you go first."

Button stood. "My gift is quintessential Button Jackson and should be easy to guess. The Widow Clicquot was the ultimate survivor. She kept swimming through all adversity and became the grande dame of fabulous and single. A celebration of Dawn's birthday and the end of Single Girl Summer wouldn't be complete without a bottle of Veuve."

Button reached into a gift bag under the table and pulled out two yellow label bottles embellished with lavish, pink bows. Dawn and Meghan applauded.

"Meg, now it's your turn," Dawn said.

"Finally. Button always provides the booze and so I'm going to provide the tunes. My gift is called 'A Soundtrack for Single Girl Summer.'" Meghan reached into a gift bag and produced two jewel cases which she handed to Button and Dawn. She continued, "The song list is on the cover. There are eighteen songs total. Six songs for each of us that represent, embody, and capture our Single Girl Summers," Meghan beamed.

Button laughed loudly. "*Meghan, this is so great*! My favorites are 'Sponsor' and 'He Loves Me (Henry in E-Flat)'. Henry will like that."

Dawn read her CD list. "You definitely had to have 'Confessions Part 2' on here. And the Beyoncé tribute is a nice touch. My songs completely capture the highs and lows of my Single Girl Summer and I wouldn't change a thing. Thanks, Meg. I hear you too."

"And my Single Girl Summer started 'Like a Virgin' and is ending with a move 'On to the Next One.'" Meghan winked at her friends and laughed.

"This is fantastic, Meg. Okay, now it's my turn." Dawn retrieved her purse from the back of her chair. She put the CD inside and pulled out two white envelopes which she passed to Button and Meghan. Button ripped open her envelope and pulled out a postcard that read "Black Girls Rock and Black Girls

Ride" at the top. Underneath was a picture of a shapely black woman riding a Harley-Davidson.

Button shouted and danced in her chair, "Whoa, that's what I'm talking about. You got us Harleys!"

Dawn shot her an incredulous look. "No, I got us rides with David's Harley club. I've never been on a motorcycle and if I'm doing it, so are you."

"You've turned into a real daredevil. I would rather have my own bike, but I'm in."

"Me, too. That'll be fun. And from what I remember, David had some cute friends," Meghan added.

"The gifts were a great idea. I'm going to miss our Single Girl Summer," Button pouted.

"Ooooh. I want to make a toast," Meghan grabbed her champagne flute and raised it high. Button and Dawn followed her lead. "Single Girl Summer bought together three women who learned from each other not to settle, to keep swimming, and that a half will never make a whole. We fought, healed, loved, cried, played, and mostly laughed. So, a toast to the end of Single Girl Summer and a toast the dawn of Single Girl Fall." Meghan looked back and forth between Button and Dawn. "We're just getting started."

***

Fr: <Button>
To: <Meghan> <Dawn>
Saturday, September 26, 2009 11:46AM
Subject: On to the Next

I've been playing my CD all day. I absolutely love it. Are you still breaking up with Phillip tonight? Do you want me and Dawn to come over later?

Fr: <Meghan>
To: <Button> <Dawn>
Saturday, September 26, 2009 12:32PM
Subject: RE: On to the Next

He sent me a text this morning suggesting I wait until the summer to start school. I texted him back "Starting in January. Be blessed." You and Dawn can come over, but I won't be here. I'm going out to celebrate SGF. I'm liberated!

Fr: <Button>
To: <Meghan> <Dawn>
Saturday, September 26, 2009 12:39PM
Subject: RE: On to the Next

Nuclear text bomb. ☺
Carpool leaves at nine.

A Soundtrack for Single Girl Summer

Button:

1. Buttons – The Pussycat Dolls
2. Sponsor – Teairra Mari
3. Champagne Life – Ne-Yo
4. The Men All Pause – Climax
5. Ego – Beyoncé
6. He Loves Me [Henry in E-Flat] – Jill Scott

Dawn:

7. (It's Not the Express) It's the J.B.'s Monaurail – The J.B.'s
8. Irreplaceable – Beyoncé
9. Confessions Part 2 – Usher
10. Freakum Dress – Beyoncé
11. Single Ladies (Put a Ring On It) – Beyoncé
12. Good Life – Kanye West

Meghan:

13. Like a Virgin – Madonna
14. The New Workout Plan – Kayne West
15. Mary Jane – Rick James
16. The Music Sounds Better With You – Stardust
17. Tell Me All About It (White Label Mix) – Natalie Cole
18. On To the Next One – Jay-Z

Acknowledgements

Thank you, God, for blessing me with creativity, inspiration, prosperity, and angels who lovingly sustain and assist me. They constantly push me to gather all my ideas and bind them together. My angels encourage me to write especially when I don't feel like it. My angels remind me that I have talents that need to be shared. My angels read revision after revision and graciously let me pick their brains. My angels have impeccable timing, accommodating flexibility, wonderful advice, and the patience of Job. My angels are my Mommy, Daddy, Granny, Poppy, Delena, Benitta, Keisha, Natasha, Tanji, Marcus, Ayanna, Tim & Joi, Micaeh, Stephanie, Chevonne, St. Louis Ben, Khari, Rooney, Art, Jenise, Rebecca, Rachelle, Sika, Daniel, Ken, Leilani, the Evanston Writers Workshop, my Christ Universal Temple family, the Women of the Written Word, and my Clear Channel family. Thank you for your suggestions, support, and enthusiasm.

I also must give an enormous thank you to my editor extraordinaire Ruth Beach and my all-girl teams at Windy City Publishers and MNJ Public Relations. It takes a lot to render me speechless and your dedication to my dream and attention to detail has done just that so I'm going to borrow these words to express my gratitude: I'm a movement by myself, but I'm a force when we're together. You make me better.

giving2green

The giving2green symbol indicates that the user has committed to giving monies to the many organizations dedicated to the fight against global warming, decreasing greenhouse gas emissions, saving our rainforests and wetlands, and fighting water and air pollution.

giving2green gives 100 percent of its proceeds to supporting the organizations fighting these battles. Because we feel that saving our planet and the people, plants, and animals inhabiting it is one of the most critical challenges we face today, we request that all our authors commit their support as well.

We feel good about making a difference. Every little bit helps, and today's businesses should step up to the challenge of not only doing their part, but setting an example—not just because it's good for our environment, but because it's the right thing to do.

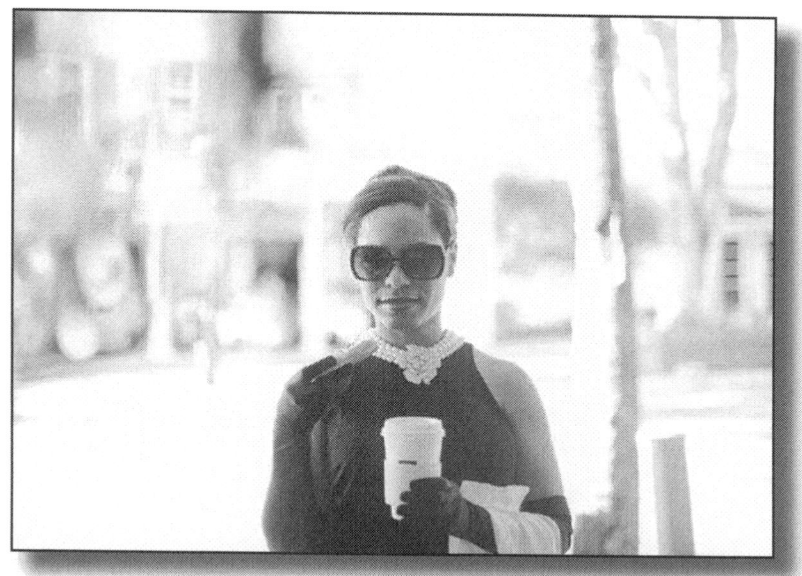

Daniel Lateulade, Photographer

Deanna Kimberly Burrell is a successful businesswoman, published author, and popular speaker. Her first book, *Voted Most Creative: Perspectives on Life, Love, and the Pursuit of Happiness*, is a collection of poems and essays that inspire creativity, growth, and self-expression. *Single Girl Summer* is her first novel and it's more than just a collection of words for Deanna. *Single Girl Summer* is a celebration of free, bold, and clever women who love and embrace life. Deanna is a graduate of Northwestern University, lives in Chicago, and is currently writing a book on advertising.

Website

www.SingleGirlSummer.com

Email

info@SingleGirlSummer.com

Made in the USA
Lexington, KY
18 September 2011